THE WINTER WIVES

Also by Linden MacIntyre

THE
WINTER
WIVES

A novel

LINDEN MACINTYRE

RANDOM HOUSE CANADA

PUBLISHED BY RANDOM HOUSE CANADA

LIBRARY AND ARCHIVES CANADA CATALOGUING
IN PUBLICATION

Title: The Winter wives / Linden MacIntyre.
Names: MacIntyre, Linden, author.
Identifiers: Canadiana (print) 20200343793 |
Canadiana (ebook) 20200343807 | ISBN 9780735282056 (hardcover) | ISBN
9780735282063 (EPUB)
Classification: LCC PS8575.I655 W56 2021 | DDC C813/.54—dc23

Text design: Terri Nimmo
Jacket design: Terri Nimmo
Image credits: Cover images: (couple) PixelsEffect; (smoke) Jose A. Bernat
Bacete; (wedding ring) Evgeniya Lystsova / EyeEm; all Getty Images

Printed in Canada

2 4 6 8 9 7 5 3 1

Penguin
Random House
RANDOM HOUSE CANADA

In

memory

of

E.A.T.

1942–2016

This is the age of oddities let loose.
—LORD BYRON, *Don Juan*

... human reality is constituted as a being
which is what it is not and which is not what it is.
—J.-P. SARTRE, *Being and Nothingness*

BYRON

My name is Angus, but almost everybody calls me Byron because I limp.

Peggy Winter was the first to call me Byron. We were in a high school English class studying Romantic poets. Byron was a poet and he limped. She said that I reminded her of Byron. We were very young when she decided that she knew me better than she knew anybody, knew me better than I knew myself, knew that I was special, which is how I came to think of her.

We were both so very wrong.

PART ONE

ALL FALL DOWN

When Allan fell, we were at the tee on the tenth hole of a golf course. It would take a long time to absorb the full impact of what happened there. Up close, death is like a mountain we happen to be standing on. Maybe we can see a piece of it, but the whole remains unreal until there's distance.

In the moment, it was almost funny, Allan staggering as if he was clowning. I assumed that he was gasping to recover from a fit of laughter. Then he fell, sort of in slow motion.

Perhaps I should have noticed what was coming when we were on the ninth green. Three strokes and he was still four inches from the cup. Even his final angry backhand swat, guaranteed to sink the ball, failed. The ball, in defiance of all the laws of physics, not to mention his forty-something years of dedication to the game, swirled around the rim, then lurched away from it.

Finally, he used his foot to nudge it in.

–This fuckin game, he said.

–Nobody's keeping score, I said.

He laughed.

I clapped him on the shoulder as we stored our putters in the golf bags. But climbing back into the cart, his face was flushed and he fell into a deep golfer silence as we raced along. He needed a distraction.

I remembered the two little bottles I'd taken from the mini-bar in our hotel. It was ten o'clock in the morning, but so what. We were on vacation.

The day was warm and close, slightly overcast—the kind of day you'd expect a lot of insects. One of the charms of a golf course, I find, is the absence of insects. Absence of almost any form of life, actually. Just grass and other golfers who seem so far away there's no danger of engagement. And, of course, the inconvenient trees.

And so it was on that day—no bugs, no other creatures near enough to see or hear, the distant highway sounds of whining cars and snarling trucks the only evidence of the world outside.

The mini-bottles were in the golf cart's cupholder. I fished them out and held them up. Allan smiled, finally.

–Hair of the dog, I said.

I snapped the caps and handed one across to him and we drove on, sipping thoughtfully.

I'm not a golfer. I played with Allan to amuse him, so he'd get the practice and the personal satisfaction of humiliating me. But that day on the ninth green I'd accidentally sunk a twenty-foot putt and beaten Allan by two strokes.

Sometimes I think that partially explains what happened on the tenth.

Allan went first, while I sat in the cart and drained the little bottle. He positioned himself carefully, stared briefly down the fairway, glared at the golf ball for a moment, then swung. There was a precise click and the ball was gone. I lost it in the haze but knew that it was headed exactly where he wanted it to go.

We saw it land and then bounce to the edge of the green.

–I'm back, he said.

My turn. I struggled out of the cart. One leg is about an inch shorter than the other and slightly weaker. Getting in and out of vehicles can be challenging. I injected a tee in the damp sod and balanced a ball on top of it. Straightened up. Tried to seem like I had some control over what was going to happen next.

I took two practice swings, then swung mightily. Missed. The ball toppled off the tee.

I forced myself to smile.

I repositioned the ball and studied it some more, glanced at Allan. He was standing, kind of leaning on his driver. His face was neutral, as if his mind was a hundred miles away.

–This is for real, I said.

–Just keep your eye on the ball, he growled.

I stared at it for a few more seconds, then swung again. This time I connected. There was the satisfying click of contact, followed by two quick whacks as the ball ricocheted off some nearby birch trees then shot back between us, narrowly missing Allan's head, and landed inside the golf cart, where I found it in the cupholder.

I plucked it out and held it up.

–A hole-in-one, I said.

Allan uttered what I thought was a loud guffaw, but when I turned toward him, he was stumbling and then he was on his knees, hands planted palms down in the grass. I assumed he'd lost his balance when he ducked. The sound that he was making could have passed for laughter had he not then rolled slowly onto his side and curled up, twitching, grimacing.

I dropped down beside him. One of the happier consequences of my disability—or I should say one of my abilities—is upper-body strength from the time I spent periodically on crutches and in gyms. Slinging heavy lobster traps and bales of hay when I was younger. I gently sat him up, held him in my arms.

His head rolled back, his eyes panicky and wild. He was struggling to speak, but the sounds he made were meaningless. He was drooling.

I could hear the whine of a golf cart and the sound of someone running. Then there was a stranger crouching on the other side of Allan, clutching at his wrist, fingers on his neck.

–Lie him flat, he ordered.

I gently lowered Allan to the grass and struggled to my feet.

–I'm a doctor, said the stranger. He was already scrolling through a cellphone.

The ambulance couldn't have been far away. In what seemed like a couple of minutes, I heard a little whoop of urgency, saw it trundling down the fairway toward where we were waiting. By then there was a small cluster of golf carts gathered around us and a dozen golfers watching silently.

–What's your connection with this guy? the doctor asked.

–We're family. We're in business. Our wives are sisters.

–Maybe you should call his wife.

–What can I say?

–It's too early to say anything.

–But he's going to be okay, right?

The doctor didn't answer.

He stepped aside as the paramedics carefully positioned Allan on a stretcher then hoisted him and slid him into the back of the ambulance. The doctor clambered in and squatted down, bent close to Allan's face, checked his eyes and pulse again. Then he hopped out nimbly, retrieving his golf gloves from his pocket.

One of the paramedics slammed the back doors, hustled toward the front. The ambulance whooped once more as it started up.

I watched it roll away down the hill toward the main road. I saw a foursome on a fairway stop to watch it pass. Nearing the highway, the lights began to flash and the siren began its terrifying, urgent screaming.

I remembered the sensations, being trapped inside an ambulance while the external wailing just goes on and on and on.

Unknown destination. The future rapidly unravelling.

I sat in the golf cart, struggling to grasp the implications of what had just occurred. The doctor paused beside me to ask if I was okay. I nodded. One by one the other golf carts slowly wheeled away, the unexpected interruption over.

Then I remembered Peggy, Allan's wife, and the need to call her, and the potential gravity of what was happening almost took my voice away.

I managed to call my wife, Annie, Peggy's sister. It's been years since we've lived together, Annie and I, but I know her number off by heart.

–I need to get in touch with Peggy. Do you have her number handy?

–Is there something wrong?

–Yes, there might be something very wrong. But if you see her before I talk to her, don't say anything. Allan is in an ambulance, on his way to a hospital.

–Oh Christ. What happened?

–He collapsed. I need Peggy's cellphone number.

–Should I be there?

–Sit tight for now. It's probably just stress.

When Peggy picked up, I tried to be tactful without diminishing what, from my perspective, was potentially momentous. Peggy has always been unflappable and she seemed to be taking it all in stride.

–There was a doctor near, I said.

–That's a relief, she said.

–Hey, everything is going to be fine. Okay?

I was working hard to sound upbeat, but there's something about falling down. Never a sign of good things to come.

–What do you think? she asked.

–Probably nothing serious. He was having a great game. He's as strong as a horse.

–I'm on my way, she said.

–You can find the hospital okay?

–Yes. And he told me the address of the hotel where you guys are staying. I have it somewhere.

–I'll see you there, I said.

–Or at the hospital?

–Yes. The hospital. I'll try to be there.

I returned the golf cart and my rented gear to the pro shop. Everything was starting to sink in, but in a kind of haze. My head was full of vague imperatives. Get back to the hotel. Find the hospital. Figure out the next few days. Perhaps the next few decades. We were getting old, but there was still a future to navigate.

And then I thought of our hotel room, where all his stuff was still scattered as he left it. The half-full water glass on the little bedside table, beside the half-read book. Things we start, assuming that we'll finish. The nearly empty liquor bottle. Trousers sprawled across a chair, a sock dangling from an empty leg. Unlived life left messy. A job for someone else.

2

Allan and Peggy had arrived in Halifax from Toronto the day before our golf game. I met them at the airport. Peggy planned to visit old friends first, and then her sister Annie, who, at the time, was still living mostly in Nova Scotia, in her own place, not far from where I live and practise law.

Allan and I headed off to the golf course, which was several hours' drive from the city.

I was the one who checked us into the hotel. Allan had a phobia about signing anything, even something as innocuous as a small-town hotel registry. You could hunt forever, but you'd never find my partner's name on a bureaucratic document, not even on our letterhead. I handled most of his official business.

Actually, Allan had many names—inventions he could use when necessary then leave behind, as irrelevant as worn-out shoes. A name is a persona, he'd say, and a persona has no substance. It was one of his many eccentricities, but I had come to understand his reasons. A name is only a name. Identity is something else, something deep and private, shared only with those who, over time, we come to trust. I took for granted that the list of people he trusted was very short. Me and Annie. And, obviously, Peggy.

I sat down on the bed in the room and searched my phone to find the number for the nearby hospital. But then I realized that if I called to ask about him, I wouldn't know what name to ask for.

That was the Allan we knew. Or thought we knew.

I met him during our first year in university, back in the late seventies. I'd seen him around, usually wearing the distinctive dark wool jacket that identified him as part of the varsity football team. I basically ignored him. They were a cult unto themselves, the athletes.

Then one evening we both found ourselves sitting in a stairwell outside the university dining hall waiting for the place to open. I had a book, and pretended to be engrossed.

–What's that? he asked.

–A book, I said.

–No kidding.

I handed it over.

–It's for English, I said.

–*The Collected Works of Thomas Carlyle*, eh.

–What are you taking?

–Science. You?

–Arts, I said.

He flipped through the pages, then paused and read for maybe two minutes, then handed it back.

–So. The pigs were Cedric's?

–What?

He took the book back, flipped it open again, read aloud.

–Gurth with the brass collar around his neck, tending Cedric's pigs in the glades of the wood. Catchy.

–I'm not that far in yet. All I know is that Cedric was Gurth's master. A Saxon nobleman. He owned the pigs.

–Gurth was a slave . . .

–A swineherd. The point is . . .

–I'm Allan.

–Yes. Allan Chase, I said.

Everybody knew Allan Chase.

–The Great Chase, I added, smiling.

His eyes narrowed. He shrugged. The Great Chase was a middle linebacker. They called him Great because he was very good at chasing people down and flattening them. Halfbacks, quarterbacks. He'd go through an offensive line like a truck.

–And who are you?

–Byron.

–As in Lord Byron.

–The very same.

–Let me see that again.

I handed him the book and he kept flicking through the pages, killing time, waiting for the door to open.

–Interesting, he said when he handed it back again.

–Well, I wouldn't go that far.

–You play any sports?

–Not all that interested.

–A poet.

–I wish.

We were teasing each other. I don't think he was accustomed to that, making personal jokes that were a little edgy but not going anywhere near larger challenges. He seemed to be enjoying the experience.

–You've got some shoulders, he said.

–Don't we all.

–I think I've seen you in the weight room.

–Could be.

There was the clack of a lock and the squawk of a door opening above us.

I was surprised when he stayed with me in the food line, because by then there were other guys around wearing football jackets. But he also came and sat with me.

–You're limping, he said.

–I should tell you that it's one thing I'm very good at. I have a great deal of experience limping.

He blushed.

–So, like, that's permanent. What happened?

–An accident, I said.

–Really? What kind of accident?

–I fell down.

–Off a horse or what?

–No. I just tripped and fell. Then my mother ran over me.

–You're shitting me. With what?

–I was only five. I don't remember much. Where are you from?

–Toronto.

–And how did you end up in Nova Scotia?

–I got recruited.

–I hardly ever follow football.

–Byron, eh?

–It's a nickname. I was born Angus.

–Angus, huh. I like Angus. It has character.

–An old name in the family. I'd rather you called me Byron if you don't mind.

My mother had named me for her younger brother. She always called me Angus. My father didn't like my mother's younger brother. I was Boy to him. He never called me Angus.

I've never really understood why we became friends. Allan was a city guy. I was seriously rural. I was still living on the farm where I was born. He had the air of someone who was well-to-do, never stuck for spending money. Mom and I scraped by, living off the land and a commercial fishing licence we inherited after Dad died suddenly, not long before I first met Allan. I was earnest about learning. I was disciplined. Education was my ticket out of poverty. He had no academic interest at all. He worked hard enough to achieve the grades to let him keep on playing football.

He was big physically, unlike me. He was strong, good-looking. He strode the campus and the town, comfortably indifferent to how he was perceived by lesser mortals. We were noticed, I suppose, when we were together, because of the contrast.

I knew the Winter sisters from high school. We moved in different circles at university, but I'd see one or both from time to time and, like everybody else, they seemed to be intrigued by my apparent friendship with the Great Chase.

If I could have seen the future, it wouldn't have surprised me that, one day, he and Peggy Winter would be close. They were beings from the same genetic pool. Like Allan, she was tall, athletic. She followed sports, and could discuss team standings as if they really mattered to her.

She was, physically, unlike her sister, Annie, who was classically blond with startling blue eyes. Peggy's hair was auburn, her eyes deep-set and dark, some days green and some days hazel, depending on the light. Allan never seemed to notice Peggy at the time, which I found odd. Then I discovered that feigning indifference is sometimes a subtle tactic to get attention.

And it worked for Allan. Peggy wasn't used to being overlooked.

One day in the university bookstore, she sidled up and tugged my sleeve.

–How do you know that football guy?

–What football guy?

–The big fella. The Great Chase.

–Oh. Allan. Why?

–You should introduce us. He looks interesting.

–Sure, I said.

And I did, but nothing came of it. Not then. There was no chemistry, I guess. Now that I think of it, the chemistry people talk about was always missing, even after they became a couple. It never occurred to me, back then, to ask Allan what he thought of Peggy.

–He's an odd one, that friend of yours, she said to me some days after I'd arranged the introductions.

–What friend?

–That one you set me up with. That Allan.

–Set you up?

–You know what I mean.

–No.

I was laughing at her and her cheeks went red.

–How do you know he isn't queer? she said.

–Queer?

–Don't act stupid.

–How would I know?

–You're together all the time. I wouldn't be surprised if people thought that.

The front desk confirmed that Peggy had checked in, but she didn't answer when I called the room and she wasn't in the dining room or at the bar. I called her cellphone, but the call went straight to voice mail. I concluded she'd gone directly to the hospital.

I hate hospitals. I spent so much time in hospital when I was just a boy, I grow physically weak whenever I'm near one. But I got into my car and drove there anyway.

I found Peggy sitting on the side of Allan's bed. His eyes were closed, and a plastic oxygen mask covered his mouth and nose. I nodded in her direction, feeling faint. Allan opened his eyes and smiled, lifted a limp hand then let it drop. The cheek on the right side of his face was drooping, the corner of his mouth slightly twisted downward.

–I can come back another time, I said.

But he shook his head, removed the plastic mask and

slurred out a word that sounded like "stay." Then he gestured weakly toward the chair.

–Zzzzit, he instructed.

Spittle trickled from the corner of his mouth. I sat. He closed his eyes again.

Soon, he snored.

Peggy said, I'm glad you came. It was important for him to see you.

She stood.

–I know how hospitals affect you. Let's step outside.

She tilted her chin toward the door.

And in the corridor, she informed me that, according to the specialist, Allan had suffered brain damage. It was going to take a lot of rehab just to restore minimal mobility. The doctor thought he'd regain his speech, but the right side of his body would likely always be a problem.

–The worst thing will be no more golf, she said.

–If that's the worst thing . . .

–I specifically asked, and the doctor told me Allan will be lucky if he gets enough mobility to walk around the house.

She shook her head, rubbed her hands over her face.

–It'll kill him, she said. It will slowly destroy him.

I put my arms around her and she leaned in.

–When can he go home? I asked.

–They think he can travel in a few days.

–Will he be okay in a car?

–I think so. I know that's what he'd want. The thought of another ambulance. Jesus. But I dread getting him through the airport.

–I'll go with you, I said.

–Would you?

She stepped back and studied my face hard, reading my thoughts. *Allan in a bed. Allan unlikely to ever again be far away from bed.*

–He's going to be all right, she said.

I looked back at him, wired and tubed, and I was thinking of my father and what he'd been spared—what we'd all been spared. Sudden death seemed not so bad in comparison.

–He'll bounce back like he always does, Peggy said.

–For sure, I said.

But I was thinking about gravity and falling down. How Dad and eventually Mom fell down and bounced into oblivion. And my uncle, Angus, falling down, off the Angus L. Macdonald Bridge in Halifax.

How I fell down and, yes, bounced back. Improved in so many ways. But, as I see it, bouncing back is the exception.

Before I left the hospital, Peggy asked if we could meet for dinner back at the hotel.

3.

The thing about Allan is that he really believed what he often used to say: you have to live as though you're never going to die. That means taking care of yourself. Staying fit. Everything in moderation.

He'd say, We can't stay young, but we can stay mobile. It just takes work.

Death is the absence of mobility, he'd say. Or the other way around: mobility is the denial of death.

I might have been offended by his obsession with physical mobility, except that I knew he saw me as he saw himself. He never viewed me as the lame guy, the guy who grew up with the reality of falling down. The guy who, for a large part of his young life, lived under the control of other people, not to mention drugs.

For Allan, drugs were optional, part of the existential experience he craved. It seemed he couldn't get enough experience. He seemed to think there isn't any bad experience, that we should look at it all as education.

–Lucky you, I'd say.

–The quality of life is all in how we look at things, he told me once.

The first time I saw anybody roll a joint, experienced the weed smoke second-hand, it was with Allan and his teammates.

He'd say, Life is just a big buffet.

I'd say something like, That's deep, Allan, I'm going to write that down. I'm going to use that.

He'd ignore the sarcasm: We're all hostages, prisoners in time. It's our duty to resist.

—Resist what exactly?

—Everything. But time and gravity, especially. It's gravity that knocks us down.

—So you should be careful about getting high.

—Very droll, Byron.

It was Easter weekend the first time he visited our farm. The big ice was still in and the gulf looked like the winter prairie. It sprawled forever, flat and white. The winds that swept across the ice from the north and northwest were bitter. The fields were all dead grass and dirty snow, the nearby forest menacing. The sky was iron grim.

—What's this place called if it's on the map?

—Malignant Cove, I said.

—Seriously?

—Seriously.

—Where did that name come from?

—Not a clue, I said.

—So what happens to all that ice? It just melts away?

—I'm not sure. One morning you wake up and it's gone.

I think the wind must take it. It usually breaks up by the first of May, when the fishing starts.

–Hard to imagine. Your father was a fisherman?

–Among other things.

–I guess you miss him.

–I got over it.

–Uh huh.

–Yours? You never talk about him. You get along?

Hard to say. He's too busy being busy to talk much about anything.

Our fishing boat, the *Immaculata*, was propped up on barrels beside the shed where we stored the lobster traps in winter. It was a big boat, thirty-eight feet long with an imposing cab, an open workspace from cab to transom. A Northumberland with flowing lines.

–So, what's with the *Immaculata*?

–We fish for lobsters every spring. My mother is religious. Believes a name like that will keep us safe.

–You can drive that thing?

–I can.

–Impressive.

–It's pretty simple. It's like a wheelbarrow. Steers from the rear. You turn right by swinging the arse-end left.

–Aha. Diesel engine?

–Hundred and thirty-five horsepower Ford. Cheap to run. You know diesels?

–I know trucks. My dad owns a bunch of them. I'll be driving one this summer. So, what did your dad die of?

–A stroke, I guess.

–You don't know?

–Don't know for sure. He went to town one day. Never came home. Just dropped.

–I often wonder how I'd react if my old man popped off like that.

He snapped his fingers.

–What do you think, Byron?

–I think it's different for everybody.

–Where did it happen? The accident. When your mother . . .

–Over there. There used to be a barn.

–Where did the barn go?

–It burned down, not long after.

–So, she ran over you, your mom, where there used to be a barn.

–Right.

–Ran over you with what? You've never said.

–A snowmobile.

–A what?

–A Ski-Doo. Okay?

–Like. How?

–Like, she just did.

–And the barn burned down, just like that?

–We don't talk about it.

–I hear you.

We walked around the boat. There was still hard, crusty snow beneath the keel and the hull was marked and battered where the traps come bumping up out of the water over the side.

–So you and your mom go out together, fishing on that thing?

–We do.

–Cool, he said.

–There's a lot of work every spring, just getting it ready for the water. Scraping and painting. Repairing traps. We'll be at that soon.

–Just you and your mom.

–Just us.

–*No shit.*

Allan set me up with my first "educational" drug experience, as he called it. The beginning of the road to dissipation, I told him. Luckily for me, it was a short road. I'd had enough of drugs. In my case, painkillers, but they're all the same. He said he understood. Whatever turns you on or off, he said. It was just a few weeks after we'd first met, just past the end of the football season.

I think by then Allan had tried them all—pot, coke, meth, LSD, et cetera. He later claimed he once drove a truck all the way from Toronto to Florida stoned on acid. Just experimenting, he assured me.

There had been a fall field trip for the geologists to another country place not far from town and someone in the group discovered mushrooms, the magic kind, growing wild in a farmer's field. The geologist, who was also a football player, kept quiet about it, and one night shortly afterwards Allan went along with him to harvest those mushrooms.

I had qualms. With the drugs I knew, anxiety always cancelled out euphoria. I tried the mushroom. Didn't like it.

–Mushrooms just make me hungry, I told Allan. Make me think of meat. Big, thick, juicy slabs of red meat.

–So what's not to like? he asked, frowning.

–I like to keep my wits about me.

–Exactly. That's where drugs come in.

–Knock yourself out, I said.

I've seen photos of myself before my accident. Happy little face, squinting in the sunshine, a mop of curls. A chubby little torso on two sturdy legs. Mom and Dad looked happy then.

I struggle not to think about all that.

I didn't know the Winter sisters before high school. I didn't really know anybody before high school. After my accident, my parents decided that the world was much too dangerous for me. Even if they had wanted me to go to school, for a long time I spent part of every year in hospitals and rehab. My formal education, such as it was, happened mostly in a hospital or at our kitchen table on the farm.

By the time I got to high school, I was more than ready for the formal academic challenges. But I wasn't ready for the social part of normal life. I had no friends. I had never really spoken to a girl.

I might have seen the sisters on the street in town or at the mall when my mother and I went shopping. I'm sure they'd have noticed me, given I was either on crutches or in a brace or wearing the big shoe. But I had no specific memory of them.

I'd heard the name, Winter. Their dad was in real estate. You'd see his face on roadside signs. Their mom was politically active. But to us country people, the Winters were from another planet, another species.

They seemed so much older than I was, Peggy and her sister, even though we were about the same age. Looking back, all girls seemed wiser and more sophisticated than I was. Even the little ones. To me, the female world was little girls and older women, every one of them a mystery.

The Winter sisters and I ended up in the same English class. It was when we started studying the early nineteenth-century poets, their works and their interesting lives, that Peggy started with the Byron.

She would seek me out on breaks. We'd stroll around the schoolgrounds, or the streets around the school, and we'd talk. She acted like I was just another girlfriend. Though I noticed that, except for her sister, Annie, Peggy didn't seem to have a lot of girlfriends. I think she intimidated other girls. I know that at first she intimidated me.

Then I decided that, way down deep, we were just the same. She was just like me. Or maybe I was like her. Whatever. And it was around then that I started having complicated feelings for Peggy Winter, first the scary things you feel when you like and trust someone a lot but don't know very much about them. Then the longing started—deep and unfamiliar and, I soon realized, unwelcome.

I had expected harassment from the boys, because of all the time I spent with Peggy Winter. Jealousy, perhaps, maybe even bullying, but it never happened. I now owned my father's truck and that alone was status. Everybody seemed to know I drove a fishing boat. Maybe I was lame, but at seventeen I had the shoulders and the biceps and the hands of a lobster fisherman. Which also might have helped.

And then, when we moved on to university, the chemistry between me and Peggy Winter became diluted in a way. I was immersed in studies. She made new friends, found a new social circuit. Strangely, it would be Allan Chase who brought us back together.

Allan seemed fascinated by our boat and persuaded me to take him out at some point that October. It was still football season. The team was doing well, to a large degree because of him. There was lots of admiring talk about the lethal linebacker from Toronto. The day was calm and sunny, but it was cold out on the water. His eyes were runny from the breeze.

I found a secluded bay and shut her down. Let her drift. I had a six-pack, and cracked a couple of beers. He rolled a joint. Lit up, waved it in my direction. I declined.

He puffed, gazing off. Then out of nowhere he asked me why a guy with all of this would bother with university at all. What more could I want when I had everything already?

I told him what my father always used to say: *You can't eat scenery, out here you need the life support called money.*

–Surely there's money to be made with a boat like this, more than you could make catching fish.

–Like how? Taking tourists out for boat rides?

–There's smuggling.

–Smuggling what? Those days are long gone when fishermen were hauling booze around for the rum-runners.

–There's always something people need.

–I guess you should know. What people need mostly gets to them in trucks.

–Lots of what's in trucks comes off the water.

–Not from lobster boats. Unless it's lobsters.

–I hear there's fishermen here on the coast who make lots of money with boats like this. You go out a way and meet a bigger boat. Get a big payday for very little effort.

–Nothing like that around here.

–You could always be the first.

–I wouldn't have the stomach for it.

–Chances of getting caught are lower than zero . . .

–That's not what I hear.

–Look around you. This is the middle of nowhere. A couple of trips and you'd be in clover.

I laughed. Opened two more beers.

–You should think about it, he said.

–I'm thinking about law school, I said.

–Well, okay. The law and crime go hand in hand.

We clinked our bottles. A sudden breeze chased ripples across the water, a dimpled swell was gently rocking us. The sky was darkening.

–We should go in.

I started up. He came and stood by me at the wheel. He had to almost shout over the noise of the engine.

–The secret is to only work with people you can trust. The hard part is finding them.

After we'd tied up, dockside, I cracked the last two beers. He rolled another spliff, still chattering about smuggling. It was a theoretical discussion, I thought. For Allan, consequences were abstractions. For me, they've always been too real.

–What if you get caught? The remote possibility is enough to keep me on the straight and narrow.

–That's because you're a fatalist, Byron.

–I've never seen myself that way.

–I'd bet that growing up here makes everything that hasn't happened yet feel threatening, like you could lose some of this.

–Some of what?

–Paradise.

–I could tell you about paradise.

–Yes, and I'm sure it would be all negative shit, coloured by your fatalism.

–But what *if* we got caught?

–The key is consistency. Truth has a structure, Byron. When people see a consistent structure, they see the truth. A lie has no structure. That's why a lie will always fall apart.

–Man. That's some dope you're smoking.

–The secret is to construct a solid structure for your lie.

–Whoa.

–You say you're going to be a lawyer? You're going to need that insight, my friend. Remember, consistency is the skeleton. The bones of truth and, if you're smart enough, the bones of a successful lie.

4.

I was waiting for Peggy as she emerged from the hotel elevator. She spotted me and waved.

We pecked each other's cheeks. She was nearing sixty and had allowed her auburn hair to reveal subtle streaks of grey. She smelled slightly soapy, like she was still a country girl.

–He was asking where you went, she said.

–I get fidgety in hospitals. I had to get out of there.

–He didn't really expect you to stay.

We both noticed simultaneously that our fingers were still entwined as we walked toward the dining room. By some mutual, unspoken agreement, we found other things for our hands to do. I checked my jacket pocket to make sure I had my wallet and key card. She dug her phone out of her bag and checked for messages.

The place was empty but for us and a single waiter. I gestured toward a table. The waiter nodded. Brought us menus.

–So, you guys must have had quite the night, she said, head cocked to one side, after we were settled.

–Why do you say that?

–He muttered something. About how much Scotch he had . . .

–Oh, I said, my eyes on the menu. I didn't think it was that much.

He'd been sitting silent for a while. He could be like that, one minute all piss and vinegar and jokes, the next sunk in gloom. He'd been talking about Peggy when the brooding started.

He'd just poured another whisky into one of those plastic hotel drinking glasses when his hand involuntarily contracted. The thing cracked and there was whisky running down his forearm, into his sleeve. He licked at his wrist, then drank straight from the bottle. Gasped. Put the bottle down.

–I never met a woman I couldn't disappoint, he said.

–That's extreme, I said, reaching for the bottle.

–Peggy used to think I was queer. Sometimes I think she still does.

–You know her better than I do.

–Don't patronize. I'm just saying . . .

I fetched two fresh plastic glasses, poured for both of us.

–I often wish that I *was* queer.

I stared at the ceiling. I shrugged.

–Life without the women. *Un*-complicated. I'd draw the line at sex, of course.

–So what would be the point?

–There you go, Byron. You're like everybody. It's all about sex.

–Okay. What are we really talking about here?

He was sitting on the side of the bed, leaning forward with his elbows on his knees, rocking slightly.

–Peggy, I suppose. And how I turned out to be such a disappointment to her. You know what, Byron?

–What?

–A woman's disappointment is where her power comes from. You gotta keep an eye on them. All the time.

–Women?

–Peggy in particular.

Peggy was frowning into her wineglass. It was late now, and she seemed weary, wearing down.

–Did you have any forewarning at all? she asked.

Our conversation had gone on and on, avoiding the realities of here and now. Reminiscing about school, the early days, feeling light and optimistic for as long as possible. Avoiding business, mortality. Avoiding Allan. Her question caught me by surprise.

–The doctor was asking, she said.

–What kind of forewarning?

–I'm thinking about the silences and moods over the last couple of years. Maybe it was some condition coming on. Did you have any idea?

–I haven't seen him much in person the last while. We've been doing things by phone and Skype.

–He had an affair, you know.

–What am I supposed to say?

–It was a while ago, with Grace. I don't think you met her, but you might have heard the name.

–The bookkeeper.

–Yes. She worked from home. He'd go over there. We thought it was for work. I'd be amazed if he hadn't told you.

–God no. When was it?

–It doesn't matter. When I found out, he broke it off. She left the company. Then she fucking died.

–She died?

–Yes. The rumour was that she took her own life. Not over Allan, you can be sure. There had to be more to it than that. I knew it wasn't serious as far as Allan was concerned. It was just a fling. He's had more than one, as you probably know.

–I had no idea.

–Boys and flings. Boys and their stiff little peckers. Pathetic girls.

We both laughed.

–I don't believe you ever disappointed anyone, I told Allan the night before.

–Hah. I've never been up to the mark.

He took another swallow.

–My old man had a mistress on the side for years.

–Really?

–He did. Even when he couldn't get it up anymore. That was when I realized there's more to it than . . . you know.

–The physical, you mean.

–Yes. The fuckin physical. Exactly what I mean. But that's where they communicate the disappointment. The physical.

He handed me the bottle. I poured. I pretended to sip.

–That's where Grace was different.

–Grace? Who's Grace?

He ignored me.

–And when *they* think *you* think they're disappointed in you? That's when they've got you by the balls.

I laughed.

–It isn't fuckin funny, man. They become your fuckin mother. *I'm disappointed in you. How could you let me down?* I don't believe you never heard the schtick.

–I think I'll go to bed now.

–No, wait. Did you ever think about the way people use the word "impotent"?

–Not specifically. No.

–I mean power, always associated with the weapon. It makes sense. Theoretically.

–Who calls it a weapon?

–You never heard that?

–I'm trying to think.

–You've led a sheltered life, my friend.

–True enough. I think I'm going to turn in now.

–No. Hang on for a fuckin minute. We don't get to do this very often. So, guess what happens.

–I have no idea.

–Ha. Lucky you. Well, I'll tell you. Guy gets insecure. Guy fucks around. Right? Needs reassurance. You recover a little bit of self-confidence. Then, boom.

I yawned. Could have suppressed it if I'd wanted to. Slapped his knee.

–Wait, he said. And *then* . . . that's when they really got you where they want you. And you know how?

–Too much information, buddy.

–Guilt, my friend. That's the last phase of the campaign.

–Campaign?

–For control. But remember. There is another kind of power. And it lasts longer than your dick.

–And that would be?

–Money, he said.

I stood.

–That's the one important thing I learned from my old man. When all is said and done, money is the only power that matters.

I stretched. Yawned again, this time loudly. I walked into the bathroom, studied myself in the mirror, wishing I had blown some money on my own hotel room.

His stuff was everywhere. He was everywhere. He tried to be invisible. But he was unavoidable, all shoulders and elbows, knee-sprawl. Loud, fantastic proclamations about the world. He was still sitting there when I came out, looking grim. Waiting for me. I mussed his hair.

–Let's pick up where we left off in the morning. The golf course always restores clarity. Real perspective.

–It's morning now. Fuck it.

–Well, I'm off to bed.

–You fuckin think about what I said.

He grabbed the bottle.

–And I'll say something else since we're talking man to man.

I braced myself.

–You're half the problem, my friend.

–Am I now? Which half?

–You know what I'm fuckin talking about.

–I'm afraid I do not.

–She compares me to you, and I don't cut it.

–She doesn't fucking know me.

–Bullshit. She knows you better than I do.

I laughed, grabbed his shoulders, tried to topple him so he'd maybe go to sleep. But he popped back up again.

–Me and Peggy, hah. Good night, Allan.

–Good night, buddy. Don't take any of that the wrong way. We both love you, man. Maybe more than one another.

I turned the light out, but he was still sitting there, hunched over the bottle and his knees, when I drifted off.

Peggy was fidgeting while we were waiting for the elevator. She suddenly seemed uncomfortable with me.

–You believe me, I hope. I knew nothing about this . . . fling.

–I don't know why I brought that up, about poor Grace.

We both stared off into space. The elevator seemed to be stuck on the fourth floor.

I squeezed her elbow. She sighed.

–I'm afraid I made it sound more important than it was. By then, there really wasn't much between us anyway, me and Allan. I shouldn't have begrudged him a little bit of. I dunno. Something on the side. Warmth. Pleasure. Then again, I'm human.

–To be truthful . . .

–The problem, Byron, is when I heard there might be someone else, I couldn't help thinking about me. About it being some kind of judgment about me and my, what. My adequacy.

She laughed, then said, If it ever mattered, it sure as hell doesn't matter now.

The elevator dinged and the door slid open. Inside, she leaned casually against the wall, arms folded, thoughts adrift. I poked the button for my floor.

–You?

–Same floor. There will be talk.

I tried to smile. After what felt like an interminable journey, the elevator stopped. We both stepped out, looking off in opposite directions.

–I often think of our Sunday afternoons, she said then.

–Were there so many?

–On your boat, remember. I think there was a whole summer of Sunday afternoons out on that boat. Sunny Sundays. Warm air and cold water. Nobody else in the world but you and me. What was it called?

–The *Immaculata*.

–The summer of 1980.

–That sounds right.

–Tell me you remember those Sundays.

She had turned to me, eyes boring into my brain, intent on verifying the memory.

I nodded.

–We don't see half enough of each other, you know, she said quietly, then leaned in and kissed me. Softly. On the lips.

–Good night, Peggy, I said, and turned away.

I knew she was watching me walk away and I was terribly conscious of my limp. It isn't such a terrible limp anymore, since the surgeries and rehab. Mostly I forget about it now. But at that moment, on that long hallway trek, her eyes on my limp defined me once again.

My mother never would call me Byron.

–They're only making fun of you, she'd say.

Of course, I knew even then that it was Peggy she disapproved of. Peggy embodied a world she didn't want to think about, perhaps a future she didn't want to face alone.

Before entering my room, I stole a furtive glance back the way I'd come. Peggy was standing at her door, key card in hand. She caught me looking, raised a hand, waved, then busied herself with fitting the electronic card into the furtive slot and turning the reluctant doorknob.

I shoved hard against the heavy door, which felt like the entry to a dungeon. I eased it shut behind me, leaned back against it, exhaled.

I lay on the bed with my clothes on, the room in darkness. I tried to remember the last time I had been with anyone the way I really needed to be with someone at that moment. I realized I had no clear memory of the last time.

I struggled out of bed. Allan's nearly empty Scotch bottle was on the bedside table. I found a coffee mug. Emptied the bottle into it. I've never been much of a drinker. Wine for social lubrication mostly. Hard liquor for despair. A ticket out of an unwelcome moment or a perilous emotion.

It was entirely possible that Peggy was sitting there in the darkness just like I was, sipping an unsatisfying cocktail, craving something normal. I could venture down that hallway with some certainty.

But certainty of what? Of disappointment?

Yes, of course. The inevitable disappointment.

Something I would say to Allan now if he was here: The answer isn't only money. Sometimes it's just common sense, an instinct that kicks in to save us *before* the disappointments happen.

Sometimes it's the probability of disappointment that saves us from ourselves.

5.

That summer, the summer of all the Sundays on the boat, there were, I think, only two Sundays.

It was an odd summer for my part of the Atlantic coast in memory a kind of golden wall of unusual weather, an endless warmth. A long, long sunny day, unbroken. The spring before that summer, Allan had gone home to Toronto with no intention, I'd discover, of coming back to university. He was sick of books and classrooms. He was even sick of football. He decided it was time to get his education elsewhere, out in the real world.

Annie Winter, Peggy's sister, had gone to Boston, where an aunt had offered her a summer job in her high-end accounting practice—an experience that would turn into a career.

Since Peggy took her cues from Annie, who was practical, especially with money, she inevitably became an accountant too, a specialist in the arcane world of taxes—managing the financial interests of mostly honest people before she went to work for Allan.

It was a Saturday afternoon, in late July, I think, or early August, when I ran into her in a liquor store. She saw me first.

–What are you getting?

–Wine for Mom.

–What about Byron?

–What about Byron?

–What does Byron like?

–Byron doesn't drink much. What does Peggy like?

–Peggy also likes a glass of wine.

–Red or white?

–White mostly. Nicely chilled.

–Mom wants red.

–I go by the price, she said, studying the shelf.

–Mom wrote down what she wants so I won't get it wrong.

–Let me see.

She took the slip of paper from my hand.

–Right.

She reached for a bottle and handed it to me, folded her arms and strolled away. I followed.

–Man, will I be glad when summer's over. This place is like a graveyard. I can hardly wait for September. What happened with your friend, the football player? I heard he's going to skip a year.

–Not only that—he isn't coming back, I said.

She turned, eyes wide.

–Really.

–He's done, I said.

–Wow. I thought he lived for football.

–Nope. Done with that. And books.

–And you?

–Same old.

We separated to scan different aisles. Met at an intersection.

–What have you been doing all summer? she asked.

–Working around the farm. Fished until the end of June. It was a good season.

–Right. I forgot. You fish. You have a boat.

–Yes ma'am.

–I think I saw your boat once. Down at the harbour. Someone was telling me about this young guy and his mother, fishing. That would have had to be you? Yes?

–Probably.

–Like, you go out together on the boat, just you and your mom?

–Yup.

–Boy. I'd like to meet that mother of yours.

–I'm sure you will, someday.

She raised her eyebrows. I could feel the familiar awkwardness return.

I love the look of fishing boats, Peggy said.

–Really? You like the water?

–Of course. You could take me out sometime, on your boat. If you were nice.

–I could.

That first Sunday dawned warm and still and pink. By mid-morning it was hot and there was a breeze stirring, but I knew it would die down. By two o'clock it did.

I expected her to arrive with at least part of her crowd, but she was at the wharf ahead of me, alone, leaning against the fender of a car, staring out over the water through large sunglasses.

She was wearing a ball cap, red shorts, sandals, a black halter top with a white sweater draped over her shoulders, the arms of the sweater hanging down her front.

When she noticed me, she grabbed a bag from the back seat of the car and climbed aboard. I followed her. Started up the engine with a sudden roar, like from a dump truck. I could see that she was laughing, her hands against her cheeks like a child.

–Can you get the ropes, I shouted.

And I watched as she scrambled back up to the wharf and released the stern line then untied the bow, coiled the rope and tossed it on, then clambered down again, passing close enough that I could smell her sunblock.

We left the harbour slowly. She was looking back, watching the wake as it foamed and sparkled, spreading out behind like lace on the flat black sea. I could tell that she was still smiling.

When we were about two miles offshore, I set the autopilot so we could just idle along. I left the wheel, walked back to where she was standing with her arms folded.

–You're okay?

–Perfect, she said.

–There's a little cove I go to, and just drift there.

She nodded rapidly.

–Yes?

I cut the engine and the silence settled all around us. A soft breeze now rippled the dark water. The blinding sun. An eagle high on an ancient, balding pine. Half a dozen gulls came flapping by, anticipating food, then flew off, squawking disappointment.

–Beautiful, she said.

She was peering over the side, hands on the washboard.

–You could swim here, she said.

–I'm not much for swimming.

–Really?

She picked up the bag she'd brought and fished out a bottle.

–Red, she said, and showed me.

–I thought you were into white.

–I assumed you shared your mom's taste in wine.

–I'll drink anything, I said.

–I bet.

A seal surfaced nearby, his round black head glinting as he stared at us. Then he twitched and vanished with an almost soundless splash.

–Fishermen hate those things, she said.

–You know a lot of fishermen?

–My uncle, she said.

–Ah.

–He keeps a rifle on the boat. Blames the seals for eating all the codfish. What do you think?

–I think people are eating all the codfish.

–Right on, she said.

We were relaxed in canvas lawn chairs, sipping the wine. She'd brought some cheese and crackers. Some fruit. We chatted about school. That's when she told me she had switched from arts to commerce.

–We're going to both be accountants, me and Annie. Maybe open our own business.

–Here in town?

–God no.

It would be somewhere large and interesting. Somewhere far away. But she'd be back for sure someday, once she and Annie made their fortunes.

–I can't imagine living without this for very long, she said.

–This? I said.

–Yes, this.

She leaned forward, gesturing toward the sea, the sky.

–You know what I mean, she said, and sat back.

–Yes.

–Do you think you'll go away? she asked.

–I would have to have a pretty good reason.

–Interesting, she said.

–How so?

–For me there would have to be a reason *not* to go away. Nothing ever happens here.

–Nothing happening isn't necessarily a bad thing, I said.

–Maybe when we're old.

The wine was nearly gone. She closed her eyes and I thought soon that she was dozing. But then she sat up, alert again, and peered down into the water.

–I feel like swimming. Do you mind?

–Not a bit.

–I didn't bring anything to wear.

I shrugged.

She climbed up on the washboard and wriggled out of her shorts. Dropped them, turned to look at me. She was wearing tiny underwear.

–Don't mind me, she said, and struggled out of her top. She was wearing nothing under it. She jumped into the water, screaming.

I stood and went to look. Just to be sure that she was okay.

She was floating on her back, her white flesh shimmering. Her breasts bobbed, buoyant in the water, small brown nipples staring back at me.

–How can you resist? she shouted.

–Someone has to stay with the boat.

–You don't know what you're missing.

And then she flopped over and quickly duck-dived, and I was transfixed as her legs and feet slipped out of sight. For what seemed like minutes, she was gone. Then she surfaced far off, swimming backwards, hair swept back, face luminous in sunshine.

She was alone in her afternoon, free there in the vastness of the elements, as natural to her as if she were a seal.

I returned to my glass of wine, still only half-finished, sat in the lawn chair and wondered about the peculiar clash of hopelessness and longing I was feeling.

Stop this, I instructed. The sun was hovering near the western horizon. Expanding shadows cooled the air.

There was a homemade ladder on board, designed for climbing in and out when the boat was high and dry at home. I got up and set it in place. I scanned the surface of the little cove, but she was nowhere to be seen. I felt a flutter of anxiety, but then I spotted her sitting on the shore, knees drawn up, chin resting on a kneecap, one hand shielding her eyes. I followed her sightline and there was another boat in the distance. We both watched it growing smaller.

I looked away, sat. Stood again. Restless suddenly. Moved my chair out of a shadow, back into sunshine. I felt sad and wondered why. Was it her comfortable solitude—as if I wasn't there at all?

There was a little breeze. I could hear water gently slapping at the boat. Then I heard her calling.

–Hey, are you still there?

She was somewhere near the boat.

–There's a beach towel in my bag. Can you get it for me?

I retrieved it, and there she was at the foot of the ladder, looking up at me.

–Hold up the towel till I can't see your face.

I lifted the towel.

–Higher. No peeking.

I raised the towel, and then I could hear the ladder bumping as she clambered back on board, feel her cold hands on mine as she grabbed the towel.

–Okay. You can look now.

I looked. She was swaddled in the towel, water streaming from her hair. It was a face like I had never seen before, a completely naked face.

–Man, you missed out. Can we do this again someday?

–Next Sunday?

–Could we really?

–Weather permitting, I said.

6.

Allan was in the hospital for four days. They moved a cot into his room for Peggy on day two.

I'm going to stay with him, she said at breakfast.

—They allow that for adults?

—They prefer that, she said. Makes it easier for the nurses, having someone in the room full-time.

—If you can think of any reason why I should be there, just let me know, I said.

—Don't worry about it, she said. And, by the way, Annie's coming down to spend the day. Aren't you glad that we behaved ourselves last night?

She patted my cheek and walked away, laughing.

I saw Annie before she noticed me. I was on my way back to my room after taking a morning walk. She was at the front desk, talking to the receptionist. I watched her until she turned and saw me.

—If you're checking in, you don't really need your own room, I said.

She cocked her head to one side and raised an eyebrow.

–I'm only here for the day, dear. I was just checking messages for Peggy.

We sat down for coffee. I find small talk awkward with Annie, whose every word and every gesture has a purpose behind it.

–Peggy is handling it well, I said.

–I'm not worried about Peggy. I'm more worried about you.

–Me?

–Yes, you. The way Allan has structured everything, this could get messy. If this is as bad as it could be, you're going to be busy.

–I don't think it's that bad, I said.

She sipped her coffee, stared into space for a while. Sighed.

–Ever since your call, I've been thinking we don't really know very much about Allan, do we.

–I've known him almost all my life, I said.

–Well, we've all known one another almost all our lives. But how much do we really know? How well does anyone know anybody?

–You know his finances. That should be enough for now.

She put her cup down and stood.

–Take care of yourself, Byron, we can't afford to lose you both.

Two days later, I went to pick Peggy and Allan up at the hospital, as promised. They were outside when I got there, both of them obviously impatient, waiting at a distance from a little knot of patients who were leaning on IV poles in their dressing gowns, sweats and johnny shirts, chattering and smoking cigarettes.

Allan was parked in a wheelchair, while Peggy alternately paced and stopped to fuss with his clothes.

I saw him brush her hand away as I came out of the parking lot.

–For fuck sake, he said. And then, to me as I got close enough, Help me up.

He tried to stand with me on one side and Peggy on the other, but the wheelchair kept getting in the way.

–Why don't you just stay sitting until Byron brings the car around, Peggy said.

He didn't answer, just hauled on us until he was standing and gave the wheelchair an angry shove.

–Look at that asshole, with the oxygen and the ci-cigarette, he said, staring at the patients and shaking his head.

His right hand was folded limply by his side and the right side of his face had the expression of someone who wasn't quite awake yet. He was unshaven and his hair was tousled. His speech was clearer, though halting.

–You have my . . . clubs?

–Yes, I have your clubs.

He grunted and began moving toward my car, leaning heavily, his right foot dragging not unlike the way my own once did.

We settled him in the front seat of the car and did up his seatbelt as he struggled to find a comfortable position.

–You're looking good, I said. He didn't answer.

Peggy got into the back seat and I put the car in gear.

–All set?

–Just drive, he said.

–Airport, here we come.

–I can hardly wait.

As we passed the golf course forty minutes later, he remained silent, staring straight ahead. But I knew what he was thinking. The one true passion in his life now finished.

–There's a place just ahead where we could get some coffee, I suggested.

Peggy spoke up sleepily from the back seat.

–We should try to avoid the coffee. It's a diuretic. Not so good just now.

Of course. The inconvenient bathroom, a looming factor in his future life. Needing help with toilets, dignity diminishing with every call from nature.

The airport was frantic, people arriving, people departing, drivers attempting to steal a few illegal minutes in the drop-off zone, traffic cops busy hustling them away. I pulled into a space reserved for the handicapped, and in a flash there was a woman in a yellow vest at the window on Allan's side.

He rolled the window down.

–Buzz off, he said before she had a chance to speak.

I clambered out as quickly as I could.

–We need a wheelchair, I said across the roof of the car.

Peggy was now out, heading for the terminal entrance.

The traffic enforcer had a walkie-talkie in her hand, and looked me up and down as I approached.

–You need a wheelchair?

–It's for him, I said, nodding toward Allan, who was red-faced, struggling with the car door.

–You got five minutes, she said, and walked away.

Allan had lifted his right foot out but was having trouble with the other one.

–Where the fuck is Peggy?

–She went inside to get a wheelchair. Take it easy.

–I don't need a wheelchair.

–Probably not. But let's just play along with this for Peggy's sake. Okay?

–This is fucking. Weird. Man.

I saw Peggy then, pushing the wheelchair through the crowd.

Driving home, I replayed the scene of their departure. Allan in his wheelchair, Peggy hovering, solicitous, a slight edge of resentment in every movement.

Peggy had hugged me hard before they headed toward security.

–I wish you were coming with us.

–You'll be fine. I'll be up to check on things before you know it. We have a lot of business to deal with.

She released me, then stepped back, chewing the inside of her lip.

–Yes. Business.

–I had a brief chat with Annie. I told her we'll have to make some changes.

–There will be a lot of changes.

–Yes. Change can be good.

She raised her eyebrows. Smiled. Then she turned and started wheeling Allan toward an elevator.

All the way home I replayed her words, the tone of her voice. *There will be a lot of changes.* I have always been like this with Peggy, trying to read the meaning in her words. To me, reading Peggy Winter has always been like reading poetry.

7

On the second summer Sunday, there was more sunshine and another cloudless sky, but a slight cooling breeze. And another bottle of wine.

–Have you ever had a girlfriend? she asked.

–No.

She smiled and gazed off into the distance.

–I figured.

I could feel the heat in my face.

–Oh? It's so obvious?

–You're very serious about everything, Byron.

–Girlfriends can be serious, I said.

–When we're older.

We were sitting side by side on the back of the boat, sipping the wine from plastic glasses.

–I plan to get serious when I'm thirty, she said.

–Why bother then?

–It's important to be serious when you're old.

–So maybe I'll get a girlfriend when I'm thirty.

–What's wrong with now?

–I wouldn't know what to do with a girlfriend.

–Well, that's good, she said, and grabbed my hand and squeezed it.

–If you ask me, too many boys think they know what to do with a girlfriend when they haven't got a clue.

–I guess you've had a few. Boyfriends.

–Don't get me started.

She stood.

–I'm going swimming. You?

–I don't think so.

–You don't mind if I . . .

She gyrated slightly, the motions of undressing.

–I don't mind, I said.

She turned her back, shimmied out of everything, hopped up on the washboard and vanished with a shriek.

I sat there sipping on the wine, wondering: What is normal? How can I not know?

I looked around me. The little pile of clothing on the deck. The wicker bag where I knew there would be a towel and who-knows-what-else.

She trusts me, I thought. Or maybe she just thinks I'm harmless. She could be right on both counts. She trusts me because I'm nothing. The thought was suffocating.

Why can't I be normal?

Normal would be naked in the water with her. Normal would be reckless.

I imagined I could hear the rumble of the engine, the belching water from the wet exhaust. The silent boat was rocking gently.

I felt a sudden chill, and when I tried to move, one leg was paralyzed. Then I thought I heard the bump of traps against the hull. I looked to where my mother always stood, but of course there was no one there. It was just the ladder moving with the swell.

Another bump against the hull. Then Peggy, slowly rising into view.

–I'll get the towel.

–Never mind.

She leaned back against the cab door, hands on her hips, closing her eyes as she tilted her face toward the sun. I accepted the implied permission to stare at her. I longed to touch her. I longed to taste the salty water that was running from her hair into her eye sockets, into the hollows between her shoulders and her breastbone. Between her breasts. I looked away. I looked around. We were alone. We were not alone. There was silence, but there was the whispering of wind, the hollow thump of water on the hull.

Alone. Not alone. Invisible but under observation. Scrawny evergreens on shore shimmering in the heat, oozing spicy fragrances.

My mouth was dry. I sipped my wine, warm as spit.

–Hand me my towel, she said at last.

I pulled it from the bag. I felt chilled. I felt hot.

Then she had the towel but was using it to fluff her hair, head to one side.

–There's nothing like the feeling of the hot sun on cold skin, she said.

I swallowed hard. Nodded. She grinned and ran her fingers through her hair, shook it loose.

–Maybe *almost* nothing.

–Whatever you say, I said.

–I was just thinking, if we were in a movie, I guess this would be the sex scene.

–I suppose it is, in a weird way, I said.

She stopped fluffing, stared hard at me for a moment, then she giggled.

–Very weird.

–I didn't mean . . .

–It doesn't matter what you meant. Why won't you come swimming with me?

–I can't . . .

–Swim? Okay, I believe that. How come so many fishermen can't swim?

–I don't know.

–I'll teach you, she said.

–It's a deal. Boat rides in exchange for swimming lessons.

–Shake on it, she said, reaching out. Her hand was cold, her face was radiant.

–You're on, I said, feeling a bolt of panic.

I turned away, stared off toward the shore. An onshore breeze was now rising and the waves were dashing lightly against the rocks. The boat would soon be perilously near those rocks. If I was normal, I'd remove my clothes. But then what?

I needed to start the engine and back out a bit, to deeper water. But that would also be a statement.

–Where did you go? Peggy asked.

–Nowhere. I'm right here.

–I embarrassed you. I'm sorry.

–No, you didn't. Not at all. I just . . .

–You just nothing, she said.

–No. Yes. I'm thinking you don't think I'm normal.

I turned to face her. She was now wrapped in the towel.

–Shut up, she said, but she was smiling.

–You don't understand, I said.

–You're the one who doesn't understand. Normal isn't everything it's cracked up to be. Feeling safe is what's important. I feel safe with you.

We fell silent. Feeling safe, she needed nothing more from me.

When I was home, Mom asked, So what have you been up to?

–Took the boat out, down along the shore. Peggy Winter came along. She's into boats. She was curious about you and me fishing.

–Peggy Winter.

–Yes.

–The Winter girls. I hear they're quite . . . vivacious.

She was sitting at the kitchen table, the seat of her authority. Teacher, skipper, mom. Inquisitor. I remained quiet, and after a long time, she sighed.

–I'm sure she's lovely. Oh, yes, your friend Allan called and wants you to call him back. He told me he's done with higher education.

–So he says.

–You knew this? That he was dropping out?

–I figured.

I turned to leave the room, but she stopped me with a gentle hand.

–Don't go getting any bright ideas.

59

8.

Allan wanted me to visit. Time to get a look at the Big City, he said. He had a feeling in his gut that I had Big City lurking somewhere in my future.

–That's a reach, me in the Big City, I said.

–So, are you coming up or what?

–I don't think so. I really can't afford it. I've been saving up for law school.

–Never mind that. The trip'll be on me. I'm earning money now. Rolling in it.

–Doing what?

–I'll tell you when I see you. You can stay with me for as long as you want.

–What about your folks?

–No need to bother them. I've got my own place now.

Allan was tanned and lean, taller than almost everybody at Arrivals. And he looked glamorous in his sunglasses and sandals, a white linen shirt hanging out over jeans, like someone out of the movies.

I can imagine I appeared lost and overwhelmed. He

shook my hand, grabbed my little suitcase. The handshake was surprising, grown-up, businesslike.

–Follow me, he said.

His car was a 1959 Impala, he informed me. I vaguely recognized the grinning snout, the bat wings.

–Whoa, I said.

The spiral ramp down from where he'd parked seemed to go round and round forever. And then we were outside in brilliant sunshine and cars were rushing all around at shocking speeds, and the vast highways were merging and dividing and running off on ramps in all directions.

I rolled down the car window and the wind rushed in, tearing at me, filling the car with the gassy city air. I wanted to ask him to slow down but knew, of course, that survival required keeping up with everyone around us in the hurtling trucks and cars and buses.

–What's our plan? I asked.

–No plan. Play everything by ear. Maybe Ontario Place for a concert. I hear Kenny Rogers is in town.

And then we were heading through a maze of busy side streets into a neighbourhood with signs in Chinese.

–Kensington Market, he said.

–There used to be a television show.

–This is the place. I own a house here.

–You. Own. A house.

–Everyone should own a house. And what are *you* talking about? You own a fucking farm. And a giant boat. Any fixed asset is an investment.

–An investment.

–All right. A place to hide your money.

–So you have money to hide.

–I'm working on it.

We turned into a quiet street and he pulled over, then pointed at a long row of identical houses, all painted different colours.

–That's it. What do you think?

–Which one?

–Number twelve. The red one.

The front door was green. The concrete doorstep was cracked and tilting. Dried-out weeds grew up along the front.

–It's old, he said, dangling a bunch of keys. I'm not sure how old. But you can tell by the quality of the work. The little details. They don't make them like this anymore.

He led me inside. From the musty smell of it, the stained carpeting was damp. There were odours from past lives, stale cigarette smoke, cooking oil, a vague whiff of cat piss. The basement was full of cobwebs and junk left behind by former occupants. I counted three old stoves, two dead refrigerators. A laundry tub, black scab scaling off its enamel. I swatted cobwebs off my face.

–A fixer-upper, Allan said.

–Excellent. You did okay.

He showed me to a small room upstairs, pointed to an unmade bed, left briefly. He came back with a sleeping bag and tossed it in.

–Your quarters, he said with a sweeping gesture.

I retrieved the sleeping bag from the floor, brushed the dust off, placed it on the bed.

–You tired?

–Not a bit.
–Then let's go out.

The weather was astonishing. Blue skies filled the gaps between tall buildings. The clot of traffic and the frequent, startling screams of police cars, fire trucks, ambulances. The racket of perpetual excitement.

I was thinking: I could get used to this. There was hustle, but there were also hordes of people just ambling along, chattering and smiling. People on perpetual vacation by the look of them. Guys wearing muscle shirts and shorts and flip flops. Girls leaving nothing to the imagination.

Allan was walking slowly, for my benefit.

–What do you think of the Big City so far? he asked.

–It could grow on me.

The sidewalks in the market were jammed with produce. Great bins full of fruit and vegetables. Hanging carcasses in shop windows. Golden chickens shimmering on turning spits. No way could anybody buy and consume all this.

–I can't imagine all this stuff getting used, I said.

He laughed, and said something about the land of plenty. I thought of waste. I thought of Mom and her refusal to throw anything away, reminding me of all the starving people in the world. If she could see this, man, she'd have a fit.

Allan only laughed again.

I also noticed cooking odours everywhere. Perpetual dinnertime, by the smell of it. Everywhere you turned, a restaurant or bar or tavern. Just walking through the streets made me hungry, tired and thirsty all at once.

–You're probably starved, Allan said after we'd been walking for at least an hour.

Allan obviously didn't eat at home. A minimal amount of cookware in his kitchen. Milk and beer, cheese and pepperoni in the fridge. Wilted lettuce. A plastic bag full of what looked like marijuana buds. Cupboards conspicuously bare, except for breakfast cereal. I thought of home: pantry like a grocery store; cupboards crammed with dishes; deep drawers stuffed with pots; pans dangling from hooks.

–You must eat out a lot, I said.

–My treat, he said.

We were in a little bistro, drinking beer and eating pizza.

–It doesn't look like you plan to come back any time soon, I ventured.

–Back where?

–School.

He snorted.

–Get real.

–So, when exactly did you decide?

–Decide what?

–To drop out.

–Actually, I didn't drop out of anything. I see it as dropping in. Dropping into reality.

–I thought science was about reality.

–Not my kind of reality.

–So why didn't you just switch to arts or commerce?

–Actually, I switched to the Arts of Making It.

–Making what?

–A life, okay?

He was staring at me hard.

–It's the eighties, man. The seventies were for fun. The eighties are for business.

He looked away, resumed chewing. A late afternoon crowd had gathered in the pub, their babble blending with the music. A song came on that I remembered from the seventies. I can still hear it. *Teach your parents well . . . their children's hell will slowly . . .*

Allan had drifted off, and I wanted to haul him back.

–So, the eighties are for business. What's beyond the eighties?

–The harvest, he said.

–The harvest?

–In the year 2000, I turn forty. I plan to be on cruise control by then.

After about two silent minutes, he laughed.

–Look at them, he said.

I looked around, but I saw nothing but people who seemed happy in the moment.

–The herd, Allan said. He pushed his plate away, lit a cigarette. Frowned briefly in the smoke then looked at me.

–Let's get out of here. I have a little job to do. You can come with me if you want to. Or you can find your way back to the house and crash for a while.

–I'll tag along, I said.

Soon we were back in the car, humming along on the expressway. Allan still seemed lost in thought and I was starting to regret coming with him.

Off to our left I saw the glittering lake, a white forest of sails billowing, bicycles skimming along a narrow trail beside the shore that could have been an ocean.

–That place there, he said, pointing.

It looked like a hotel.

–Mafia, he said.

I laughed.

–Mafia?

–Of course. They're everywhere.

–You know people in the Mafia?

–Ohho-noooo. Not personally. Not me, man.

–So, what do they do there, in a hotel?

–They don't go near the place. They just own it and pay people to run it. That's the thing about having money. You have to keep it somewhere safe.

–What about banks?

–For some folks, banks are anything but safe. Unless you own the bank. Property. That's the ticket.

Then we were on another ramp and on another street that ran parallel to the freeway.

–Speaking of Mafia, you're about to see part of my dad's empire, Allan announced.

–Am I going to meet him?

–Probably not. I work for him, but we don't have a lot of contact.

–His empire is what? Remind me.

–Trucking. Long haul.

He wheeled into the back entrance to a large complex of warehouses, tractor-trailers backed up to yawning doorways, forklifts flitting.

–Where are we?

–Ontario Food Terminal, he said.

–So what's the Mafia got to do with this place?

–You do not want to know.

He stopped, backed into a loading dock near a large semi-trailer.

–Wait here.

Then he was out of the car, trotting up a stairway onto a platform, where he disappeared through a wide-open doorway. I felt weary. Overstimulation, I was thinking. All the new impressions.

Maybe I dozed briefly.

When Allan opened the car door, he was carrying a green garbage bag, which he threw over the seat, into the back.

–What's in the bag? I asked.

–Laundry, he said, and laughed.

Laundry, I said.

–Drivers drop it here. I pick it up.

–You do laundry?

–Laundry? Not me. I deliver. One of my many little services.

He turned onto the street that would take us back to the freeway. And then there was another ramp to yet another freeway, this one heading north. Allan kept checking his rear-view mirror. Soon I could see airplanes drifting down to earth through pink smog. The airport was somewhere near. He lit a cigarette and shoved a cassette into the car stereo. Music blared.

–What do you think?

–Great, I said.

–The Clash, he said.

–Ah, the Clash.

–You never heard of them?

–Of course I've heard of them, I lied.

He was pounding out the beat on the steering wheel.

–Cost me as much as the car, having that sound system installed.

He cranked it up.

I lost track of all the ramps and sudden changes in direction. I knew we were still driving north because I could see the sun sinking on the left, a great red fireball on the horizon. And then we were on more side streets, darkened by tall buildings. He parked and we sat for a minute or two in shadows that were lengthening around us. He smoked another cigarette. Like he was killing time. He checked his watch. He gestured with the cigarette package.

–You've never been tempted?

–No, I said.

–I started when I was fourteen. Everybody smoked. There was none of this talk about your health. Anyway, I don't plan to be around long enough for it to matter.

I laughed.

–Really. By the time we're forty, there's nothing left anyway.

–After the harvest, I said.

–Ah. The harvest. That makes all the difference.

He seemed distracted, watching something in the rearview mirror. I turned my head, looked behind. There was nothing there.

–Are we waiting for someone?

He didn't answer, just leaned forward and looked upwards. There were maybe half a dozen high-rise buildings clustered around us. There were balconies. Plastic chairs and kids' toys. I could see what looked like a car seat. Blankets and sleeping bags and clothing draped over railings. No people.

–What's this place? I asked.

–Apartments. Imagine living in a dump like this.

He coughed slightly.

–I'd rather be fucking dead.

He nodded agreement with himself then ground the cigarette to nothing in the ashtray.

–Let's go.

He opened the car door.

–Where?

–This is the guy who takes care of the laundry.

–It doesn't look like a laundry.

–Well, that's how the less fortunate get by. Jobs on the side. He's well paid for it.

He hauled the garbage bag out of the back seat. Locked the car doors. We entered a lobby that smelled like boiled cabbage where a couple of black guys lounged, watching us.

–Hey, said Allan, smiling.

–Hey, my man. One walked toward us, clasped Allan's hand. There was lots of wringing hand business, nudging, laughing.

–Guys you know? I said as we walked to the elevator.

–Just guys I see around.

We rode up twenty floors. I felt my ears pop. We emerged in a noisy hallway, loud music, a baby screaming, angry voices and more steamy cooking smells.

Allan strode ahead of me, garbage bag under his arm. When he stopped in front of a door, he turned to me before he knocked and leaned close.

–When we're inside, you stand by the door with your hand in your pocket and don't say anything. Okay?

–I guess so. Why?

–I never know who's going to be here.

He rapped lightly. There was the sound of a deadbolt and the door opened slightly. Then a chain sliding.

A very thin guy with a ponytail hanging out the back of a ball cap cracked the door about eight inches wide and stared at me for what felt like a long time.

–He's okay, said Allan.

We followed the ponytail into a living room. He was wearing a Blue Jays sweatshirt and baggy sweatpants. There were two women on a sofa, watching television. Above them hung a lurid picture of a doe and a speckled faun by a pond, a sunset in the distance. They were staring at something. A hunter maybe.

One of the women was leaning back into the corner of the couch, legs tucked underneath her, leaning her head on a hand.

The other, who seemed a lot younger, was applying blue polish to her toenails. Neither acknowledged me or Allan. I stayed near the door as I'd been instructed. Right hand in my pocket.

–Who's this? asked the guy with the ponytail, nodding toward me.

–East coast buddy, Allan said, and handed him the garbage bag.

I shrugged. Said nothing.

–Where on the east coast?

–Nova Scotia, Allan said.

–Nova Scotia, the guy repeated.

–We're in a bit of a rush, said Allan.

The guy carried the bag toward a recliner and sat, dropping the bag at his feet. Sized me up and down.

–Buddy got no tongue?

–Tell him, Byron, Allan said.

–Country place. You never heard of it, I said.

–Why is it important? Allan asked the guy.

–Just bein' friendly. Always like to know who's in my house. An east coast thing. Right? You should know. Didn't you go to college there or something?

Ponytail stood then and walked toward me. He was a bit taller than me. He reached out. I removed my hand from my pocket and he grasped it, squeezing hard, kind of drawing me toward him.

–Byron, is it?

–Yes.

He released my hand.

–Name's Mike, he said.

–Good to meet you, Mike, I said.

–There you go. East coast formalities completed.

–Where on the east coast? I asked.

Allan chuckled, then rolled his eyes.

–Is this important?

–St. John's, the guy said.

–*SinJans*, said Allan, mimicking.

Mike left the room. Allan turned toward the women.

–You guys from *SinJans* too?

–We're from here, but our folks came from there, said the younger one, leaning down, blowing on her toenails.

Mike returned with a large brown envelope. Allan held out his hand.

–First things first, said Mike. And he upended the garbage bag.

I'd guess at least twenty-five large, bulging zip-lock bags flopped out on the floor. Allan looked at me, stricken, and his face flushed red.

–Jesus Christ, Mike.

Mike picked up a bag, fondled it and opened it, sniffed.

–Nice, he said, then handed Allan the package.

–You didn't have to fucking do that. Allan was furious.

–Whaa? said Mike.

–Wicked laundry, I said when we were back in the car, Allan driving fast down the freeway toward the city centre.

–You weren't supposed to see that. The fucker has no common sense.

–You worried I'm going to tell somebody?

–No.

A sign said *Gardiner Expressway*. Sunset glittered on the looming skyline. Sailboats stood almost stationary on the lake, leaning north, away from the soft south wind.

–However, if you were ever asked, I don't think you've ever been a good liar, Byron.

–So who's going to ask me?

He ignored the question.

Next he took me to a tavern. It was dark, an all-male place. Couple of guys noisily playing shuffleboard. Allan was in a funk, crowding our small table with sprawling elbows, hulking shoulders, peeling the label off a sweaty beer bottle.

–That was so fucking not cool.

–What?

–What happened in that shithole of an apartment. I have a good mind to . . .

–To what? Replace your laundry guy?

He stared at me. His expression was unfamiliar. Cold. Then he smiled.

–Is that what you'd do? Replace the dick-brain?

–Just making small talk, I said.

–But you've got the right instinct.

He sat back, drank. Waved at the waiter, held up two fingers.

–So, what's this bullshit all about? I asked.

–Need to know, Byron. We should only know what we need to know.

–What do I need to know?

–I guess the truth, man. But only because we go back. I trust you, okay?

–Okay.

–The guy I work for isn't really my dad. He's kind of like my foster dad. It's a complicated thing. I come, I go. I drive trucks for him all over North America. He doesn't give a shit what's on the trucks.

–But you do.

–Ninety-nine percent of it legit.

–And the other one percent?

–Hey, there's a little risk in everything.

–I told you I don't have the stomach . . .

–But that's the life for me. The open road. My own wheels and a wallet full of cash. All I want for now. Okay?

–Crossing the border?

–So?

–That's gotta be tense.

–No sweat. Pop a Valium fifteen minutes before you get to the booth. Calm as calm can be, that's the key. Look at me. Friendly. Preppy.

I looked at him. Close-cropped blond hair. A spray of freckles. Wide-set blue eyes. The ready, all-inclusive smile.

–I hold up the manifest. They see a friendly white guy. They see themselves. Their sons and brothers. They wave me through.

Then he was peeling the bottle again, once again adrift, distant.

–No. That was definitely *not* cool back there. Gonna have to have a word with Mike.

Saturday morning, he drove me back to the airport.

–You should consider moving to Toronto, he said.

–I'm going to law school, man.

–They got law schools here. But why not forget about the law schools for a while?

–It isn't that simple. After dropping out, it isn't always easy to drop back in.

–Sure it is. You make it how you want it. Work here for a while and make some real money. Then go back to school.

–Work in the laundry business.

–You'd always have clean clothes.

His smile was innocent, the smile that always served him well.

–I've got all the money I need, I said.

–But the point is to have *more* than you need. Because you never know how much you're *gonna* need. Life is full of surprises. Money cushions many stumbles.

–So, this is you, then. No more school?

–I'm thinking of heading for the States, man. Centre of the universe is where I want to be. Preferably Florida. I've had enough northern winter to last a lifetime. You could come.

I'm going to law school, remember?

He laughed.

–You'll never be without work. Lawyers live off criminals.

–There are many kinds of law.

–Whatever you decide, I'll be here. Or, better still, down in the Sunshine State.

As I was dragging my bag from the back seat, he said,

–Whatever became of that little Peggy?

–She's around, I said.

–Tell her I said hi. We got some unfinished business, me and Peggy.

He winked.

–Let me help you with the bag, he said as he tried to take it from me.

–Thanks for everything. I can handle it from here. Catch you later, Allan.

–Don't be a stranger, Byron.

Don't be a stranger? Such a common phrase. *Have a nice day! Safe travels! Don't be a stranger!*

Empty words to me, for I have always been a stranger. I was a stranger then, as I am now. In other people's faces I still see puzzlement, perhaps a reflection of my own uncertainty.

What was it that Peggy saw in me? What did Allan see?

Maybe that's what bonded us for life, strangers with nothing more than curiosity in common. What is love but an extreme curiosity, an insatiable craving, to truly know a stranger?

Byron. Annie. Peggy. Allan. Always strangers to each other, always strangers to ourselves. Who are we? Who am I?

9.

The man who lurks in the shadows of my memory was a stranger too, even though I wore his name until Peggy Winter casually replaced it.

–I can't see you as an Angus.

That was how she said it. A declaration.

–From now on, I'm going to call you Byron.

And soon everybody but Mom called me Byron. Maybe Peggy didn't know that the name, Angus, was precious to my mother. He was her only sibling, a constant presence in our lives.

In my memory of Uncle Angus, golden shafts of light and dust are suspended in illuminated air. I remember the musk of domestic animals, dry hay, and sounds that make my stomach churn.

I don't remember the specific violence, but I feel it, as an impenetrable darkness. I feel it now as I have always felt it. Violence leaves the deepest imprint on all the senses. Sound, smell, jumbled images. Indelible.

We were in the barn. He fell down. My uncle Angus fell down hard.

I remember arms flailing to find balance. A man who is struggling to stand, failing, falling down again. Laughing at himself. Or crying.

I remember laughing and crying and confusion. Snot and drool and blood trickling from some impact.

I was only five years old, but it hit me like the punch that felled my uncle, sprawled and helpless, suddenly an empty thing.

He was only trying to be nice to me.

My father stood over him, breathing hard, hands clenched into ugly fists, one fist slightly bleeding, blood smeared on his boot.

He was only trying to be nice.

I remember my uncle Angus struggling to rise, and the crunch of bone as he's knocked back down. And I remember running toward the door, running toward the daylight, the brilliant sunshine glittering on snow.

Running blindly through the door. And the sudden deafening machine. And then I'm the one falling down. The snowmobile was like a living thing, rearing up, then crashing down. I can see my mother's face, blinded by excitement.

I think I remember the feeling of the snow on my face. I didn't feel the weight on top of me. Voices. I remember voices shouting, and adults crying, and how it just went on and on and on. I couldn't feel the leg at all.

Then I heard the fire truck, and I remember looking for the fire, thinking that's why everybody was excited. There must be a fire somewhere. And then someone picked me up, and started running, and I was bouncing in his arms as he stumbled toward the fire truck, then past it, to another vehicle behind, red, just like a fire truck, with flashing lights on top.

I know my father blamed my mother and her brother. My mother blamed herself. But wasn't I the one to blame? Wasn't it all my fault?

He was only trying to be nice.

My father hit my uncle and my uncle fell.

I ran toward the daylight. And I fell. And everybody suddenly was falling down.

Forever.

PART TWO

MALIGNANT COVE

10.

I don't remember when my uncle Angus died. Many years would pass before I'd know the details, the when, the where, the how. I still struggle with the why.

Some of what I now think I know came out in bits and pieces when Annie lived here, in Malignant Cove, with me and Mom. The two of them would talk in low voices at the kitchen sink, or in Mom's bedroom, or strolling in the yard. I'd see them gesturing toward where the barn once stood. Annie was discreet any time I'd ask her what Mom was telling her.

–She imagines things, I warned.

–Have you asked her directly about the accident?

–What would I ask?

–What she remembers. I think there are things she'd like to talk to you about.

–There really isn't all that much I need to know, I said.

–You both were there, she said.

–Yes and no.

–Distant memories come back unexpectedly sometimes. Someday you and your mom will need to put your memories together.

–That's what I'm afraid of. Memories are subjective, Annie. Memories can lead to conflict. Memories cause wars.

–Oh dear, Byron. Then we must never reminisce, you and I.

After watching Allan and Peggy vanish into the airport, I drove home in a fog of memory. In the circumstances, I was glad to see Annie's car parked where it always used to be when she lived here and basically ran the farm, ran my life. The long, slow years of our marriage.

Annie left Malignant Cove when, like her sister, she became absorbed by Allan's enterprises. She moved to town, half an hour away, for the conveniences. It's what I told myself, when she was gone. It wasn't about me. It was about the business.

But though we lived apart, that same business kept us close for more than twenty years.

She was at the stove when I came in, stirring something aromatic.

–Don't mind me, she said.

I poured two drinks without asking if she wanted one. She accepted without comment.

–So, you saw them off.

–I did.

–How was Peggy?

–You spent a day with her at the hospital. You tell me.

She put a lid on the pot she'd been stirring.

–We'll just let that simmer, she said.

She sipped her drink.

–Peggy's going to be okay, she said.

—

We watched the sun go down that evening. It's part of why I've been rooted here for my whole life, days measured out by blazing sunsets. Hot as hell in summer; icy brittle in the winter.

–I miss this, Annie said.

–It's always here, I said.

–I think the time is coming when we'll have to live without it for a while.

–We?

–Surely it's as obvious to you as it is to me.

–Toronto.

It's unavoidable.

–I hope you're wrong.

I wanted to ask her to stay the night, but the answer would have spoiled a quiet moment. The embrace she gave me before she left was genuine.

–You'll be okay here?

–I'm always okay here.

–We have a lot to talk about, you and I. About the future.

–Yes indeed, we do, I said. But we're in reasonably good shape. Right?

–Up to a point. I think we're soon going to have to make a bold assumption.

–Meaning . . .

–The Allan we remember will soon be gone.

Allan wrote occasionally when he first moved to the States. Florida was exactly what he had hoped for. Warmth, basically, year-round. He didn't miss the snow, or maybe just a little bit at Christmastime.

He loved being on the road. He loved the States. Everybody was on the make down there, was how he put it. Buzz. A word I'd never heard before applied to a location other than a beehive or a wasps' nest. He loved the buzz.

–It's the land of milk and honey, especially for lawyers, he wrote.

More than once, while struggling through law school, I remembered how casually I'd dismissed Allan's suggestion that I take time off from my studies to earn some easy money with him. We needed money. But Mom and I decided to sell the boat and fishing gear, and use the money for tuition and living expenses while I'd be in the city studying. I had no more time for fishing anyway. The licence to fish lobsters was worth more than I'd expected. We sold some land, and our few remaining animals, and I also borrowed money.

I moved to the city, came home on weekends. I focused exclusively on my studies. I did well, and in my final year I was recruited by a well-connected city law firm.

At some point Allan wrote that he'd been seeing quite a lot of Peggy Winter, and that she asked him about me all the time.

They'd reconnected in Toronto. The chemistry was obviously clicking this time. He'd tried to persuade her to move down south with him. But she was stubborn. No way was she moving to Florida. Unlike him, she loved the cold. Well-named she was, he wrote. Peggy Winter. She liked Toronto. Didn't like Americans all that much.

She was working for a large real estate developer. Doing great. A crackerjack accountant. Qualifications up the ying-yang. Sharp. As. A. Tack.

Occasionally she'd visit Allan in Fort Lauderdale. We three should arrange a get-together here, he said. For old times' sake.

I'd stopped reading his letter for a moment. I was trying to remember where she was when I'd last thought about her.

At the end of one of his letters, he added a PS: *Get laid. It's fun. You're overdue. It's easy. Really.*

That stung. I put the letter down, then picked it up and reread the line.

Me getting laid? Peggy getting laid? By Allan? By other men besides Allan?

Why did it sting? Eventually I concluded my upset wasn't about them at all. It was about me. I just didn't understand the lives of other people.

I began to pay more attention to the world around me. Even people I thought I knew now mystified me. People are inscrutable surfaces. They are social fabrications, *concealing* private lives that are unknowable to me.

Perhaps it was just as well that my private life was equally unknowable to almost everyone. It was suddenly weird to me that, for one thing, I was a twenty-five-year-old virgin, living mostly with my mom. It seemed unimaginable and, looking back, I suppose it was. Not just the virginity. But my lack of awareness, before that moment, that I was really different—a difference that was only indirectly related to my limp.

I had tried once to be normal, at least as I understood it to be "normal" from overheard high school conversations. I was probably about nineteen. The girl and I had parked somewhere private, a place where, according to the gossip, normalcy was always going on.

A warm summer evening on a hillside from where you could see the glitter of the town, the dark nothingness of the sea beyond, perhaps a slash of moonlight in the distance. A hill on which virginity could die unnoticed.

I was in the midst of trying, but when I seemed to be getting close, the girl whispered in a breathless way, Please. Don't.

I'd been told by someone with experience—maybe it was Allan—that most girls will say *please don't* to satisfy their conscience, and that you had to push past that. But I didn't.

I put the brakes on right away.

–Sorry, I said.

–That's okay.

And then there was a roaring sound.

–What's that?

She'd been fumbling in her purse for her pack of cigarettes, but she was suddenly very still, listening.

The sound grew louder, came closer, seemingly from nowhere. A winter sound, but it was summer. I was confused, clammy with adrenalin.

She straightened up, and moved away from me.

–You don't happen to have matches?

–Aren't you hearing that?

–Yes, she said.

–You can really hear that?

–God yes.

–It sounds like a snowmobile.

–A snowmobile? No, for God's sake, it's—

Bouncing headlights moved quickly, wildly, in our direction. Jesus, I said, and got out of the truck, hobbling toward the lights and the noise. I could see now there was more than one machine, coming straight at me. I stumbled and fell, deafened by the sound. And just before they were on top of me, they spun away. A volley of small stones rattled off the truck.

She came to me where I was sitting on the ground and helped me to my feet.

We stared into the darkness until the noise was gone and there was nothing left to look at but the twinkle in the sky, the distant glow of town. I had a pounding headache.

—Guys on dirt bikes, she said. They come up here all the time. Just to see who's here. I think I know them.

I nodded.

I drove her home. Hugged her in the porch. Interpreted her silence as gratitude. Later, someone told me she was telling people I was strange, that I was cold.

It was the summer just before the summer Sundays on the boat with Peggy.

Mom was surprised when I started coming home from work in Halifax on Friday evenings. Then she came to expect me. I felt normal in Malignant Cove. I felt safer here, in control. There were no social pressures on the farm. And, increasingly, I realized that I was needed here. Mom was getting older and I suppose she really started *feeling* old once we'd given up the farming and fishing. She had been in her late thirties when she married Dad, early forties when I came along. So, she was already well on in her sixties when I became a lawyer.

She now had too much time for looking back. Until then she'd been mostly preoccupied with the here and now, and perhaps a future that still held pleasant possibilities. Now she had only the unalterable past to stew about. I now can see it's where many of her future problems started.

One Friday night, just after I got that letter from Allan, Mom mentioned Peggy for the first time in years.

–I hear that the young one you used to hang around with, that Peggy Winter, she's away in the city somewhere. Halifax, I imagine. You must see her there.

–She's in Toronto.

–I suppose she writes.

–Not to me.

–I was just wondering, is all. I understand her sister came back from Boston some time ago.

–Annie. That makes sense. I've heard she has a business here, in town.

–What kind of business?

–She's an accountant.

–Do tell.

–I don't know her very well, I said.

–They say she and Peggy are complete opposites. You'd never know they were related.

–That could be, I said.

–I'm sure they've turned into lovely people, the both of them.

The senior guys at the law firm kept the high-profile criminal and corporate stuff for themselves and steered the intellectual property and family law in my direction. I seemed to have a way of dealing with the anxieties of ordinary people who find themselves ensnared in legal matters, people pitted against each other, pitted against power. Conflict was my bread and butter.

I think it was Hobbes who once said that conflict always boils down to domination and avoiding death, the two great driving forces in human nature. I could see it everywhere, every day. The way the office worked. The way the city worked. The posturing in courtrooms, bars, in grocery stores, in cars at the stoplights. Everybody gunning engines, positioning themselves to dominate.

Managing conflict is a more than full-time job and I suspected the partners thought that going home for weekends was self-indulgent. But they didn't have the balls to challenge me. Or maybe it was condescension: cut the lame guy a little extra slack. Like it or resent it, it worked for me.

Most of the time I kept my head down, stuck to my own files, and came and went more or less the way I wanted to.

And so I was startled when a senior partner grasped my arm one afternoon, just above the elbow, his way of saying he had something serious to discuss.

–Got a minute?

–Of course.

He followed me into my small enclosure and sat down.

–I have a client coming in half an hour, a fellow from down your way. I'd like for you to sit in.

–Sure.

He stood, smiled.

–You have a way with people. We have high hopes for you.

The client was a middle-aged lawyer, someone I remembered from home—a senior partner in a politically active firm that I had actually considered when I was looking for a place to article. He seemed relaxed, sitting at a long table in a meeting room.

–Byron, I'd like you to meet a friend of mine. Jack, this is Byron. He's from out your way. Jack and I were in law school together. Well before your time, of course.

Jack stood, stuck out his hand. He was physically impressive, tall and lean-jawed, with engaging eyes that instantly invited familiarity.

–Byron, yes. We've followed your career. I hope you're being well treated here.

–Couldn't ask for better, I said.

Jack smiled. I sat down opposite him.

–Jack needs our help clearing up a misunderstanding. I thought this would be a chance for you to spread your wings a bit, Byron.

–I'm always ready for a challenge, I said.

The partner was still standing.

–I'll let you guys chat a bit. Jack, stick your head into my office before you go. Let me know how you want to proceed.

Jack seemed curious about me, asking questions about my experience, what I had studied, who I knew back home, people prominent in business, politics, the law.

I didn't hesitate in telling him I really didn't know anybody of importance, but I was well aware of anyone who mattered.

–You're from out Malignant Cove way, I gather. Your dad was a fisherman?

I confirmed it.

–He's still with us?

–No. Dad passed. More than ten years ago.

–So sorry to hear that.

–Thank you.

–So, here's the thing, Byron. I don't know how much you've had to do with miscarriages of justice. I mean, the media is full of stories nowadays. I just never thought I'd ever be part of one of those stories. But here I am.

I sympathized.

He told me he was facing an array of charges arising from a casual relationship he'd been having with someone he believed to be a consenting female adult.

–I was in a state of personal crisis. You follow?

I followed.

He thought that he was dealing with an adult. He found out she wasn't when they became intimate. He should have stopped it then and there. But he didn't.

–She'd easily have passed for twenty-one at least. Maybe older.

She was actually thirteen.

–She has a couple of crackpot parents. They found out about us and bullied her to get evidence so they could come after me.

–What kind of evidence?

–Photographs.

–You let her take pictures?

–She set me up. She liked playing games. We took pictures of each other.

–Let me guess—with her camera.

He nodded.

–What's your status right now? I asked.

–Charged. Statutory fucking rape.

–How do you think we should proceed?

–Aggressively, for sure. I don't want anything to do with a jury.

–Juries can be persuaded.

–Not with this family. Dad's a professor of sociology. Mom's a pastor of some description.

–We can probably work with the daughter's physical appearance, I said.

–Yes. Nowadays any female over ten years old seems to want to look like a tart.

He shrugged, looked away. He seemed to drift for a moment, then said,

–How old are you, anyway?

–I'm twenty-eight.

He stared at me as if he was seeing me for the first time. He exhaled.

–Well, well. That would be about right.

–What do you mean?

–So, about twenty-two or twenty-three years ago, when I was starting out, I sat in on a trial. Some fisherman from the shore beat the shit out of his brother-in-law. But there was a lot more to it. Ring any bells?

–I'd have been five or six at the time.

I managed a smile, straightened my notepad.

–It's just such a bizarre coincidence, he said. You did have an uncle named Angus? Right?

–Yes.

He nodded.

–I don't want to seem indelicate, but did he not do away with himself, back twenty-some years ago?

–Like I said, I was five or six.

–We never know the whole story. But that never stops people from jumping to conclusions, he said.

–I'll be in touch.

II.

The coffee room at work was also the smoking room before the powers that be banished smoking to the sidewalks. Because of the relentless haze, I only went there when I was desperate for a caffeine hit. The coffee sucked. The smokers didn't give a shit about the quality—a cup of coffee was only an excuse to have a cigarette. But, for me, drinking the office sludge was easier than hobbling outside to where the non-smoking coffee snobs were always going for their special brews. One morning, as I entered the wretched little room, the chatter dropped suddenly to an awkward silence, one word still hanging in mid-air.

Pedophile.

It stopped me in my tracks. When I realized that everybody was staring, I took a deep breath and smiled around. I filled my mug and left.

Later, one of the morning's smokers came by my cubicle. She kept a hard focus on my face, my eyes, as she made small talk. Just before she turned to leave, she said, Look, I hope you didn't take that the wrong way, back there, in the coffee room.

–Not at all, I said.

–I mean, it was and it wasn't about you. But it wasn't what you think.

–And what should I think?

–We're all feeling bad for you, having to defend that bugger. We all think the world of you.

She said that with such enthusiasm it surprised me.

That Saturday evening at home, I decided it was time to ask Mom a direct question.

–What do you remember about when Dad was on trial?

–What?

–Nobody ever told me what it was all about.

–Why are you bringing this up now?

–It came up at work.

–Came up how?

–I can't talk about that, except to say it involved a client. But did the trial have something to do with my uncle Angus?

–For the love of God . . .

–I got asked if I had an uncle Angus.

She stared at me for a moment, her chin trembling.

–Some things are best forgotten.

She got up and left the room, slowly climbed the stairs.

She didn't come back down until it was suppertime, and she stayed silent as we ate, her mind a thousand miles away, it seemed. When we'd finished eating, I told her I'd clear and wash the dishes but that, afterwards, I had to go to town to see a client. A lie, of course.

She made no reply, just headed for the stairs, moving slowly. She didn't say good night.

Driving to town, my thoughts drifted back to Allan's letter three years earlier, and that I had yet to follow his advice. Get laid.

I was indifferent to the challenge but speculated as I drove toward town: What would it be like to have a date? To be conscious that someone, somewhere, was waiting for me? Looking in a mirror maybe, determined to look her best. Or his best. I doubt if it's much different one way or another.

Maybe someday. For now, I just had to get out of the house.

I headed for a quiet lounge that was part of a motel next to a strip mall and the town's liquor store. I went in. Considered the menu briefly. Ordered a drink. And then another drink.

After about three, I admitted: this place is *dead*. Stone. Cold. Dead. I asked myself: What were you expecting? Some kind of city scene? Young professionals draped over each other, chatter loaded with hot insinuation, faces shining in anticipation of late night hookups?

Soft country music hung in the air. I could make out Patsy Cline. Or maybe k.d. lang, who sounded eerily like Patsy. There was one other table occupied by a silent couple, staring off in opposite directions. In the movies, there's a bar where lonely women perch on stools and wait for interesting strangers. At this bar, there was a bartender, back to the room, arms folded, watching a hockey game on television.

What a waste of time this is, I thought. It would probably even be a waste of time if the place was full of people, because they'd all be more or less like me. Kind of lonely. Kind of needy. Kind of bored. I drained my glass.

And then, the door opened and who should arrive on a gust of merry voices but Peggy's sister. Annie. Annie Winter.

She noticed me and waved. I waved back. I paid my bill. I stopped by her table. She was with a young married couple

I recognized and another couple I had never seen before. Annie introduced me, called me a hotshot lawyer from the city. Someone asked how we knew each other. Annie told them she and I went way, way back, all the way to high school. She was all smiles. She didn't look at all like Peggy, I realized.

I was suddenly feeling loose. I made a joke about how wild the town bar scene was. We joked about how we'd managed to become strangers in a little town like this. She told me later that this was a Byron she'd never seen before, never even knew existed.

–We must have coffee sometime, I said as I got up to leave.

–I'd love that, she said.

Driving home, I wondered, Really? It's that simple?

It wasn't as if Annie was a substitute for Peggy. Not at all. They couldn't be more different. But Allan was so right. It was fun.

12.

A few weeks after my first meeting with Jack, his friend, the senior partner, stopped by my cubicle again.

—Come by my office when you have a chance.

I closed the file I'd been reading, which was the Crown's disclosure in Jack's case. It wasn't pretty.

—Close the door, he said.

When I was seated, he came around the desk and sat beside me.

—We've never really talked, he said.

—It's a busy place, I replied.

—Yes. But we should make time for lunch. I need to get your perspective on how this place works. How the *world* works, from the point of view of your generation. You boomers.

I laughed, and said, That would be great.

He stood, hands in pockets, and stepped away to stare briefly out a window.

—These charges against Jack. What's your thinking?

—I think it's a hard case to defend.

—I agree. Where would you focus?

—Obviously, entrapment. Overzealous prosecution. We take the position he thought she was as old as she said she was. When her parents found out, they could have got in touch with Jack and said, "Hey Jack, do you know how old she is?" Jack shits his pants. The end.

–Exactly. But these parents obviously know Jack. They have an agenda. Don't ask me what it was. Maybe they have history with Jack? Some old grudge? Do they want to shake him down? Anyway, once the cops get involved, and then the Crown, our Jack is no friend of Crown prosecutors, the fat is in the fire for Jack.

–The grey area is what Jack knew and when . . .

–Jack says he thought she was old enough to make her own choices. Her parents *know* how old she is. Instead of stopping it, they *assume* he's a pedophile.

–Is he a pedophile?

–What do you think?

I hesitated, then said,

–I guess it doesn't matter what I think. The Crown will make the case that he is a pedophile and a predator. Which is what we'll have to overcome.

–So how do you go about defending an accused pedophile?

–I would emphasize Jack's frame of mind. What he knew and when. What he intended, which was a normal . . .

The partner held up a hand to stop me.

–You attack the accuser, is what you do.

I said nothing. I could feel some unseen peril, looming.

–You go for the accuser's throat, because, in our adversarial system, the accuser is *always* a fucking liar. Would you have a problem with that?

–What makes you think I would?

–Your body language. I'm watching your reactions.

I was about to stand and get out of there, and yes, he read my body language.

–Just stay for a minute. I should tell you Jack called the other day. And we had this exact discussion.

I wasn't able to read his expression. There was a long silence.

–He's been doing some thinking. And he thinks you might be conflicted about his case. Do you have any idea what I'm talking about?

–Not a clue, I said.

–Jack claims that you've been a victim of sexual abuse. You don't have to respond.

–I'm listening.

–So, what do you *think*?

–About what?

He sighed. Maybe I imagined it, but I think he rolled his eyes.

–About your objectivity in a case like this. A lot will hang on the credibility of this female, and we'll have to play hardball.

–I don't know what Jack is driving at. But if he has qualms about me . . .

I looked him in the eye. He stared back. Neither of us blinked.

–I guess you aren't about to answer the elephant-in-the-room question, he said.

–And that would be?

He chuckled.

–You're good at this.

–Thank you.

–So here it is. Have you, at any time, been sexually abused? By anyone?

–My honest answer? I don't know. So I don't know how Jack is sure I was.

–Excuse my French, but how the fuck could you not know? Come on.

I stared at him, unblinking. It surprised me how cold I felt. How outside the moment.

–Frankly, I don't see the relevance, I said at last.

–I disagree. There's like an epidemic of these bullshit sex crimes. Victims are starting to come out of the woodwork everywhere. I need to know where you stand.

As far as I was concerned, there was nothing left to discuss. I stood.

He looked away from me, then said,

–I might have to put someone else on this. I think Jack would be more comfortable.

–Your call.

I left.

All the way to Malignant Cove that Friday evening, I rehearsed my questions.

Mom, what happened just before the accident? Before Dad came along? Before you arrived on the snowmobile?

Now or never. It was important that I know. Finally.

But I never asked. That weekend, it was as if she wasn't there at all. Physically present, physically familiar, but in every other way, she was a stranger. I couldn't ask a stranger.

Soon after that conversation with Jack's friend, my boss, I sensed a change in how I was perceived by the more senior lawyers in the firm. I felt no longer up-and-coming. Maybe down-and-going.

I decided that what I needed was a break, even just a long weekend away. It was early April, and spring was beginning everywhere, it seemed, but here. The wolf months, the old people would call February and March. Once upon a time, it was when the food would be running out, in the forest, in the homes. Wolves, emboldened, skulking around the villages. Now it's just the skulking wolf-winter, hovering and hungry. Then April, the cruellest month.

I said to Annie,

–Allan keeps inviting me to Florida.

–Nice. Why don't you go?

–Would you come with me?

–Who'd look after your mom?

Good question, and now that Annie was part of our lives, she was the one to ask it.

–I think she'd be all right.

Annie was quiet for a while. And then she said,

–Byron, I think you're in denial. Maybe you don't see it. But your mom shouldn't be alone. Ever again.

–Come on.

–I'm serious.

–Okay. I don't really like Florida anyway.

–No, you should go. Go for Easter. I'll look after her.

–Not a chance. I wouldn't have that, Annie. You go to Florida. Maybe coordinate with Peggy. I hear she goes down to visit Allan.

–Byron, do us all a favour. Me, your mom, yourself. Just get out of here for a few days. Just go.

I did.

Florida struck me as an ideal place to kill yourself. There's something ominous in the searing climate when the sun shines and maybe in the atmospheric pressure when it doesn't. The humidity. Every bit of fabric faintly mouldy after rain, everywhere the heavy musk of decaying vegetation.

Allan met me at the airport. He was wearing a sports jacket, which caught me by surprise. I'd been expecting shorts and flip-flops.

–What's with the jacket? I asked.

–What about the jacket?

–I don't think I've ever seen you in a jacket.

–You haven't seen me period for what . . . light years.

–It looks good on you.

–I have a business meeting after I drop you off.

–Isn't trucking your business?

–I'm diversifying. There's a nice little motel I have my eye on. Not far from the beach. Basically, an investment.

–So, you're prospering.

–Couldn't ask for more.

He dropped me at his house, in a residential neighbourhood nowhere near the ocean.

–We'll get you to the beach later.

–Don't worry about it, I said.

—

The house was perched on top of what seemed to be a large garage. It was spacious, from what I could see from the outside. The yard was large, surrounded by trees that mostly blocked the view of the other houses in the area. I wondered what he needed all the space for. Or a three-car garage.

Allan seemed much older. There was crinkling around his eyes and at the corners of his mouth, and he was developing a belly. He now projected a certain edgy toughness, not the adolescent bravado I remembered. I recognized in it a trace of the performed aggression I encountered in the business people I sometimes had to represent, not to mention other lawyers.

The more we talked that weekend, the more I sensed that Allan had hardened on the inside too.

–Beach day, he announced on Saturday.

I protested. I'm not much for beaches, and especially bathing suits.

–I have this leg, I said.

Allan insisted. He told me he had to meet some people at the beach and talk some more business and I should come along. The business wouldn't take long. But when we got there, I didn't see anybody who seemed to be on the beach for business.

–Bring a book, he'd said.

He'd brought an umbrella and I settled under it with the book while he changed into a bathing suit then waded off into the ocean.

He was an impressive swimmer, like a water mammal, completely at home in the element—long arms drawing him along, head turning in perfect synchronicity as he breathed. I could never swim like that. I grew up beside the sea, but I can barely keep myself afloat. I avoided it, except for work. Loved and feared it. He acted like he owned it.

The next time I looked up, I saw him standing neck deep in the middle of a little group about fifty yards from shore, deeply engaged in conversation. I only noticed because there were no other bathers near them and one person in the group was wearing a hat. Then the guy in the hat was wading ashore and he dropped the hat in the sand beside a young woman who was sitting not far away from me, fully dressed, browsing through a glossy magazine. Then he returned, bare-headed, to Allan and the others.

They talked a bit longer, then Allan flopped backwards and backstroked away from them. The others—I counted four—continued talking for another minute, then waded ashore. They were all older fat guys who looked ridiculous in Speedos. When the owner of the hat reached her, the woman with the magazine stood, picked it up, shook the sand off and passed it over, and they all walked off together toward the changing rooms.

Allan eventually waded out of the surf, then sprawled on the sand beside me.

–What was that about? I asked at last.

–What?

–Those guys you were talking to.

–A business meeting, he said. I told you I had business here.

–In the water?

–Why not?

–The motel deal?

–This is something else.

–So what was with the guy and the hat?

–We were all supposed to be in bathing suits. Somebody got paranoid, so he had to lose the hat. Down here, nobody in business trusts anybody else. You understand?

–But a hat?

–A hat can be a lot of things besides a hat. Right?

–I don't get it.

–Never mind. It's not important. Aren't you going in?

–Not me.

Back at the house, he poured some wine. His place was cool and spacious. Minimally furnished. Expensive-looking art.

–You're into art now, I see.

–What do you think?

–I'm not much of an expert.

–That one there, the Emily Carr? It's an original. You'd be shocked how much I paid for it.

To my eye it was a moody cluster of woozy trees. Still, I nodded appreciatively.

–It's an investment, he said.

–I'm trying to imagine Peggy in this scene. I suspect she's a beach person. I know she loves to swim.

He shrugged.

–She doesn't like it much down here. The humidity, I guess.

–I can relate to that, I said.

–So, what about all that—me and Peggy?

–What about it?

–Come on. You must have thoughts. Feelings.

–About Peggy? Give me a break.

–You know she obsesses about you?

–I doubt that very much.

–Well, your name keeps coming up in conversations. Byron this and Byron that.

–Get out. Trust me. She's all yours.

He was staring at me hard, consciously projecting disbelief. A lawyer's trick I'd learned.

Then he said,

–I wouldn't want anything to come between us, Byron. You and me, I mean.

–Actually, Allan, I'm seeing someone. Nothing serious. I didn't plan to mention it.

I had been studying my glass but now looked at him. His eyebrows were arched in disbelief.

–Anyone I know?

–Probably.

He hooted, then stood up, towering over me.

–Okay, man. You've come this far. So spill.

–Annie.

–Annie?

–Annie Winter. Peggy's . . .

–Fuck. Right. Off.

He slapped his forehead, did a kind of pirouette.

–You've got to tell me . . . Have you . . .?

–Have I what?

–You know what. Have you done the deed?

Something else I learned in a courtroom: how to say no while making someone think you said yes.

–You gotta be kidding me. No way. You must remember how straitlaced she is . . .

–You son of a gun. You sneaky bugger.

He headed for the kitchen, then returned with another bottle in his hand. A German white of some kind. Poured.

–Well, well, well. We're kind of half-related now.

I suppose I expected a longer conversation, but he soon returned to some deep and private place.

After a considerable silence, I looked up to see him staring at me now as if my presence was somehow inconvenient. I've always had a knack for finding information in a face, and he had something on his mind that was even more important than the Winter sisters.

–I should tell you, it might get a little busy around here tonight, he said at last. There could be some noise.

–Oh.

–I'm in the trucking business, right? Shipments often arrive at night and we have to break down the cargo and load it into smaller trucks for delivery. I just got word today. There's a tandem coming tonight.

–No problem. Can I help?

He lit a cigarette. Blew a smoke ring.

–I don't think so.

–So this is your trucking terminal, right here.

–You could say that.

–What about the neighbours?

–It doesn't happen often. They put up with it.

And just as he predicted, it did get noisy at about two in the morning. Motors. Voices. Truck doors clunking. I got up and looked out. I cracked the window just a bit. Low voices, people speaking what I thought was Spanish.

A short guy with a smouldering cigar, wearing the hat I recognized from the beach, walked through the glare from some headlights, intensely talking to the man beside him. The other, taller, guy was Allan.

I went back to bed and fell asleep. One gift I have is the ability to sleep in the midst of institutional commotion. A legacy from so many nights in hospitals.

Of course, I knew what they were doing out there. Laundry on a larger scale.

Allan slept in the next morning, so I went for a long walk. When I got back, he was making breakfast.

−I hope the commotion didn't bother you, he said.

−Didn't hear a thing, I said.

Monday, on the way to the airport, I said,

−I've often wondered about Mike.

−Mike?

−Mike, the Newfoundlander. In Toronto. The laundry guy?

He frowned.

−I don't talk about Mike.

−Sure.

−He crossed the wrong people. I suspect he had an accident. What brought that up?

−I'm thinking you're in a dangerous line of work.

I'd expected him to just drop me, but as we were approaching the departure zone, he suddenly wheeled onto a ramp and raced up into the parking garage. There was an angry car horn, rubber tire squeal, a cut-off taxi close behind us. He parked on a nearly empty level, cut the engine, then lit a cigarette, and checked the rear-view mirrors.

—I'll find my way all right, I said.

—Just sit a sec. I want to talk about something.

—Okay.

—I'm planning to move back to Toronto, eventually. Florida is too goddam complicated for my simple tastes.

—I think that's a good plan. When?

—Down the road a bit. There are a few more things I want to do before I settle down. Maybe travel. Try living in another culture while I'm still young. I'm thinking Mexico.

He jammed his cigarette into the ashtray. Sat back, studied the car roof.

—I'm going to want a partner I can count on back in Canada.

—Who'd you have in mind?

He ignored the question.

—You're a bright guy, Byron. You got sense. Okay? You're an attorney, right? I think we'd make a great team.

—Yes, I'm a lawyer, Allan. A *law*-man. Remember?

—I wouldn't ask you to do anything that was wrong. I know you too well for that. Anyway . . .

—Smuggling drugs is against the law, Allan.

He smiled.

—I admire your subtlety, Byron.

I opened the car door.

—Wait a minute. You'd be nowhere near the so-called drugs. Anyway, that's all going to change down the road.

–You can't change the past, my friend.

–I don't understand the problem, Byron. We're talking pot here, for God's sake. A *herb*. A remedy for whatever ails. It should be fuckin legal anyway. You didn't give me an answer. What do you think?

–I think I'm going to stay on the right side of the line.

–But what about down the road? Look, booze was illegal for a long time. People want this. We could be tomorrow's Bronfmans.

–Or yesterday's Capones.

Jee zus Christ . . .

He looked stricken. I noticed, for the first time, how weary he seemed.

–Okay, Allan. I'll think it over.

–I think we could do great things together.

–Like, for instance?

–Well, after I've earned a ton of money, we do great things with all the money. I mean, what else is money for, man, if not for making your mark?

–It's the earning money part that worries me.

–On that score, I might as well tell you, Peggy has already agreed to be my partner.

–Your partner? How?

–Taking care of the money end. Accounting. That's her magic. But one of these days, we'll tie the knot. So, come on. We'll be kind of like a family. Me, Peggy. You, Annie.

–I'll think about it.

–Talk to Annie.

–Why would I do that?

–Just talk to her. We'd be a killer team, the four of us.

He laughed, punched my shoulder. Guys are always doing that for whatever reason. My arm was almost useless for the next half-hour.

His suggestion was more intriguing than I wanted him to know. Not then. But I would spend many sleepless nights after that, struggling with questions that I'm sure have troubled lawyers since forever. About the fine line between protecting and enabling.

And it wasn't just an ethical dilemma. Peggy being in the mix made it also about chemistry.

13.

It was after that trip to Florida that I noticed the confusion Annie had been warning me about. Mom started getting mixed up about basic things. Even who I was, at times mistaking me for her dead brother.

She also became argumentative, using expressions I hadn't heard for years.

−*Your hole is out,* she shouted once in the middle of an argument about how to make the tea. *The fucking water* has to be boiling when you pour it on the tea bag.

−The *what* water?

−You heard me. A *rolling boil.*

And then there was her first fall. That might have been another clue. Actually, when you think about it, a clue only becomes a clue in retrospect. A clue only explains something that has already happened. In the moment, her fall told me nothing about what was coming down the pike.

I heard a crash. And then I heard her swear.

−FFFFFFU-KH.

I chuckled. I went to see what happened. I found her on the floor beside a chair she took down with her. Not even trying to get up. *You're going to have to help me.*

Shocking, unprecedented words.

–You're going to have to help me. I think I broke something. I stood there, braced against the table.

–My fuck-king hip.

Now I spent my weekends cleaning up the house, preparing meals to last her for the coming week. Annie's visits became frequent, then regular, pitching in. She'd spend whole weekends. On Monday morning she'd go back to her place in town and I'd return to my city obligations. Mom managed in our absence with the help of home care people.

In the law office, increasingly I'd opt for routine assignments. Paperwork. Simple cases.

Mom became my child, a childhood working in reverse, revealed in moments of unconscious transparency. Mental stumbles that drew even more attention to her growing physical unsteadiness. As she became more childlike, it was easy to forget that, like any child, she was destined to be gone one day in the not so distant future. Unlike the child, when she was gone, she wouldn't be returning.

The day the doctors sat us all down and told us the prognosis and what we should expect was one of Mom's good days. When we were back home and settled in, Annie poured drinks. Mom declined, which was unusual.

–I'll be able to get away with anything now, she said. Say exactly what I think. All the people I've always considered arseholes, now I can just say. People will be just, "There she goes again . . . it's only the dementia."

–Maybe the doctors are wrong. They can't know for sure, I said.

Annie gave me what I took to be a warning glance.

–However it turns out, we'll all be here together, looking out for one another, she said.

Mom was quiet.

–I don't think a glass of wine would kill me, she said at last.

–You've always preferred a dry red, I said.

I poured a glass of Malbec.

–Maybe.

–You like Malbec. There was a while it was hard to find around here. We thought it was exotic.

She nodded, but I could tell from her expression that she didn't have a clue what I was talking about. She sighed.

–It's the one thing we never had in our family. Senility, or whatever. I don't think anybody ever lived long enough to get dementia.

She laughed.

The first time I heard someone mention Alzheimer's, I thought he said "old-timers." Old-timers' disease.

She sipped. Shifted slightly. Stared at the ceiling.

–Who knew that dying young was really a blessing in disguise?

She had a second glass and then she went to bed. I don't think she ever used that word again. Dementia.

When the house was quiet, Annie said,

–You need somebody here, Byron.

–I've got the home care people coming in.

–No. You need someone full-time. You need to keep working, so it can't be you.

–Work and worry, I said.

–I know a woman. Someone she knows.

She removed a piece of notepaper from her pocket, placed it on the table. I could see a name and a telephone number written on it.

—I know she'd be glad to, for little or nothing. You guys are famous up the shore, you and your mom, from the fishing. They still talk about how you carried on after your dad died.

—That would be the problem, the talking. The weird woman and her weird lame son who just happens to be a lawyer.

—The one I have in mind is my aunt, Shirley. You wouldn't have to worry about gossip. I can talk to her. Better still, you should call her.

She pushed the little sheet of paper toward me.

—So what about the nights?

—I could come, she said.

—I wouldn't hear of it. Nor would herself.

—I think she likes me. Or approves, at least. It would be no big deal. And, like you said, you'd be here on weekends.

—It would be too much to ask.

—It would actually be easier for me. I worry about her when I'm not here. And I can work from here.

And so I made the phone call.

Whole years, maybe even decades, can be summarized in special moments. I'm remembering a violent storm. It was on a Saturday night. Annie had taken a rare weekend off. It was just the two of us, Mom and me.

I was standing at my bedroom window. I love bad weather and was hoping it would last for days.

The old house was alive with sounds. Outside, trees were thrashing and dark clouds were rioting around the moon.

Then I heard an object landing on a floor. Not a heavy object. But the clatter was unmistakable, a small object striking hard tile. It was in the kitchen. I checked the clock: 3:20.

I found her bent over, braced against the kitchen counter, reaching down, fumbling.

–What's wrong?

–I dropped it.

I put a light on. It was a hairbrush.

–What do you want that for?

–Just give it to me.

–It's late.

–I know it's late.

–What do you need with a hairbrush at whatever time it is?

–I'll get it myself, then.

She was on the brink of toppling.

–Whoa.

I stooped and grabbed it and handed it to her.

–Put out the light, she said.

She fumbled with a button near her throat, then another, loosened her dressing gown, shoved it off her shoulders. Then she stuck the hairbrush down her back, began to scratch.

–My back is itchy, she said.

–Come on. Put that thing away. I'll scratch your back for you.

And so she leaned her elbows on the counter, staring out the window above the sink as the storm raged. She was developing a hump, or maybe it was just her posture, leaning forward. I scratched gently.

–A bad night on the water, she said.

–A good night to be in the house, I said.

And then we were both absorbed into the outside spectacle, the roaring wind, the furious trees and the galloping stars flashing on and off among stampeding shadows.

On an otherwise unremarkable Friday afternoon in early summer, I was clearing off my desk before a two-week holiday. The routine at home had recently been much improved, thanks to Annie's aunt Shirley, who, from day one, didn't hesitate to take charge.

She was younger than Mom, but they had been in school together. They knew all the same people. They could have passed for relatives to hear them talking.

One annoying habit that Shirley had was to repeat herself— in particular telling me how much I reminded her of my mother's long-dead brother. Angus. Over and over and over.

Just before I left the office that Friday afternoon, one of the junior partners stuck his head around the corner of the cubicle.

–You're not joining us for drinks?

–What are we celebrating?

–We won a tricky case.

–Which one?

–The lawyer. The guy accused of statutory rape. Heard before a judge alone.

–Really?

–The Crown is threatening to appeal, but I think we nailed it. I think we laid down a marker for defending other sex-related cases. Important jurisprudence, man, challenging a so-called victim's motivation.

–I see. That actually worked.

–The Crown put the poor girl on the stand. Big mistake. Our man made a mess of her. Made her look way older than her age, the way Jack saw her. She could have fooled anybody. And that was the point. She was trying to be grown-up and Jack got sucked in like anybody would.

–Did Jack testify?

–No fucking way.

I returned to the pile of documents I'd been sorting, shuffling the papers until I could think of something else to say.

–So are you coming?

–I think I'll pass.

Somewhere on the long drive to the farm that Friday evening, I collided with reality: you really aren't cut out for that kind of lawyering.

But what kind of lawyering was I cut out for? Just thinking about legal aid and all its virtuous assumptions, the hard slogging for hardly any compensation, exhausted me. Specializing in corporate litigation, with all its compromises and double standards?

I laughed out loud.

Allan?

Perhaps. He'd been trying to tell me that everything we do is compromised at some point. We survive by compromise, by moral flexibility. The ethical constraints I felt at getting involved with his enterprise were fraying rapidly.

But if I went with Allan, there was Peggy. Always Peggy.

14.

When I look back in time, there are gaps when I seem to have disappeared from my own memory.

I know that I eventually resigned my position with the law firm. I get depressed calculating just how long I spent there. Nine stagnant years, at least. The stagnation, of course, was my own doing. My work became tedious because it was always overshadowed by personal obligations on the farm.

But late one afternoon it struck me that I'd been in a cubicle for nearly a decade. Other associates had joined the practice and before you knew it had their own offices, their own assistants. Two of them had become partners.

More important, I realized I no longer had the stomach for the office culture, if I ever did.

So, finally, I told the partners I was leaving to set out on my own. Hang out my shingle in a smaller place. They seemed pleased. I didn't tell them that the smaller place would be a kitchen table in a farmhouse.

I think there was a small send-off in a bar by people I'd never really known, a brief, conclusive encounter with a city landlord who seemed glad to terminate an undervalued lease.

I remember I felt an almost instant sense of liberation.

The early part of the new experience is clear enough, as is the ending of it. It's the in-between part that feels lost, and, consequently, wasted. Life remembered in disconnected episodes lacks substance. But those days were misplaced, I think, because of Mom's confusion and how it spread to everyone and everything around her.

I would tell myself often: one day it will all make sense.

I do remember that, somewhere in that gap, Peggy married Allan, and they disappeared together. I think that's how it often happens. Unfinished lives, united, become complete, at least temporarily. Briefly, people don't need other people because they're so completely wrapped up in one another.

For the longest time I didn't hear a word from Allan. I think they lived in California for a while. Then Mexico. Then, maybe, New York. Annie heard from Peggy every now and then, and she mentioned something about a condo in Manhattan. I remember that because I thought, *Condo in Manhattan? They're doing okay, then.*

It feels like this middle period went on for years, even an entire lifetime, and perhaps it was a lifetime. A mostly memorable lifetime, even if I don't remember most of it.

And then one day Annie declared,

–You know I'm doing work for Allan and Peggy now.

–I didn't know. Doing what?

–Mostly bookkeeping. They pay me a retainer.

–Where are they now?

She seemed puzzled.

–Toronto. You know that.

–I had no idea.

–Byron, we discussed it.

–Last I heard, it was California. Or New York.

–It's been Toronto for the past four years.

–Maybe dementia is contagious.

I thought she'd laugh, but she just shook her head and sighed.

–So, they're still together?

–They are. And on that subject, we should talk about the future. Where all this is going.

–Where all what is going?

–You know what I mean.

–I know exactly what you mean.

–Well then?

–I guess we should get married, I said.

–We definitely should.

–Low-key.

–There's no other way.

That's the way it has always been with Annie. No drama. And that was how we did it, before a local judge, with his secretary and a paralegal for our witnesses.

One day I got around to asking her how much she knew about Allan's business.

–Why the sudden interest?

–Just wondering.

–He makes a lot of money from a lot of sources. I look at numbers and make sure that everything adds up.

–I see.

–Byron, you know Allan better than anybody. You've known him for many years. If there's something specific you want to know, just ask. I'll decide whether or not I can answer. Better still, ask Allan.

–Allan is my oldest friend. I'd trust him with my life. But Allan is a criminal. Or was.

–And your point?

–Are you okay with that? What does Peggy think about his businesses?

–I'm not sure what you mean by criminal. To the best of my knowledge, he has never been in trouble with the law.

–I wonder how he's managed that. I suspect there are many Allans.

–Let's just say, there are many legal entities. I do the numbers for legal entities. Numbers don't belong to moral categories. Numbers are pristine. That's the beauty of them, Byron.

–And Peggy?

–Talk to her yourself. We're all family.

Then Mom fell down again, and that changed everything.

She was on the tile floor in the kitchen when I got there. Annie was sitting beside her, cradling her head and shoulders. Mom's face was white. She seemed to be unconscious. Annie was weeping quietly.

–*Call 911*, she whispered.

15.

Allan and Peggy came for the funeral. It had been years since I'd laid eyes on either of them. Peggy hadn't changed. Allan was even bigger, flabby padding added to what had once been an athletic frame.

By then, Annie was working pretty well full-time for Allan. She still did taxes for a few university profs who lived locally, some old farmers and fishermen and service station operators in town. But basically, she worked with her sister, looking after Allan's books. Her trips to Toronto had become frequent.

We held a small funeral that was, according to Mom's instructions, non-religious. Afterwards, a brief gathering at a funeral home, a few memories shared among old friends.

Shirley spoke of all the sadness that Mom had endured in her long lifetime. She was appropriately vague, but nobody was in doubt about her meaning. My awful accident. The barn mysteriously burning a few months afterwards. Dad's sudden death. How Mom and I had bravely carried on the struggle to keep the little farm alive. Shirley only choked up once, when she mentioned Mom's younger brother, Angus, so tragically taken so many years before.

When she said his name, I felt the prickle of uneasiness

that flashed around the quiet room—and knew, even though I didn't raise my gaze from the glossy floor of the funeral parlour, that everybody in the room was staring at me.

Late that evening, when we were back at home and the women had left us with our drinks, Allan talked about his business.

—Have you ever wondered where you'd be now if you had taken me up on the offer I made when you came to visit me in Florida, years ago?

—Pointless to speculate, I said.

—Probably. But it's all worked out. For me, at least.

—Maybe we'd both be in jail. Maybe I'd have brought bad karma.

He smiled, swirled his glass.

—Byron, Byron.

—Or we'd all be crazy wealthy. We'll never know, right?

—The secret, Byron, is in the accounting. I can sleep at night because I have two of the best accountants in the world.

He sat back, studied my expression, then launched into what became a speech.

He explained the basics. He owned part of an American casino, which was on tribal territory somewhere in the south-western United States. New Mexico, I think. The location, he told me, was irrelevant. Unless I was interested in learning more.

He smiled.

He also owned part of a bank in the Caribbean. That bank had relationships with a couple of the big Canadian financial institutions. But again, the details were irrelevant in what was just a chat.

–And the laundry business?

He winced.

–That's pretty well behind me.

–Pretty well?

–I'm a full-time capitalist these days.

He was busily turning cash into real estate.

–Why am I still thinking laundry? I said, and chuckled.

He frowned at me.

–What are you getting at?

–Just making a joke, I said.

He wagged a finger.

–Jokes, as you would know better than anybody, can be in bad taste.

He sat back, sipped his drink, then, after a moment, resumed his recitation. He told me he was investing aggressively in housing estates, parking garages, condo buildings et cetera.

–Shopping malls?

–We avoid mall development. Too many . . . entanglements.

–What kind of entanglements?

–Don't get me started. If you want to talk cutthroat, we can talk about mall development. Basically, we just buy rundown real estate, fix it up and resell. But surely you know all this from Annie. Don't you two talk?

–We don't talk about work.

–I admire that, he said, and drained his glass.

And then he assumed the troubled frown I know so well from watching masters of negotiation, signalling the sharp turn toward where you want to take a listener.

–I'm going to be straight with you, old friend. I want your

wife in Toronto. Helping with the business. On the inside, with me and Peggy.

I noticed that his right eye was twitching, probably a trick he had developed. I doubted very much that he was really nervous.

I fetched the whisky bottle.

–You?

–I'm good, he said.

I poured for myself and sat. And waited.

–So, what do you think?

–I think you should be talking to Annie.

He smiled. He reached for the bottle. Paused.

–I should know better than to fuck with you, Byron. I shouldn't beat around the bush.

He poured heavily into his glass. The cork squeaked as he jammed it back in place.

–Here's the situation. Life is getting very complicated thanks to 9/11. The fucking wars on everything.

–The war on drugs was going on long before 9/11, I said.

–Now it's terrorism too. Anything transborder that involves the USA is a nightmare now. Drugs and crime and terrorism. It's turning into a police state on a wartime footing down there. Half the country is in prison.

–I thought you were out of there.

–I am, more or less. But I still have financial interests. And that's where you come in. I want out of there completely. Full stop. I need you now, more than ever.

–Let me think it over, I said.

—

Annie, predictably, was pragmatic when I told her the next morning.

–He wants me to work with him.

–Well, what's the problem with that? I have no trouble working with him.

–I guess there isn't one.

–He needs you. We all need you. We're entering a highly sensitive phase of . . . growth. We need your steady hand and common sense.

We, she said. It was kind of stunning, actually. Like I'd just walked in and discovered that I was way behind the action. Like coming home and finding the doors locked. And then a friendly stranger lets you in.

She explained the details Allan had left unspoken.

In a nutshell, he was repatriating money. Tons of money. He was hauling it home through a maze of offshore financial institutions and putting it in property. The kind of property people live in, work in, invest their hard-earned money in so it can grow more money to invest.

–That's all there is to it, Annie said.

I studied her face for hidden meanings.

–It's how the world works, Byron. Allan has a lot of money stashed in safe places abroad. But he's bringing it all home now, which is great for the economy.

–I got that much.

–Right. He'll gradually roll it all into a dozen or so mid-size commercial properties. Eventually, it'll all be consolidated in one big holding company, then reinvested through some kind of partnership he's now working on.

–Why does he need me to do that?

–He needs a legal brain that he can trust. His secret of survival is to stay deep in the background and let other people do the hands-on work. He needs people he can trust absolutely. He trusts you, Byron.

–He wants me to be a front man.

–Isn't that what lawyers do?

–Annie, do you not worry about how Allan got so much money?

–I don't care how Allan got his money. He has already lined up a group of reliable people who will be company directors when the time comes. All respectable. Lawyers, a couple of doctors. A well-known ex-politician.

–What do you mean by reliable?

–They all owe Allan, one way or another.

–So, Allan basically owns a bunch of power brokers who will provide cover for him.

–That's one way of looking at it, Byron. Another way is that they lend *gravitas* and respectability to a new business venture.

–And we bring?

–We're family.

I sat up alone that night, nursing the last drink of a long day. Allan and Peggy had spent the day in town, reconnecting with their distant past. Annie managed to avoid me. I knew it was all a strategy: let him stew; let him reach his own conclusions; life is short; we don't often get new and interesting opportunities in middle age; let him think about the money.

Allan and Peggy came home with Chinese food. Dinner was quiet, our conversation about how much town and the university had changed, how nothing seemed familiar anymore.

When they briefly mentioned pressing business matters that needed to be dealt with, I felt like an outsider. It was clear that my wife had already gone into a world I could barely imagine.

Allan's world. Their world. Peggy's world and Annie's world. Now, for some reason, they needed me.

Maybe it was time to leave history and all her secrets behind me. Mom was gone and I was free. But free from what? Free to do what? Free to make choices that are difficult, if not impossible. But what kind of freedom is that?

And then I heard footsteps.

–So you can't sleep either?

–Peggy?

I was sitting on the sofa, watching the night sky through the front window. She came and sat beside me.

–It's a lovely night, she said.

–It is.

And it was. There was a high full moon, casting a bright stillness on the landscape.

–I'm having a nightcap. Would you care for one?

–I'd love to get some fresh air, she said.

–You aren't dressed for it, I said.

–I'll get a coat. Will you come with me?

I stood.

We walked up the lane toward the highway.

–That moon. Those stars. In the city, you don't notice, she said.

There was no sound louder than our breathing.

–I feel good just being here, she said.

–Mom had a theory about crystals in the bedrock below the topsoil. She said they created positive energy.

–I can feel it, she said.

She took my hand and we just walked.

–You talked to Allan?

–Yes.

–So what do *you* think?

–I think I'm thinking.

She stopped and turned to me, moving close.

–I don't think you've ever kissed me, Byron.

–I think that I'd remember if I did.

–Don't you think it's time?

I was suddenly light-headed. Speechless. She placed her hands flat on my chest. I leaned down and kissed her lightly.

–Don't be afraid, she said, and cupped my face between her hands and kissed me long and deeply. Then she put her arms around me and nestled her head into my shoulder.

–Maybe that wasn't such a great idea, she said.

–Sorry, I said.

–Oh. The last thing I want is for you to be sorry.

She stepped back, grasped my hands. Maybe it was an effect of the moonlight, but her face seemed to be illuminated from within.

–Have I ever told you that you are perfect? she said.

–Not that I recall. A perfect what?

She laughed, and she wheeled away, running toward the house, shouting back at me,

–You can't catch me.

And, with my bad leg, I knew I couldn't.

In the morning, just before they left Malignant Cove, Allan asked for my decision.

I told him he could count me in, but with some conditions.

–Anything, he said.

–I will not move to Toronto. Annie and I can do from here anything you need, given the state of modern communications. Does that work for you?

–Look, I mean it when I say Annie and Peggy are the heart and soul of the business. But I also need you. I need you more than I need either of them.

–Why do you need me so badly, all of a sudden, Al? Why now?

–Once you're on board, you'll get the picture. You'll know exactly where you fit. Basically, Byron, I want you to be me.

I really can't explain why I agreed. Maybe it was the money. Or the death of my idealism about justice and the law. Or something simpler, like boredom. Or Peggy's kiss.

Or maybe, way down deep, it was what I'd always wanted. To be him.

PART THREE

DEMENTIA

16.

The house felt strangely empty after Allan and Peggy went back to Toronto. I told myself it was to be expected. Mom's needs had kept the place alive. How often I'd craved silence, the luxury of idleness.

I knew Annie felt the same. It wasn't something that we talked about. But we had shared an unspoken understanding, throughout Mom's illness, that after we reached the inevitable, predetermined ending, we'd have time to focus on each other. It didn't work out that way.

I now realize that Annie had been adrift for years. But it was only when the household was reduced to just the two of us that I understood it was Mom's illness that had held the place together all along. Annie was physically present, but we were worlds apart.

Is it really Annie's absence that you're noticing?

In my mind, I replayed the moonlight walk with Peggy, the conversation. The kiss. And it opened up the memory to other moments, a flood of feelings from the past.

At suppertime, maybe a week after the funeral, Annie suggested I fix something for myself from leftovers. She wasn't hungry. And so, I asked,

–Annie, what does all this mean for us?

–In what way?

–I was thinking, now that Mom is gone, there will be more time for us. It's pretty well been all about Mom since day one.

–So it matters to you? The "us"? Sometimes it's hard to tell.

–It matters more than I can say.

–Do you love me, Byron?

Such a simple question. I guess she misunderstood the hesitation before I said, Of course I do.

That was just a month before she left me. Left the farm to live in town.

One quiet evening, after a week in which we'd hardly spoken to each other, she announced, in a completely normal tone of voice,

–I can't live out here anymore, Byron. It's like living on an island.

–An island?

–Yes. A desert island.

So, when did this brilliant insight sink in? That we're off the beaten path here? That we're nobodies in the middle of nowhere? That we've been living on a frigging farm?

I let the words spin silently inside me until they lost momentum.

–What are you thinking?

I could only shrug.

I understood. I gradually convinced myself that this moment, like Mom's death, had been predetermined by circumstances beyond anyone's control. *It isn't about me.*

Since she'd teamed up with Allan and her sister, everything

around us in the country, on the farm, had become a reminder of her isolation. The Internet was slow. The couriers were always getting lost. Nervous about mail delivery, she'd opened a post office box in town. Didn't trust the phones.

I had noticed how happy she was when she'd return from business trips, how alive she seemed while Peggy and Allan were visiting.

Eventually, we talked. Rationally. That is how it has always been with Annie. Reason over passion.

–You'll be fine, she said.

–I'll cope.

–You'll more than cope. You don't need me, Byron. You don't need me anymore, not since your mom died. Actually, my love, you don't need anybody.

How could I explain to her how wrong she was when I was unable to admit it to myself?

We reached an understanding. The deal, after she'd decided to move out, was that we'd work from where we lived. Me on the farm, Annie not far away—a place in town, where services were more efficient. But, no matter what, we'd stay close. No static. Still partners.

That's how it was for years, I guess.

It all changed, of course, halfway through a round of golf, the day that Allan, the indestructible Great Chase, became physically dependent on everyone around him, and his sudden needs revealed the limits of our freedom.

17

Allan was felled in mid-August by the stroke. It was now almost November. You could feel the early chill of winter in the evenings.

I was in the backyard wrapping burlap around the trunk of an oak tree that Mom and I had planted just before she broke her hip, way back before she lost her independence and her mind.

—Let's leave something that's more permanent than us, she said.

—Something noble?

—Precisely. Anything worthwhile takes time.

I tried to remember exactly when we'd planted it. She'd dug the hole. She had researched how to plant an oak tree. She explained a taproot, how it was different from other roots.

Our little oak was now three times as tall as I was. But now there were tiny fissures in the bark and the woman at the nursery suggested wrapping it before the frost. Water gets in behind the bark through the cracks, it seems, and freezes there. Over time it can do a lot of damage.

It was worth a try. Anything to mitigate the wear and tear of growing old.

Take a break, I told myself. Take a load off. I sat on the edge of the deck. My cellphone started jumping on the railing. I made a sudden move to grab it, but my tricky leg was uncooperative and I almost toppled.

Fuck it. If it's important, it will ring again.

I put the phone beside me.

A dozen years ago, when I first went to work for Allan, I'd be in a panic now. When the phone rang, it was almost always about something urgent. Allan or Peggy with a critical assignment. A company to be registered or dissolved, titles searched, property transferred, an affidavit to be sworn somewhere, dictated by some stranger, often in the middle of the night. A meeting, hastily arranged with a client I knew I'd never see again or with another lawyer or with Allan's servile board.

The meetings were usually just a few hours' drive away, in Halifax, not so often in Toronto. Allan had kept his word, and never pressed me to relocate.

I could pretend I was a farmer while letting other people do the farming, pasturing their cattle on my land, harvesting my hay to feed their animals.

I maintained my membership in the Nova Scotia bar society, and took care of a manageable list of respectable rural and small-town clients. I developed strong professional contacts in Ontario, to whom I carefully doled out the legal work I couldn't do myself.

Until recently, it was more or less the same for Annie. She worked from town, only visited Toronto when she wanted to. We'd meet for lunch from time to time.

The lifestyle suited me. Halfway through my fifties I'd become more conscious of my limits. I went through a phase where I'd wake up in the middle of the night, obsessed with death. Thinking, apropos of nothing: *Death really happens. There will be a moment just as real as this one, but it will be my last conscious moment.*

Like someone running low on money, I obsessively checked the existential bank account. Every day a debit.

Then one day on a golf course, when life seemed to have transcended time, time caught up with Allan.

The phone began to vibrate again, then the ringing started. I could see Allan's number in the call display.

It was Peggy.

–Hey!

Her usual hello.

–Hey yourself. What's up?

–He asked me to get you on the line. Am I interrupting something? You sound like you're outside.

–I am outside. Just puttering. How is he?

–I'll let you draw your own conclusions. Here he comes.

Allan's voice was strong, but powered by a kind of urgency that said the strength was temporary.

–Is that you? he said.

–The one and only.

–I thought you'd have your bony ass up here by now. We've got stuff to talk about.

–Is something wrong?

–Everything is wrong. I need you here.

–I can come by the end of the week, if it's urgent.

–You still talk to Annie?

–When I need to. You know she's been in Toronto, mostly, since you got sick. I thought it would be temporary.

–You think me being laid up is temporary?

–Who knows?

–I damn well know. So you didn't know she planned to stay?

–No.

–It's something you'd better think about yourself. There's fuck all to keep you down there now, and you're needed here. It's one of the things we have to talk about. You being here.

Give me a couple of days.

–I know you and your couple of days. I've had Annie book you on a flight tomorrow. Check your phone. You should have an e-mail, confirming.

And Peggy on the line again.

–You can stay with us.

–Is he beside you?

–No. He's gone back to his room.

–He sounds strong.

–It comes and goes. We can talk. Basically, things are okay. The business, I mean. The rest . . .

–Is Annie staying with you guys?

–She's at the condo. You know that nice place on the harbourfront? The one we bought from the American? The guy with the girlfriend?

One of our companies had bought the apartment from a businessman who had kept a mistress there. When the woman moved on to an even wealthier Australian, the American put it on the market at a price that I'd considered to be outrageous. Allan bought it without haggling, and paid for it in cash.

–I know the one, I said.

–Well, I think she's going to take it over.

–So she's decided to live up there.

–For now, at least. But there isn't much there, at the condo, hardly any furniture. So stay with us. Okay?

When I called her, Annie said she'd pick me up at the airport.

–We'll have time for a drink while I'm there, I hope. I'm not staying long.

–Maybe you should get someone to shut the water off. Suspend the services while you'll be gone.

–You think that I'll be up there for a while? Think again.

–You'll see for yourself when you get here.

–So why didn't you let me know that *you* were staying on?

–Because, Byron, I didn't know myself. I wasn't ready for what I found here. You should be prepared.

After she'd hung up, there was the sound of a distant truck. And then nothing.

I returned to the oak tree. I was moving slowly but felt breathless just the same. When I crouched to tie the burlap, pain shot through the knee of my good leg. All part of a new reality.

Lately, I'd begun to feel a little flash of panic if I moved too quickly. It wasn't about the limp, which has always been so much a part of who I am.

I'd tell myself: You're only in your fifties. What will your sixties feel like? Don't even think about the seventies.

And now I heard myself admitting to the oak tree how much I missed another human presence.

Is it involuntary solitude that makes us prematurely old?

I went inside and poured a drink, carried it out to the deck and sat studying my burlap-swaddled oak. Almost all the trees and shrubbery around me had been planted and nurtured by my mother. An optimistic statement, I suppose, acknowledging our limitations but conscious of the continuity of life.

The sun was setting, promising tomorrow. A promise and a threat, the way I saw it. I felt the chill of the gathering darkness.

I stood. My body ached. Old sensations working now in tandem with the new aches and pains, from which there will be no recovery.

I can live with dying. Everybody must. But what about that other possibility? The one that robs us of our ability to know anything? Mom stayed silent on that score.

At first she did try to welcome her dementia as a gift of spontaneity, the freedom to be herself, say anything she wanted without consequences, say anything to anyone, about anyone. I believe the reality I witnessed was something else, an imprisonment.

I went inside, turned on a light and turned up the heat. I considered pouring another drink. Maybe not a great idea, I told myself.

I sat in front of my computer, the reliable escape hatch, entryway to everywhere. The compensation for everything that everybody isn't, for everything that isn't spoken when and where it should be, isn't heard or understood when and where we need the knowledge.

I typed in "dementia" and waited for the predictable avalanche of information.

And in the middle of it all, I read that there are facilities where, for a surprisingly modest sum of money, experts will track the secrets lurking in our genetic code, where time stores all her strategies, where destiny lies dormant, waiting to surprise us.

I made notes. I made up my mind.

18.

I called Annie as soon as the plane touched down. She said she was waiting for me in the car just outside the Arrivals door.

—What kind of car am I looking for?

—I'll stand outside it with the trunk open so you can spot me. It's black and shiny, like a limo. A Mercedes.

Allan's only self-indulgence was his car. He wasn't into Jags or Beemers like the ostentatious near rich, but he had a passion for Mercedes. Annie was hard to miss.

—So, he let you take the S-550, I said when I was settled into the passenger seat.

—Who?

—Allan.

—This is mine, she said.

I could tell that she was watching me for a reaction, but I stared straight ahead. My reaction was anxiety. I don't know why, or, more accurately, didn't then. I was also processing her appearance. Hair, makeup, wardrobe. She might have been heading for a film shoot. She wore a heavy, not unpleasant scent that was new to me.

—You seem different, I said.

—You make it sound like not a good thing.

When we were finally in the flow of downtown traffic, I asked her when she got the car.

–When it became apparent that I was going to be here for an indefinite period.

–And when was that?

–Not long after I arrived.

–A gift from Allan.

–More like a bonus. Or a bribe.

–Extortion, huh.

–You're travelling light, she said.

–I told you, I don't plan to be here for long.

–We'll see.

We were at an intersection, not far from Union Station, watching the human throng clotting on the corners, straggling across even when their light was turning red. I could never get accustomed to this morning scene.

–Do you remember that song from the seventies? The Fugs, if I recall.

–What song?

–"River of shit."

She laughed.

–I can't imagine you doing this all the time, I said.

She shrugged.

–I thought you were happy on the farm, I said after a fairly long silence.

–I think I was. From time to time. Anyway, happy is just a recurring episode, if we're lucky. Right? You do know that?

–Yes. Happy is a meaningless concept. I must remind Allan someday.

I watched the people surging into crosswalks.

–Daytime vampires, I said.

She patted my thigh.

–Get used to it, she said.

–So, how is Allan doing?

–Taking care of Allan is a big part of the job now.

–He sounded fine on the phone yesterday.

–He can put it on when he has to.

–You're depressing me, I said.

–Life is linear.

–Which means what?

–Which means we need to focus on what might happen next, plan for the end point and avoid regrets about what's past. Done is done.

–Concentrate on going forward, I said.

I felt her staring at me, frowning.

–Man, I hate that phrase, she said. Going forward. As opposed to what? Standing still? Going backwards?

She leaned on the car horn briefly when the light turned green and the car in front of us didn't move.

–Going forward, as if it just happens. As if . . . Come on, move, asshole! Put away the fucking phone! Go forward!

How I regretted coming. How I dreaded seeing Allan. He and Peggy lived in an expensive corner of a middle-class neighbourhood, not far from an ethnic strip that Allan liked for the anonymity it provided. The ambience was a mix of old-stock Europeans and Asians of a more recent vintage. Lots of women wearing black, many of them covered head to toe.

–Okay, so why am I here?

–You don't know?

–Help me out.

–Christ, Byron. Sometimes I wonder about you, you seem so out of it. Estate planning. You're here for estate planning.

I laughed.

–Aren't we jumping the gun a bit? Also, sorting out estates isn't really my specialty, certainly not ones on Allan's scale. Surely there are outfits here that . . .

–You're forgetting the need for some discretion when it comes to Allan's ventures. It's about separating his future, such as it is, from his past. Do I really have to explain?

–I thought that you helped him to take care of that years ago. Sealing off the past.

–There's a whole new set of imperatives.

Peggy held my hand warmly at the door, then led me inside. She looked weary, and Annie was anxious to get away, claiming something pressing at the office.

–He's been waiting for you, Peggy said.

I asked how she was coping. She mentioned interrupted sleep, hardly ever getting out. Being there for Allan, his many needs, his changing moods.

–He sleeps a lot, but this is his best time. Mid-morning. Don't be surprised, though, if he begins to fade.

She rapped lightly on a closed door just off the entranceway.

–We turned his office into a downstairs bedroom, she explained. I'll leave you guys alone, she said, opening the door.

—

The first thing that struck me was the hospital bed, which occupied one side of Allan's cavernous office. The whiteness of it. Gleaming stainless steel. The crank. More machine than bed. The protective side rail dropped.

–Better here than in the living room, Peggy said. She didn't have to explain that Allan was no longer able to get upstairs.

Mom had refused to allow a hospital bed in the house. She had her reasons, I assume, locked somewhere in her memory. Something ominous about where a bed should never be. Like in a living room. She'd say, Sooner or later, every living room *becomes* a funeral parlour, which is why the doors are almost always closed.

He wasn't in the bed, though. He was at his desk, looking like someone who'd been parked there temporarily. Uncomfortable. His smile was just teeth, nothing in the eyes.

–Did she get you anything?

–Like what?

–Coffee?

–I'm good.

He looked me up and down.

–Have you been trying to lose weight?

–I didn't realize. Speaking of which, you're looking kind of lean yourself.

–Clean living. So what's the plan?

–You're the one who insisted that I come up here right away.

–I think the women more or less have everything under control.

He winked. I wasn't quite sure what the wink meant.

–We can deal with any loose ends. When you're here for good, he said.

–And when might that be?

–The sooner the better, Allan said, then lapsed into a long silence, staring toward a window. At last, speaking as if from a great distance, he said he was sure that I'd been giving a lot of thought to the few things left to be decided.

–Actually, I'm not a hundred percent sure what those things are.

–Aha, he said, and shifted in his chair, grimacing. Well. We're going through another transition phase. It was in the works, which you should know, given what you've been doing the last few years. But we have to speed it up now. You'll be busy.

–I understand. But I'd like to make this stay a short one.

He grinned, then sucked his teeth. Found a toothpick on the desktop, picked briefly, examined something.

–I need you here, he said, still staring at the toothpick.

–But you said the women . . .

–That's *why* I need you here.

He scanned the room, cleared his throat, then stared hard into my face.

–They're great, aren't they, our ladies? But with me kind of out of it, they can use your help.

He winked again.

–Come here and help me up.

He was already lifting himself out of the chair, hands braced on the edge of his desk, arms trembling.

I went to him and placed an arm around his waist.

–Where do you want to go?

–Over to the bed. Come around.

He grabbed the lapel of my jacket and I almost lost my balance. And then I felt his hand inside my jacket, fumbling with my inside pocket. And then he seemed to steady himself.

–Just give me your arm, he said.

When we were beside the bed, he turned, placed his arms around my neck.

–Now you'll have to do a little lifting, he said.

I placed my hands below his armpits, to raise him. He had his hands on my shoulders, face pressed against my ear, and he was whispering.

–*They hear everything*, he said.

–Hmmm?

–*Every word. They're listening. They're watching.*

I lowered him to the bedside.

–This is great, he declared.

Then, with his head cocked to one side, he again whispered:

–*The fucking room is wired.*

I stared at him as he settled back against the pillows. Then he instructed me to make mechanical adjustments so he was sitting almost upright. The door opened. Peggy arrived with a tray, on it two mugs of coffee, cookies.

–How are we doing? she asked cheerfully.

–Catching up, I said.

–I'll leave you to it.

And she did.

Allan lapsed into silence when we were alone again. His hand trembled as he raised his mug. I thought of Mom as he struggled, lips pursed, leaning toward the mug to get a sip.

She had bouts of paranoia too, days when she'd convince herself that Shirley was spying on her, or that I was snooping in her purse.

Coffee slopped onto his shirt, but he didn't seem to notice.

–So, this transition, I said.

–Well, we had things pretty well set up before all this.

–Yes, the reorganization. But I'm not sure about the stuff before I came on board.

–The dark ages. Forget about them. That's history.

–The casino?

–I handed everything over to the Indians. There was a reasonable agreement about money. You can forget about that casino.

–There's another?

He nibbled on a cookie, stared some more at me.

–I'm a little out of touch, I said.

–That makes two of us, he said, and laughed. Hold this.

He handed me his mug, struggled to sit up straighter.

–That's better, he said.

I handed it back and he sipped at it for a while.

–How are you, anyway? he said. What's going on with you? The women don't tell me anything.

–Nothing much happens on the farm.

–You can see what I've been dealing with, he said, gesturing around the room.

–Understandable, I said.

–I suppose the wives have told you all about the big affair.

–Actually, no. I don't know anything about a big affair.

–No one mentioned Grace?

–You mentioned Grace, I think? At the hotel. Before the . . . golf.

–Yes.

–I heard she passed away.

–Well, if you heard that . . .

–That's all I heard.

–But you didn't hear how?

–No.

I see. Well. She took her own life.

–Man. That's . . .

–With my help.

I stared at him, processing the words. Allan had a flair for the dramatic.

–That was the big affair, he said, and laughed again.

He told me that he and Grace had been close, but just as friends. Maybe it was deeper, emotionally, but it never progressed beyond deep conversation. Intimate disclosure.

–Which is, I suppose, a kind of infidelity . . . but what the hell. If people can't talk to one another, what's the point. Peggy had her suspicions, though. She has a nose for anything threatening.

Then Grace got sick with ALS.

–I read up on it. There are cases where it goes really slow. Sometimes it stops. But not for her. It was . . . galloping. She didn't want anybody to know. I was the only one. Nobody at work. She had family out on the west coast, a couple of kids from a marriage.

–And she didn't tell *them*?

–Nope. I considered going behind her back, then I told her I was going to tell them. It was unfair to them not to know, not to be able to help. But she said, "If they know, they'll make me want to die." I didn't really get it. Not then. But I went along with her. Now I can understand.

–Not sure I do.

–Some people don't like to be a burden. And the distress of the people who care about you makes you want to get it over with. It's how she saw it, anyway, and I couldn't argue with her.

He and Grace spent a lot of time together in her final months. She had always worked from home. When she fell ill, he'd visit every day. And so, it was presumed that they were having an affair. For her, that was easier to live with than the truth. Illness had become a more complicated problem than infidelity. The lie was simpler and Allan went along with it.

–You think it through. If you're a good person, it's easier to suffer than to cause suffering. You don't have to agree with her. But that was her thinking.

–You never told Peggy.

–I'll tell her. Sooner or later. But I haven't yet.

He winked at me again, hinting at something. The wired room, perhaps.

–What?

–Nothing. Nothing. Where was I?

–You said you helped her end it.

–Yes. I let her down big time. Like I turned into one of her worst fears.

–I don't understand.

–It got to me, watching her go downhill, and of course she noticed. That was too much for her, watching me watching her.

His face was grim, eyes wet.

–She expected me to be stronger, and I wasn't. I became part of what she warned about. What I've always been. A fucking disappointment to the women.

–Come on . . .

–So she asked me to help her get it over with. She wanted a contact. And she asked me to be with her at the end. I couldn't refuse, could I?

–What kind of contact?

–A doctor I knew from way back. Smoked a lot of weed. The least I could do was step up. Be there for what she needed even if I hated like hell the thing she needed.

–You set it up.

–Yes. And she was right, you know. She basically just fell asleep. It was a relief, actually, after watching her . . . disintegrating. That was when I understood what she'd been telling me. When somebody gives up on life, it's because of what his life is doing to the lives of other people. Can you understand that?

He studied his hands. Looked away. Looked back.

–So. If it ever came to that, Byron . . .

–Fuck you.

–The guy's card . . .

–I'm not listening . . .

–It's in the top right desk drawer.

I stood.

–Allan, if that's why you dragged me up here, you're wasting my time and yours.

–It isn't the only reason. Just something you should know I'm counting on. I want you to be here.

–I'll be here when there's a sensible reason to be here.

–That won't be up to you.

Outside his office, I felt a moment of confused alarm. Had he lost his mind? For Christ's sake . . . *the room is wired*? Really? Was it paranoia now? Then I remembered he'd put something in my pocket. Something small. I reached inside my jacket and found a USB thumb drive.

Peggy was sitting back in a large recliner, feet on the footstool, ankles crossed. She had a document file open on a small table beside her.

–How did he seem?

–Feeble, physically.

I suddenly felt awkward. There was something in her tone, her expression. I was sure there was nothing I could tell her about Allan that she didn't know already. *She doesn't want to know what I think. She wants to know where I stand.*

–I had to help him getting back to bed.

She smiled.

–You should know he usually manages to get there by himself.

I shrugged.

–But, yes, he's going downhill.

She closed the file, folded her arms.

–It's partly because he won't do anything to help himself. Flatly refuses rehab. Just stays in that office day and night. But maybe he was playing with your head a bit, exaggerating a little?

–I didn't think so.

–What I notice most is the mental change. He'll say things, sometimes, that are off the wall. Did you notice that?

–No, but sitting in a room twenty-four seven will do things to anyone's head. Have you tried to get him out for a walk or something?

–He hasn't shown any interest. It would be pointless asking.

–I might, anyway.

–Be my guest. But he's pretty well given up. I think people as physical as he was have a harder time with disability. I realize I don't have to tell you . . .

I smiled.

–It takes backbone to confront adversity. As you know.

I shrugged.

–Listen to me, she said, and laughed. As if I know frig all about adversity. But, just the same, he's never really had to struggle, physically.

I said,

–The reality is that there are always people worse off, and better off.

–Which is why I hope you can stay and remind him what it takes.

She stood and stretched, folded her arms, studied the floor briefly, then asked,

–What do you know about vascular dementia?

–Not a thing. Are you saying there's more than the damage from the stroke going on?

–There are a few things I need you to sign before you go back.

–I can do it now.

–Later, maybe. Do you have plans for lunch, Byron?

–Not yet.

–Let me take you to lunch. There's a nice little place not far from here. We can walk.

It was a Greek place and she ordered for us both, including a sweaty carafe of white. A litre. It was going to be a long lunch.

I noticed that she hardly touched her salad. She drank her wine, though, and she talked a lot about Florida and southern California, the southwestern United States. A casino in New Mexico. She only mentioned Allan near the end.

We'd finished the carafe. She looked around the restaurant. The place was nearly empty, the lunch crowd long since dispersed.

–Allan is only happy at the edge of things, she said.

–A dangerous place to be sometimes.

–Almost all the time. I feel much safer at the centre, where the people are. Safety in numbers, I say.

–That's why you're an accountant?

–I never thought of it like that, but yes.

She smiled, reached across and clasped my hand.

–We've always kind of danced around each other, haven't we?

I allowed my hand to fold around hers. I stared at our two hands, imagining that they belonged to other people.

–But from here on, we're going to have to be pretty open.

She pulled her hand away.

–I'll do my best, but I'm just the lawyer, I said.

She laughed.

–So, why did you mention vascular dementia?

–It's something we should be ready for. Even now . . .

She looked away, then met my eyes.

–We have to keep in mind that, for all practical purposes, there is no Allan. This isn't something new. Officially, there never was an Allan in the business. But now it's important we find out who he really is.

–Who he *really* is?

–You, of all people, know what I mean. Allan is a fiction, a creative enterprise that he's been working on for decades.

–Aren't we all, more or less?

– Do you *know* Allan, Byron?

–I know the Allan he's always wanted me to know.

–Is that enough for you?

–Sometimes more than enough.

She wagged her head a bit in disagreement.

–Not anymore, she said.

–You've been married to him all these years. What's left for *you* to know?

She stared at me. I knew the look, the weary, hesitating expression of one who needs to share her knowledge but is afraid to.

–What are you thinking, Peggy? Spit it out.

–I'm mainly thinking about you, she said.

–Never mind that. We know that he trusts us.

She smiled.

–He trusts you, Byron. Not us.

I wanted to disagree. But I couldn't, truthfully.

After we left the restaurant, we walked a block or two, until we were on the flank of the lower Don Valley. We crossed on a pedestrian bridge over the whizzing parkway and the muddy

Don River. She slipped her arm through mine, then retracted it. And after a while she caught my hand.

–I don't want to be here, in Toronto, I said.

–It doesn't have to be forever. Just long enough to navigate the changes we have to deal with.

–Why me?

–Don't you get it, Byron? You are—for all intents and purposes, and legally—the company.

–I'm the name on a lot of documents, I know that. I guess it would be wise to make a plan in case anything happens to me. Where would you be then?

I laughed. She frowned.

–There's nothing wrong with you, she said.

I shrugged, kicked a stone. She caught my arm and turned me toward her.

–Right? And if there was, you'd say. Right?

–Yes.

–No secrets from here on, Byron.

We crossed a playing field, then climbed a steep hill. Near the top, I noticed a familiar musk in the air, barn smells, the pungency of old manure.

–There's a little hobby farm over there, she said, pointing toward a weathered fence, some barns. We can sit there for a while.

We wandered through a gate, into another century. A quaint old farmhouse. There were small groups of people, mostly children, ogling the horses, chickens. We found a sheltered place to sit.

–You know this scene, she said.

–Yes. It takes me back.

–To a good place?

–Not especially.

She put an arm around my shoulder, leaned her head close to mine.

–God forbid that anything should happen to you, she said, squeezed me and let go.

–Is it his competence you're worried about, Peggy? It seems to me he's still on top of things.

–Yes. He's still aware and engaged. But Allan isn't nearly as together as he might seem. It's why you need to stay around long enough to draw your own conclusions.

The lawyer part of me was suddenly alert. Listen carefully, it said. Weigh every word.

–He suspects that people close to him are ganging up on him, spying on him, hiding things. Paranoia, I think, might be the first clue he's headed nowhere good in terms of his mental state.

I frowned. *They hear everything.*

–He talked about disappointing people, I said.

–Disappointing Grace, you mean?

She was staring at me, her eyebrows arched. I looked away.

–I know he told you about how he helped her die, she said, and shrugged. He has a point, about disappointing people.

I was beginning to feel a deep anxiety. Perhaps it was the barn smells. The adults speaking to the children in loud, emphatic voices, like weary nurses on a ward, impatiently projecting patience.

–Can we go somewhere else?

–I thought you'd like it here, but sure, let's walk.

I headed toward the gate, leaving her behind. She caught up just as I stopped to let a crowd of children and their braying supervisor by.

–You okay, Byron?

–I'm great.

We walked back toward the expressway. From the pedestrian bridge, I could see, to the north, heavy traffic on the viaduct that spanned the valley, a long, high bridge that people used to jump from. To deter jumpers, the city installed a barrier, a tight assembly of vertical steel rods. A "veil," some people call it. The experts say a jumper needs to be deterred only briefly to experience the glimmer that might change his mind. How long did my uncle hesitate, waiting for a glimmer that clearly never came?

–The creepy viaduct, Peggy said, following my gaze.

–Yes.

–I could not imagine . . .

–You know about my uncle.

–What uncle would that be?

–My mother's kid brother. She only had the one.

She was frowning now.

–His name was Angus, I said.

–I know.

–You know. And you know they named me after him.

–I never think of you as Angus. What made you think about him?

–Looking up there.

She nodded then.

–You know the story. He jumped from the bridge across the harbour in Halifax. I think it's about that high.

–That's fucking morbid, Byron.

I stopped, turned to face her.

–Did you know about my uncle when you rechristened me?

–No, she said.

I turned away, looked back up the valley. Cars now slowing down. Rush-hour traffic clogging the viaduct and the expressway.

–I think about him now and then. What goes through someone's mind.

–Allan has a theory that suicide is an impulse of misguided mercy, she said.

–You do it for other people.

–Something like that. I think it's crazy.

–I'm not so sure.

–How could you possibly love someone that much?

–I think Allan could. I always thought that about him, in spite of what he's always tried to make people think. It's just a feeling I've always had.

–He loves you, she said.

–And he loves you.

–I only wish, she said.

I stopped to watch the traffic below us. You'd really have to be determined to do it from here, from the pedestrian overpass. You'd have to wait until the cars and trucks were really flying and then aim yourself. You'd be making a shit show out of some driver's life, but you wouldn't have to worry about things like consequences.

Peggy had kept walking. Now she stopped and called back to me.

–Are you coming, Byron?

–I think Allan has a death wish, I said.

–Allan has had a death wish for as long as I have known him. Restructuring the company is part of it.

–I'm not talking about the business . . .

–But it's all the same. You hear about suicides first killing their children . . .

–No, no . . .

–First, he wants to kill off everything he's achieved. Be prepared to hear about the grand plan. *Giving back* is his new buzz phrase. He's determined to *give something back*.

–How is that a death wish?

–Okay, call it phase one of self-destruction.

–We're talking about his money, not his life.

–It's money that belongs to all of us.

–And what is it he wants to do with the money?

–Like I said, he wants us to start giving everything away, as his atonement for all his little failures, all the disappointments he's caused, the harm he thinks he's done.

–What harm would that be? He always said, "It's only pot," like it was manna from heaven.

She looked away.

–There was more than pot, of course. At least at one stage.

–He's never told me that.

–We were in Mexico for a while.

–I see.

–There were people there. I was scared shitless half the time.

–What kind of people?

–The kind of people down there who have power. The SUVs. The bodyguards. The guns. He was careful to keep me out of it.

–Allan was never into guns.

She wagged her head back and forth, to agree and disagree.

–He isn't now, she said.

–I'm sorry.

–Don't be sorry. I was young and having fun when I wasn't terrified.

–So, you're saying that he has regrets about that now.

–Life got complicated for a while and things happened that you and I will never know about. And yes, now he has regrets and he thinks he can buy his way out of them. And, to cap it all, there's Grace.

–There are worse things than contrition.

–I didn't know you were a Catholic.

–I'm just saying, I'm here for him. I'm here for you. But I can't stay here indefinitely. Okay?

She nodded.

In the evening, Peggy and I helped Allan from his office-bedroom to the table. He was cheerful at dinner. He drank some wine. We talked mostly about the early days—safely about people we remembered but really didn't care about.

Peggy sat beside me, with Allan across the table, so she could hear him better, she explained. I suppose I should have asked myself why she insisted on a nightcap after he had gone back to his room, but it just felt normal.

Near the bottom of the drink, she said, It's wonderful talking to you, Byron. I never get to talk to anyone the way I talk to you.

And it wasn't shocking when, very late that night, I felt her slide into the bed behind me, felt the warm fullness of her body pressed against my back.

Perhaps I thought that I was dreaming, but the gentle hand was real, my face was real, my neck. And the old masculine responses, frequently forgotten now—they were real and overwhelming.

For the first time in her presence, everything felt right. She was whispering.

–We'll soon be old, Byron.

She draped her hand across my waist, laid it flat on my stomach. I was afraid she'd slide it downward, afraid she wouldn't. I put my hand on hers.

And suddenly, her hand was gone and she was propped up on one elbow.

–Hush. Listen.

–What?

–He's moving. He needs something.

And then she was gone.

I saw Allan briefly in the morning. He was at his desk and Peggy brought us coffee. He was distracted, mostly silent. I was nervous, wondering what, if anything, he might suspect about the night before.

At last he asked,

–You looked at what I gave you?

He patted his chest, winked. The thumb drive.

–Not yet, I said.

–That's okay. It's just stuff.

He was speaking loudly, as though into a microphone.

–Stuff, I said.

–Don't laugh, he said. He frowned, shook his head, a warning of some kind. Then he coughed into a paper towel. His face was flushed.

–We're getting old, he said.

–We can't help that.

–Getting old is the best-case scenario, my old man used to say. One thing I want to ask, and you can tell me it's none of my business. But I'm curious.

–Fire away.

–You and Annie.

–What about us?

–How does that work?

We live in different places. That's all.

–Life should be so simple. You lucked out with Annie. I wish I'd known her sooner.

I laughed.

–Where are we going with this?

–Nowhere. But I'll tell you straight up—if I could rewind the old odometer, you'd get a run for your money.

–What about Peggy?

He stared at me for a long moment, then nodded.

–You know more about Peggy than I do, he said.

–How can you say that?

–*How can you say that*, he mocked.

I stood.

–Annie's waiting for me in her new Mercedes. That was a nice gesture.

He waved a hand.

–A small investment. You'll be back soon, he said.

It was not a question.

He struggled to his feet, breathing heavily, leaning on the desk. Held out a hand. I reached across and grasped it and he pulled me toward him until his forehead was almost touching mine.

–Don't be worried, he said.

–Okay, I said. I forced a smile.

–*I'm just fuckin with their heads*, he whispered.

On the drive to the airport I felt a steady buzzing in my chest. Something in there seemed distressed. Conflict. I felt I shouldn't leave. I didn't really want to leave. I really didn't want to stay. I didn't know why I'd been summoned. Whose idea was it?

After a curt hello as I climbed in, Annie stayed silent. Ostensibly, she was focused on the traffic, but I felt that she was tuned in to my confusion.

What was Peggy thinking? What did Peggy mean when she said we'll soon be old? What is Peggy thinking now?

What is Annie thinking?

But perhaps her silence was nothing more than impatience. She had better things to do than transport me to the airport on what was probably a busy day.

–I thought we'd get a chance to talk more, I said at last.

–I thought you'd be staying longer. I got tied up at the office over an issue with a property.

–Something I should be worrying about?

–At some point probably.

–What's the headline?

She laughed.

–The possibility of headlines is the headline. We have an apartment building occupied by relatively rich, old white people. We planned to tear it down. There's resistance.

–From rich, old white people.

–Yes, but mostly from the neighbours, who think we want to put up a high-rise condo building. Block their sunshine.

–And we do?

–We did, but Allan waffled. Now he wants to sign the place over to the tenants. For a dollar.

–They must be overjoyed.

–They don't know yet.

–I'm sure it could be structured so that it would make sense from a tax point of view.

–That isn't the point, Byron. This is part of something more serious where Allan is concerned.

–Peggy hinted at something like this when we talked.

–Allan wants to move all our assets into something like a charitable trust. I think his mind is going.

–When did a charitable impulse become evidence of mental illness?

She sighed.

–Come on, Byron. Don't play cute. His doctors have told Peggy that the early signs of vascular dementia are there. The mood swings are hard to live with—despair, rage, weird manic ecstasy. One day he has too much energy, the next he can't hold his head up. And then there's the paranoia. I'm surprised you didn't notice, even on a short visit.

–That's why you and Peggy wanted me to come? To see this?

–You need to get more involved, Byron. He needs to be watched.

–What about the board?

–Allan owns the board. You know that.

She looked across at me, expecting a response. I looked away. *I'm fuckin with their heads.*

–He's becoming quite hostile to us, Byron. To Peggy and me. If she wasn't married to him and if she wasn't my sister, I'd just pack it in and leave.

–Strange. He practically told me that he's in love with you.

–You're joking.

–No. He seemed quite rational.

–That's what I'm talking about. Tomorrow he might rip my face off. He's losing it, Byron.

–Do you think we could live together again?

She laughed.

–There's a non sequitur if I ever heard one.

–Not really. If I'm here for a longer stretch, I'll have to live somewhere.

We were near the airport. I could see the airplanes floating down, rising lazily through haze. She reached across, caught my hand.

–I can't think of any reason why we couldn't.

–That would be a plus.

–So, you'll be coming. Soon, I hope.

She got out of the car and came to me as I dragged my suit-bag from the back. We embraced.

–It might be like starting fresh, she said.

–But coping with dementia again.

–We're good at that.

–Maybe I'm talking about myself.

She stepped back, frowned.

–Stop it, she said.

–Maybe I'm the one you should be concerned about. I have the family history.

–I'm talking about Allan, darling. I'm talking about reality. Let's keep our eyes on what's in front of us. We have to keep him true to himself by keeping him out of the picture altogether. It's what our Allan, the real Allan, would want.

I picked up my bag, turned away. Then I turned back.

–Annie?

She was at the car door, looking across the rooftop, the question in her eyes.

–I think I'm going to get my DNA tested, I said.

–Your what?

–My DNA. When I get home.

–For what?

–Guess.

She laughed.

–Safe travels, Byron. Check in when you can.

She laughed again and made a gesture my mother used to make, twiddling her forefinger in little circles by her temple.

—

Checking pockets at security—loose change, keys, the USB drive. For a moment I was baffled. USB drive?

Damn. How could I have forgotten to review this while I was there? Just stuff, he said. Allan was never in his life about "just stuff."

On the plane, I briefly considered opening my laptop and scrolling through the thing. But I grew mildly nervous about the well-groomed stranger sitting next to me. Better to leave it for when I was home.

Annie once explained her theory that memory is a parallel reality. Basically, an extended falsehood, a lifelong lie. At best, a kind of literature.

But for me, memory is embedded in sensations, not narrative. Sound and smell. Touch. Music. Aroma. Colour. Revulsion from the smell of blood. Muddy lanes and sodden fields in spring. Fresh-cut hay in summer. The tang of apples in the fall. I associate particular events with certain seasonal conditions. The sharp heat of August feels unlike the warmth of a mellow morning in September or October; autumn has its own unique sensual pungency.

And so I can, with relative certainty, "remember" that the series of events I am going to try to reconstruct happened mostly in the autumn and the winter of an extraordinary year.

Ironically, I clearly remember the moment when I was told that there was a very real possibility that I could lose important aspects of my individuality. Memory, for one. Ultimately, my independence. Specifically, I recall the particular chill of a winter rainfall.

But I also remember thinking, as I was told, I am not a victim. I have some control. The early detection of this unexpected menace meant that I might be able to deter the process of decay and mitigate the outcome, for example by doing crossword puzzles. The daily *New York Times* was recommended, for reasons I forget.

I could exercise my brain by watching game shows on TV, and bolster my memory by writing little memos to myself.

And yes, I also remember that on this wet and chilly day the last leaves on a forlorn city maple tree were drooping under the weight of the relentless drizzle.

But this is surely too much information, and much too soon. Dementia is a catastrophe that usually happens silently and in slow motion.

PART FOUR

DECLUTTERING

19.

It might have occurred to me that as Allan's role in running his affairs became more compromised by illness, life for his three partners—Peggy, Annie and myself—would become more perilous. My quiet life on the farm had been, in many ways, a kind of insulation against feelings of vulnerability in what was, realistically, a risky line of work.

But, in hindsight, I can see that our downfall began at least three years before his stroke.

As he'd told me, my job had mostly been to represent Allan— be Allan, I suppose is more accurate—in relatively minor transactions, buying properties and flipping them, creating the corporate personas that seemed to be important to him. Sometimes I had to drive to Halifax or fly to Toronto, invariably on short notice, to meet people I somehow knew I'd never see again.

Then I would come home again, to the peace and quiet of my farm, where I was relatively comfortable, in mind and body.

And then one afternoon two well-dressed men appeared at my front door, unannounced. They were friendly. One asked if I was Angus. I was briefly confused but quickly realized that these were people who knew me only through official documents. As if reading my mind, each produced a business card and handed it to me. They were policemen.

–Can you spare a minute?

–Of course. Come in.

They weren't that big, physically, but they seemed to fill the room. Their attitude would have been overwhelming if not for my understanding that, notwithstanding all the power and peril they consciously projected, in this instance they were supplicants.

–What can I do for you gentlemen? I asked when we were sitting in my office. Coffee maybe?

–No thanks. You have a nice set-up here, said the older one, presumably the designated talker.

–It suits me. How can I help you?

He produced a notebook, flipped it open.

–We're hoping you can help us locate a former client. Albert Rose. Does that name ring a bell? You set up a company for him.

I stood. Walked to a window, stared out for a while. Which reminds me that it was winter. The trees were skeletal, fields rippled with fresh snowbanks.

–Rose. He's from Toronto, I believe.

–You do a fair bit of work out of Toronto?

I shrugged and turned to face them.

–I get the odd referral. People who want to incorporate in Nova Scotia. I think I remember Rose. It was some real estate venture, wasn't it?

–I notice you don't have a shingle out.

–I try to keep things manageable. I don't get around as easily as I'd like. Travel is a problem. I don't have many clients.

They both nodded sympathetically. Even though almost nobody stares anymore, or dares to condescend, people always notice disability and they adjust.

–You seem to do quite well just the same. You go to Toronto often?

–Only when I have to.

–When was the last time you spoke with Mr. Rose?

–I'd have to look back at my records. Why don't you tell me what this is about?

The younger one was thumbing through his notebook, and spoke for the first time.

–This incorporation that we're interested in was two years ago.

–That long? I wouldn't have had anything more to do with it once the paperwork was done.

–You're still down as chairman, he said.

–Is that a fact? Remind me of the name of the company.

–Water Street Lofts, Inc.

–I'll check that out. I should have been replaced by now. Obviously, someone is being careless with the paperwork. You understand, I was there just for the incorporation. I wasn't the only lawyer.

–So when did you last have contact with Mr. Rose?

–It would have been back then.

–You have billing information? Address? Phone? E-mail?

–I want to be helpful, but we're wandering into, you know, lawyer–client territory.

The older officer raised a hand.

–Yes, with all due respect, we could go the legal route. Search warrant and all that nasty stuff. But we just thought this would be . . . simpler.

–Yes. Thank you for that. Perhaps if I knew a bit more about the issue, as it pertains to Mr. Rose. Your name is, again?

–You can call me Tom.

He was nearly my age, I guessed, though it was difficult to tell because his head was shaved to a shiny glint. There was a shadow of a hairline just above his ears, but it was difficult to discern whether the stubble was grey or sandy.

–Well, Tom, I'm just trying to imagine the grounds for searching my humble office, I said.

–At this point, it's confidential . . .

I threw my arms wide, as if crucified on a cross of principle.

–There you go. We're both kind of hamstrung by professional constraints.

–We could go off the record, on the understanding . . .

–Of course, but what good would that do, other than to satisfy my morbid curiosity?

–I gather this was your first business with Mr. Rose.

–First and only.

–You know he has some commercial properties in the Toronto area?

–I don't remember the particulars, but I think that's correct. I actually never dealt with him face to face. It was all by phone and fax.

–Seems that's how he does business. Never face to face. Do you find that unusual?

–Different, I suppose. But that's the way it is now, with all the technology. Increasingly impersonal.

–You can say that again, Tom said.

They stood then. Closed the notebooks.

–If you think of anything you'd like to share, Tom said, then he thanked me, hinting that they'd probably be back.

The quiet one stopped in the doorway, staring out across the place.

–This reminds me of where I grew up, he said.

–Somewhere near here?

He laughed.

–No. Northern Manitoba. It's bleak like this.

Even after they left, I wasn't thinking about peril. I poured a cup of coffee. Sat in the gathering darkness for a while, recalled Allan's story about taking Valium before a border crossing.

So far, I've never needed Valium.

When I'd finished my coffee, I sent a cryptic text to Allan. *I think I should come up for a meeting. I've had visitors.*

He responded moments later, asking if I could fly up to Toronto the next day. He said he'd make a booking at a hotel. I knew the one—a shabby place on Jarvis Street.

In and out, short agenda. No point getting the girls involved, he said.

The hotel reminded me of that dreary apartment building years before, and the delivery of laundry, and Mike's casual indifference to the conventions of the laundry trade.

Allan brought along a dour-looking man about our age, but he didn't introduce him.

Immediately after shaking my hand, the stranger headed for the bathroom. He didn't close the door. I could hear the clank of the toilet tank and the swish of a shower curtain.

–What's he looking for? I asked.

Allan whispered, *Don't mind him.*

Later, the stranger asked to see the business cards the cops had given me and noted down their names. Then he asked a lot of questions. Eventually I asked,

–Are you by any chance a lawyer?

–Why do you ask?

I decided not to answer. Allan, throughout this exchange, was sitting silently on a bed, elbows on his knees, staring at the floor.

–So, what did you say about Albert Rose?

–That he was a client, I said.

–And what if they come back?

–I've done my job. I'm not concerned.

–We hope.

Allan stood.

–So, what was all this about, Al?

–Due diligence, Byron. You know about due diligence.

As it turned out, my return flight was delayed. I called Allan.

–Let's have a drink. Just the two of us.

–How long is the delay?

–They're saying three hours.

–I'll meet you at the airport hotel. In the lobby bar.

We had a history of cryptic conversations, Allan and I. Maybe it was the crucial factor in the long survival of our friendship, our ability to communicate through a kind of mental telepathy. We didn't have to say much to understand each other. For long periods of time we didn't have to say anything at all.

–This was a long trip for not much, I said after we sat down.

–It was important anyway. I'm familiar with those cops and I needed to hear what they're up to from you face to face. Phones are tricky nowadays.

–What *are* they up to?

–Right now, just fishin'.

–Tell me I'm delusional, but I think I might have just met Albert Rose, I said.

He was staring around the almost empty bar.

–One of them, anyway. What did you think of him?

–Where did you find him?

–You guessed it. He's a lawyer. Or was. Got into some trouble with the Law Society over a trust account. I give him work sometimes. He used to be a cop too, or could you tell?

–Bent?

He held up a hand, thumb and forefinger almost touching.

–Give him a little slack. He's a bit paranoid, in a creative way. Checking out the bathroom was a bit over the top, though.

–No kidding.

–But Byron, this is good.

–How so? We have cops poking into things.

–They came, they sniffed, they went away. You handled it perfectly.

He shifted his weight in the chair. Signalled for two more drinks.

–I've got plans to keep you busy for a while.

–Happy to hear that.

–Albert and the other Alberts . . . we're going to be buying them out.

–Buy them out? I thought the whole point was that they weren't in.

–Okay. Pay them off. They've done their thing as stand-ins for you and me.

–Do they know that?

–I'm tired of all the Alberts. I'm going to try the big leagues for a while. We'll be placing our holdings in a new company, and then liquidate. We need cash. We'll be getting into major real estate development. We need bigger players.

–What kind of major real estate development?

–Office towers. High-rise condos. Some high-volume parking plazas. So, you're going to be busy with a lot of paper-work. After this, we'll be able to retire.

–What would you do if you retired?

–I'd dedicate my time to golf. Maybe design my own golf course, a layout that would always let me win.

–A mini-putt, perhaps.

–Ho, ho, Byron. You missed your calling. But we should make more time for fun. Life is short.

–So I hear.

He was smiling, stroking his sweaty glass with a forefinger. There was soft music, the sound of glasses tinkling at the bar. I was thinking about money, real estate, flipping property, doing mental math.

–So, you're on top of all this, Byron? Where we're heading, long term?

–No.

–Good. Just remember, the secret of survival is mobility. Keep moving. Keep the enemy confused. I'm working on some joint ventures.

–With anybody that I know?

–Unlikely. They're foreigners.

–How foreign?

–Very. Think of these arrangements as friendly one-night stands. Transactional. Among adults. Win-win for everybody.

–Good to know.

–I could use you up here full-time.

–When the time is right.

He stood. We shook hands and hugged. I left.

The transition happened slowly, and from my point of view seamlessly, over about two years. The people I'd been setting up as principals until then had been nobodies, literally. They proved easy to get rid of. Albert Rose simply disappeared, as did a number of other obscure personas and made-up identities, along with the disposable companies I created for them.

There were no self-aggrandizing announcements as the business grew. No press releases. The properties were modest, compared with the megaprojects then disfiguring the Toronto and Vancouver skylines. Hardly anyone that mattered seemed to notice what we were up to.

I used high-end lawyers from established firms in Nova Scotia and Toronto, solid outfits that were considered to be terminally dull. I deliberately avoided my old law firm. No point risking familiarity.

I knew the files. I knew the endgame. Money coming out of Nowhere, going into Nowhere. Real properties bought and sold by unreal entities.

It was actually fun to work with the other lawyers, putting up with the condescension the elite reserve for people who seem to have no grand political or public profile. Especially from some of the older ones, in Halifax, who vaguely remembered my humble origins in the profession.

Annie, on the other hand, had their full attention any time she spoke. I believe they deduced that if Annie was my wife and partner, there must be more to me than was obvious to them.

Half the time, I barely understood what she was going on about.

One meeting in particular stands out. Allan was there, which was unusual. He introduced himself as my assistant, both of us enjoying the theatre of it all. I was playing the star. The boss. And I looked the part. Allan had instructed me beforehand to get a suit made, something that actually fit me for a change, and to get a city haircut. Maybe let the whiskers grow for a day or two.

We had three other lawyers on our side of the long oval table. After I introduced our team and we got down to business, Annie did most of the talking. On the other side of the table were bankers, brokers and lawyers, and an observer who didn't introduce himself but spent a lot of time scrolling on his phone. Obviously a flunky, but there was something in his bearing that roused my curiosity.

I excused myself before the meeting ended, saying I had a plane to catch. The remaining business was for Annie and the other lawyers. Allan, my so-called assistant, stayed behind to monitor.

Passing by the man who hadn't identified himself, I overheard him talking softly in a foreign language into his phone. I had seen enough spy movies to recognize that he was speaking Russian. I paused. He turned his head, looked up, stopped talking.

I fished my cellphone from an inside pocket, said "Hello" into it, walked two more paces, stopped. Started talking to myself. The mystery man resumed his conversation. I pretended to be ending mine, held my phone out as if checking messages, reversed the selfie camera and took a picture of the man behind me.

And left.

Later, I e-mailed the photograph to Annie: *Do you know this dude?*

He never introduced himself, she replied.

Maybe you should keep an eye on him.

One thing I will not forget. Allan called me at the farm, late on a sultry August evening not long after that meeting. He was in unusually high spirits, told me to clear my schedule for the next week.

–We're going to step away from work for a few days, mate. We're going to be young again.

–Sounds good, I said.

–Peggy and I are coming down there. She's going off to do her thing and you and I, my friend, are going to play golf. Non-stop. Every day while I'm there. Until we're sick of it. Pick a golf course and book us into a hotel.

I remember thinking, *Fucking golf, again?*

20.

In retrospect, it feels as though I procrastinated for weeks before I finally retrieved the mysterious memory device Allan had stuffed into my pocket in Toronto. I knew that I should just plug it into my computer and deal with what was there. I didn't. It can wait, I thought. I was dreading another brush with his mortality and, to be honest, my own.

The most pressing business waiting for me on my return was a DUI charge against a prominent local doctor for whom I'd once handled a relatively friendly marital breakup. I eventually handed his file to one of my former colleagues in Halifax, a litigator with the kind of pit-bull tenacity that is required in such no-hope cases.

Another problem involved an insurance claim for which I had almost missed a filing deadline. My cranky client was threatening to report me to the bar society on account of it. These and other chores required most of a week of concentration and telephone tag at the expense of other things. Like looking at Allan's ominous thumb drive.

And then there was a reminder from the post office that I had a package waiting there.

It first occurred to me that I was bored while I was driving to town to fetch the package. Town people used to make a joke about country living: you might not live longer in the boondocks, but it will definitely seem longer. But what I was feeling wasn't funny. It was like a numbness spreading in my core.

It was late afternoon. The sky was dense with cloud, but there was a space between the bottom of a cloud bank and the crest of the horizon and it was suddenly ablaze. I stopped the car on the shoulder of the road to watch as the sun descended from the clouds and then melted on the burning sea.

The spectacle has always defined this place for me, the clarity of light, the infinity of sea. Could I imagine life without it?

Not easily. But for the first time ever, it didn't seem impossible.

When I turned up at her wicket, the clerk in the post office observed that I had been away. I nodded, annoyed. Yes. I'd been gone. Briefly.

–Anywhere interesting?

–Just Toronto, I said.

–Ahh, she said.

She was studying the package as she handed it to me and it wouldn't have surprised me if she'd asked me what was in it.

It was only when I had it in my hand that I remembered the genetic test kit that I'd impulsively ordered online before I'd gone off to Toronto. Then I remembered why I'd sent for it.

The instructions seemed to me to be nonsensical. And yet I followed them precisely. I filled out all the forms and provided credit card details. I refrained from food and drink for hours. I postponed brushing my teeth. Then, with some difficulty and not without spillage, I drooled saliva into a small vial.

Could it be so simple? I thought of Mom and her slow decline and our denial of all the signs we saw before us. And now Allan. It was at this moment, thinking about Allan and the state he was in, I remembered the USB drive he'd slipped into my jacket pocket.

When I opened it, I was almost relieved to realize the file made little sense to me. At the top of a single page, in boldface: **TPWC**. And then, single-spaced, in three parallel columns, short lists of numbers. Fifteen in all. It could have been a secret code. But they looked like bank accounts. But where? He had written at the bottom of the page: *In time, all things are made transparent. AND GURTH WILL HAVE HIS PAIRINGS.*

Where had I seen that enigmatic line before? Gurth? And then I remembered: in a stairwell outside the dining hall at the university, many years before, and Thomas Carlyle, the book I'd been studying the first time I'd had a conversation with the Great Chase.

TPWC. *The pigs were Cedric's!*

I took the obscurity of his message as an excuse to ignore the thing, for a little longer. I was sure I still had that book somewhere, *The Collected Works of Thomas Carlyle.* I'd have to track it down.

Allan wasn't just playing mind games with our wives, he was messing with my head too. I shut down my computer, slipped the USB drive into a drawer. A memory that was meaningless for now, deferred.

—

When, two days later, I handed the return envelope with my DNA sample to the woman in the post office, she examined the address and remarked,

–My daughter did this once and found relatives in Australia.

–Did what?

–Went looking for her ancestors.

–Great. And did she get in touch with the Australian relatives?

–She tried, I guess. But they never responded.

On the drive back, the narrow, darkened road to Malignant Cove felt dangerous. Pretty houses partly hidden by the trees now seemed melancholy.

My annoyance with the woman in the post office slowly turned to empathy. People who are nosy are basically bored. I had known her forever. But now I knew *about* her. She was obviously lonely, and her response was curiosity about other people. *Is this what lies in store for me?*

I need a change.

I was suddenly intrigued by Allan's compulsion to dispose of everything. It's a reality we all must face—decluttering, they call it—something I learned about in my law practice, helping people with their wills, helping them dispose of their possessions.

Our wives think he's going crazy. Perhaps he's just decluttering on a grand, outrageous scale. If we're wise, we control the process while we can, or someone else will do it carelessly when we're no longer competent. Considered in this new light, I, unlike Annie and Peggy, didn't feel particularly threatened by this winding down of his affairs. Of *our* affairs.

Back at home, I rang Allan's number. Peggy answered.

–He's asleep, she said quietly.

I told her I had made up my mind—I would move to the city and stay there for as long as it might take to put our business on a safe and solid footing.

–That's brilliant news. Do you know when?

–I have some things to deal with here. But soon.

21

I knew I should be packing for what might be a long-term absence. But there really wasn't much to pack. Clothing. A few files. Some books. *The Collected Works of Thomas Carlyle*, for one. Which reminded me—*where did I put Allan's thumb drive?*

Because its existence was supposed to be a secret, I'd taken pains to hide the goddamned thing. And now, in my distraction, I'd forgotten where it was. He had slipped it into an inside jacket pocket. I was sure of that. But what jacket? And then what?

I vaguely remembered having placed it in a drawer. I ransacked the kitchen before concluding logically that I would have put it in my desk. Of course.

But during the brief walk from my kitchen to my office, I found myself standing staring into a closet upstairs without knowing how I got there. There is now a blank space between remembering the desk and realizing I was now standing, confused, upstairs in what had been my mother's bedroom.

Why was I standing in a trance in my dead mother's bedroom? Fucking idiot. This, I find, is what happens when systems fail unexpectedly—I lash out, mostly at myself. And then I noticed a stack of photo albums and several shoe boxes on a closet shelf above the hangers.

A more superstitious person might have been inclined to think that she had, somehow, led me there. I dismissed the idea. I shut the closet door, turned to leave. Stopped.

I'd once spent an afternoon snooping in here at a time before the past had any meaning. I recall reading letters written by my mother's friends. Unrevealing letters to my mother from my father. But now I also remembered an old newspaper clipping among the letters.

I rummaged through the shoe boxes until I found it. There was my father's name above a larger headline: ACQUITTAL IN ASSAULT.

My father had assaulted someone. This was explicit. But whom? The victim's name had been omitted from the story because my father's lawyer had argued it could reveal the identity of an innocent third party. A minor.

I recognized the lawyer's name—he was long deceased. The judge had heard his arguments in camera and had ultimately directed the jurors to return a verdict of not guilty.

I sat down on the bed, mystified.

Who was the innocent third party?

The minor?

For God's sake, idiot, just face it.

My cellphone was ringing. I wanted to ignore it, but I pulled it out of my pocket. Allan's number.

—Allan's had another stroke, Peggy said when I answered.

It was as if I had been expecting it.

—

Annie was waiting at the usual place, in the usual Mercedes. She popped the trunk from inside the car. I heaved two heavy suitcases in, closed the lid.

–A two-bag trip. Excellent, she said when I climbed in.

–We'll see, I said. It's mostly files and books.

She focused on the surrounding traffic, smoothly executing perilous manoeuvres in the airport chaos. She swore softly.

–Fucking limos.

–They think you're one of them, I said.

A brief, tight smile. And then we were quiet until we were on the teeming southbound freeway.

–I'll take you straight to Peggy's, she said.

–How is he?

–Not good. I think you'll be staying there for a few days, at least until we can make a more permanent arrangement.

–Permanent?

–I mean longer term. Nothing's permanent.

–What about the condo?

–I think it's better all around if you're at Peggy's.

I turned my attention to the terrifying traffic, too fast, too close, too reckless. There was something in her tone. Something about where I was staying. Peggy's doing?

–So how's Peggy coping?

–Peggy always copes.

–I thought I'd be staying with you . . .

–We can talk about it later.

A roaring eighteen-wheeler passed us on the inside. After the noise died down, I asked,

–So, how bad was this stroke?

–More like a series of mini-strokes, she said. They call them transient something. TIAs. He's been online, reading up.

–If he's doing online research, it can't be all that bad.

–He says it's all about old football injuries. He thinks he's getting better.

–I thought concussion damage was permanent.

–Try telling him that.

Then we were on the side streets in a neighbourhood I recognized. The trees were stripped for winter.

–What about you, Annie? Is everything okay with you?

She laughed and reached for my hand.

–Peachy. I'm peachy.

I held her hand until she took it back.

Annie parked and walked me and my suitcases to the door, where Peggy was waiting. She hugged me and kissed Annie's cheek. I found that odd for them, the cheek kissing.

–Allan's napping. Can you stay for coffee, Annie?

She stayed, but left her coat on. But the conversation had hardly passed the chit-chat stage when she abruptly put her cup down, stood and said she had to run.

–What's with Annie? I asked when she was gone.

Peggy studied me for what felt like a long time.

–You two haven't talked.

–Not really. Just in the car.

She stood, picked up my cup.

–How about some hot?

–Sure.

After she came back and had handed me my coffee, she sat and tucked her legs underneath herself. She studied her cup for a while, then looked up at me and said,

–Annie's seeing someone.

I let the information register. It added up, explained the silences and stiffness. The only real question in my mind was why I was feeling so indifferent.

–Anybody I know?

–I have my suspicions.

–You two don't talk?

–Not about that. It might be nothing more than some new friendship. She's a very platonic individual. Unlike her sister. But she's been lonely.

I nodded. Her phone rang.

–Hey. You're awake. Byron's here. ·

Allan was in his hospital bed, still half-asleep. It seemed like he stared at me for maybe fifteen seconds before he recognized me. Then he waved a hand, and struggled up onto an elbow. I caught a distressing whiff of urine—unmistakable— and disinfectant.

–Help me out of here, he said.

–Are you sure?

–Yes, I'm sure.

We stumbled to his desk, where I lowered him into his chair. I sat across from him and we just stared at one another. His face was bonier, unshaven. Frosted whiskers, except on the upper lip, where there was the beginning of a dark moustache.

–You're looking good, I said.

He nodded. Picked up a pen.

–To what do I owe the honour?

–I hear you had another little episode?

–Who said that?

–You've obviously bounced back.

–You're not believing the horseshit about dementia and whatever. Old football stuff is all it is.

He stared off toward some distant corner of the room. Outside street sounds filled the silence. A passing car. A barking dog.

–I guess I'll be staying here for a while this time, if that's okay, I said.

–That'll be great. We can talk. Maybe we can go out.

–If you're up to it.

–I'm up for anything.

–I was hoping to stay at Annie's, but . . .

I paused, watching his expression.

–I hear she's got a boyfriend, I said finally.

–No big deal, right? We're all grown-ups.

He shrugged.

–Peggy doesn't seem to know much about him, I said.

–Peggy knows.

–Do you?

–It's a Russian, I think.

–A Russian.

–Someone she encountered at meetings who was working for the partners. But don't hold me to that. I don't know for sure.

I fished my cellphone from an inside jacket pocket. Clicked on Gallery, scrolled through photographs. Stopped on one. Passed the phone to Allan.

–Him, maybe?

–Could be. What's this from?

–Last summer, before your stroke. A meeting. You were there.

He grimaced.

–The memory isn't great, he said. Fucking football. If I knew then what I know now.

I studied the photograph. A strong face. Eyes full of curiosity. He had a solid hairline, clipped short, with a widow's peak. He was maybe in his mid-forties. Young compared to us, compared to Annie. But Annie and her sister never looked their age. Never seemed their age.

Allan took the phone again, studied the image a little longer.

–What made you photograph this fella?

–I was curious. He was the one guy who didn't introduce himself when we went around the table. Made me wonder. Then I heard him speaking Russian. So, when you said a Russian, I just guessed.

–Nick.

–His name is Nick?

–Nick something. I can't keep their names straight. Annie's been dealing with him. If you're worried, just say the word. I can get rid of him.

He tried to snap his fingers, but they just rubbed together.

–I'm not worried about anybody.

–How long are you around for?

–As long as needed.

He held his hand out. It was trembling. I grasped it.

–Someday soon, I'd like to get out of here. Maybe have a pint somewhere. Like the old days. We're overdue . . .

–Any time, I said.

The light was on in Peggy's room. I rapped gently on the door frame, looked in. She was in bed, wearing a high-necked nightgown, reading glasses on her nose. She put her book down. Patted the bed beside the book.

–Sit.

I sat. She rubbed my back.

–You're okay?

–Women ask that a lot. I often wonder if they really want to know.

–Look at me.

I swivelled so that I was facing her. She removed the glasses, placed them on a bedside table. She squirmed away, toward the far side of the bed, making room.

–Lie down, she instructed. And I did.

–Do you really think he has dementia?

–There isn't any doubt. He has very clear moments, then his concentration goes and it's like he isn't there at all.

–What would happen if we both came down with it?

–You and me?

–Him and me.

–What are the odds of that?

She laughed.

–It's in my genes, I said.

–Sure. Like cancer. We all have it in the genes. We have all kinds of garbage in our genes. We keep our fingers crossed. It's all we can do.

She kissed me lightly on the lips.

–Now go to bed. You know where your room is. I'm glad you're here.

I kissed her back, emphatically.

–He says he'd like to go out.

–Good luck with that.

–Is he able?

–Physically, yes. We have a van, you know. But he's refused to even look at it.

–How much did you know about the Russian?

She did a rather theatrical double take, but the expression on her face was cagey. She could have been a lawyer.

–What Russian?

–Never mind.

Allan was shaved, groomed, dressed for the world, sitting at his desk. He was cheerful. He banged his cane on the floor.

–Let's rock and roll.

He struggled to his feet.

–There's a nice little place not far away called Allen's. Named after a joint I used to go to in New York. How about that? I was a regular back when I was mobile.

We took the van.

He insisted on a booth and it was a struggle to get him settled. A waiter brought us menus then resumed his conversation with the bartender. It was mid-afternoon and the place was almost deserted.

–They don't remember me, Allan said.

–When were you last in here?

–Just before that golf game, last summer. I was ten feet tall then. They'd jump to attention when I came through the door. How far did we get with that game?

–Tee on the tenth hole, I said.

–Right. I remember now. For a long time I convinced myself that we'd be going back to finish it someday. That isn't going to happen.

I picked up a menu. Opened it.

–Let's have a pint and a talk before we order. We can talk here, he said.

–We can't at the house?

–The wives are all over me. Especially Peggy. You've seen it. Maybe they're just looking after me. Or. Well. They're clever women. Who the fuck knows?

The waiter came back. We ordered pints of beer.

–How much have they told you about my plans?

–Just that you want to start giving stuff away.

–That's one way of looking at it. I'm actually creating a big fund. You guys will manage it. It will offer possibilities for worthy folks who otherwise won't get to do stuff the way we did. It's all about money now. The world is different.

–That's admirable.

–Don't mock.

–I'm not. But do you really want the attention this will draw?

–You know and I know I won't be around by then.

–Still, it will be a story. A mystery story. Questions about the mystery man and his mystery money.

–You guys are smart enough to figure it out.

–For example, the apartment building.

–The old people.

–That's in the works now, I gather. You'll still be around when you give that piece of real estate to the tenants.

–So what?

–How long do you think it will be before a reporter starts asking questions about the knight in shining armour? I gather these tenants are well-off and well-connected, the kind of people who get listened to.

–So, we just tell the reporter to fuck off.

–Not that simple.

–Baloney.

He frowned and sipped his beer.

–I'll leave it up to you, he said.

–I'll try to make it happen, but discreetly. So, the next phase is what?

–Downsizing.

–Decluttering.

He laughed.

–Clutter. Good word. Look, we had to take some chances to accommodate a significant infusion of cash. So we found people who had a similar requirement and formed a temporary partnership.

–The requirement being?

–Don't play dumb, Byron. In the real world there are many

sensible reasons for churning money. The cleanest way is through property. You know that.

–Wash, spin, rinse. Repeat.

He rolled his eyes, shook his head and looked away.

–Sometimes I wonder about you, Byron.

–So you're saying we've completed that phase. When did that happen?

–Recently. I kept you out of it for your own good. Now that it doesn't matter, I was able to do the talking for myself. Let's just say there's a lot of money that has been refreshed.

–That's a change, I said.

–What is?

–You front and centre. It's been quite a long time since you've been you. How did that feel?

He smiled, wistfully, I thought.

–They'll never catch me now. The Great Chase. Remember that?

I nodded, and said, I thought you hated that name?

–The Great Chase? Yeah. I did. But it's kind of funny now. Who ever thought that kicking the bucket might be fun?

–Fuck off, Allan. Cut the morbid shit.

–Face facts, Byron. That's your job.

–Okay. Now what?

–Most of the money in the States has been liberated from that swamp.

I took the USB drive from my pocket and held it up. He nodded.

–Good. I was afraid you'd lost it.

Then he was digging impatiently through his own pockets.

–What you're trying to find is always in the last place you look.

–That makes sense, I said, teasing. But I noticed a quick flash of anger in his eyes.

–You people think I'm . . . aha, there it is.

He held up another thumb drive.

–I might be slow, but I'm not stupid. Okay?

–Okay, I said. What's on that one?

–This will help when the time comes.

He slipped it into the inside pocket of his jacket. Picked up the glass of beer.

–If anything happens, it will be easy enough for you to find in my desk. You'll need it before you can do anything with the one you have.

–Which is what?

–You know as well as I do.

–Bank accounts.

–Correct. The thing I have here in my pocket will tell you what bank they're in. It might take a trip to another part of the world. But it'll be a nice trip. Plan to make it in the winter. It'll be somewhere warm.

–How much have you told our wives?

–I've told them nothing.

–They think you don't trust them.

–They have that right.

–You mean they're correct in their assumption, or you don't care what they think?

–Both.

The waiter was hovering. Allan waved him away.

–Listen. They will try to keep the business going. They'll have control of what's still out there. But I want everything wound up. Liquidated. And I want some good to come from all the money. As simple as that. They have different ideas.

–What is still out there?

–A few million here and there. Equity in some stuff I haven't managed to get rid of.

–The rest?

–It's in your pocket.

–How much is in my pocket?

He smiled. Patted his own pocket.

–You'll know when you need to know.

He took another sip of his beer, then leaned back. I noticed that he hadn't lost the habit of regularly scanning a room, who comes in, who goes out. Who's talking, who's listening.

–Money is a queer thing, Byron. I've always figured the hardest word in the English language is "enough." It's a word that makes people crazy when it comes to money. What's enough, eh?

He sighed, drank deeply from the glass, picked up his menu.

–We should eat something.

–So, how much do you know about Nick, this Russian?

–The limo driver.

–The what?

–I didn't tell you that? He's nobody. Speaks the language is all, so they take him with them everywhere they go. He runs a high-class livery service for the wealthy. Works out of the casino.

–In Toronto.

–East of Toronto.

–A casino.

–I love casinos. One of the most important financial institutions in the system, Byron. Think of a stock exchange that lets ordinary people on the floor.

–So, this Nick is the guy who is seeing Annie.

–I didn't say that. But you just say the word and I'll have the nuts cut right off of him.

He wasn't smiling when he said it.

He picked up the tab. He paid cash, carefully counting out nearly two hundred dollars. Dropped a forty-dollar tip. He scanned the bill, folded it and put it in a bulging wallet. Then he just stared at me.

–We might not be doing this again, he said.

–Don't be so sure.

–I need to know something.

–Sure.

He looked away from me, scanned the room again. Sighed deeply.

–Peggy. You'll take care of her, right?

–I'm not sure Peggy needs . . .

–Listen to me.

He reached across the table, caught my wrist.

–Nothing bad can happen to her, right? No matter what went down in the past, and what I think now, she always stuck by me. You look out for her.

He held my wrist. He held my eyes. And I suddenly knew what it was like to be threatened by my dearest friend.

22.

That evening I found an e-mail message on my phone that was flagged *Immediate attention required.* It was from the genetic research outfit. I opened it to find that the analysis of my spit was now complete and my genetic secrets now available.

I logged on.

I scrolled through the information. I had a cousin in Prince Rupert, BC. I was 96 percent of Celtic origin and 4 percent "other." I also had a marker that presented a strong possibility that, like my mother, I'd have Alzheimer's disease before I died.

It was a flat statement, cranked out by a computer. No evidence of human input.

I stared at the jumbled explanation. High levels of ApoE4, whatever that was. Symptoms of dementia may appear abruptly or over time. And near the end, there was what seemed to be another alert, in boldface. A second assessment of my data had turned up a significant anomaly involving something called PSEN1.

The existence of the mutant gene raised the *probability* that a disease pathogenesis was already under way and it could inevitably lead to a loss of PS1 function. I was advised to consult my doctor.

I didn't know what "PS1" stood for, and there was no further explanation in the e-mail. The word "mutation" was alarming. "Pathogenesis" was a word new to me. "Disease" was all too understandable.

But the message quickly became clear to me. Reduced to its most bleak conclusion, and supported by my anxious Google searching, it was a notification that I was facing early-onset dementia and that it was possible, if not likely, the process had already started.

I stood at the bedroom window. Rain in small rivulets trickled down the glass. I could hear an occasional car swish by on nearby streets. There was a tattered maple tree in their backyard, a few red leaves clinging, soon to be defeated by the inevitable snow.

I didn't sleep much. The cryptic diagnosis was almost too incredible to be distressing and was soon overtaken by a struggle to make sense of my recent conversations with my dying friend.

Which of us is crazy? Or are we both?

I got out of bed, turned on a bedside light and texted Annie. *We need to talk. ASAP.*

I suppose that a doctor would know better, but even as a lawyer I can safely say that there is no typical reaction to news that life as we know it, and have come to take for granted, is about to end.

A young lawyer told me once how he wept uncontrollably for days after he'd received a diagnosis of multiple sclerosis.

I had a client, a 28-year-old construction worker, who found out he had leukemia just after he'd been screwed in a divorce. He would die without a marrow transplant. He told me he felt lost. Abandoned.

The life trajectory we take for granted can slip into a decline we barely notice, if we register it at all. I know that. I'm not sentimental about existence. It's like being on an airplane. Sooner or later, we feel the gentle nudge from a change in ambience. Or maybe it's a jolt. We awaken from a slumber. We raise our eyes from the book or the computer screen. We have started our descent. It is predictable, but it is unexpected just the same.

I remembered Mom's sardonic comment about the arseholes she would no longer feel obliged to tolerate. She had a glass of wine. She laughed with us. She excused herself and went to bed, though it was still the middle of the afternoon. I don't think she went to bed to grieve.

But I can now imagine that she was weary, had no energy for the tiresome conversation that Annie and I would feel compelled to have. And maybe just a bit pissed off at those of us who would survive her.

Annie's condo was a place I didn't recognize, though I'd stayed there occasionally on business trips before she took possession. It was an older building, perched on the lakeside, its back to the city. Relatively low-rise, it could ignore the cluster of newer towers that had grown up behind it, and it would probably outlive them all because of the location and the view and the quality of its original construction. Before my DNA analysis, I'd have noticed only that the layout of Annie's unit was significantly different than I remembered it. Now, the unfamiliarity was ominous.

She had extended the kitchen to accommodate a huge table and seating for eight people. What was once a living room and a den was now merged into an open space with three separate configurations of stylish furniture, unified by the one feature that I did clearly recognize: the stunning view of Lake Ontario.

You don't forget what you didn't know, I told myself. *As time passes, there is much that will feel unfamiliar.*

Annie made coffee. The way she went about it gave me the feeling that she was stalling.

—So what's up? she asked when she finally sat down across from me, a tiny coffee table between us.

—Do you remember that DNA test I was thinking about?

—Refresh my memory, she said.

—I've had results.

—Maybe a drink of something with the coffee? A cognac.

I had prepared a reasonable briefing—serious disclosure without melodrama. I was thrown off by her tone. *A drink? What's up?* Questions for a client.

I thought of: *Well, for openers, I think I've started dying.*

—Nothing to drink, I said.

She sat there. Stared thoughtfully, waiting. It was her indifference, I think, that made me hesitate. *What's the point?*

It crossed my mind—*I'm talking to the wrong Winter sister. I should just leave.*

I said,

—You look well.

—Thank you.

—The place has changed a lot since I was here last.

–That must have been a long time ago, because I really haven't done much. So. Your DNA?

When she raised her mug, I swear she checked her wristwatch.

On a mantel just behind her, above her left shoulder, I noticed two framed photographs.

One was a print of the surreptitious photo I had taken of the Russian, Nick, and mailed to her. The upscale taxi driver. The other was of Nick and two women, with Niagara Falls in the background. They were partly obscured by mist, but the two women were unmistakably Annie and her sister. They were all laughing, and standing very close together.

The photos were directly in my line of sight. Nick's young, smiling face. Peggy. Annie. Beaming in the fog.

And then it was as if the mist was billowing around them, obscuring features. And then it seemed that they had vanished. And the mist was now descending around where I was sitting. And I became aware of my own voice commenting on the photographs, but it was as if the voice was coming out of someone else.

I took a gulp of the coffee and it burned.

I gagged and spat it out and heard myself say *Goddam fuck* and then the floor was rushing toward my face and it smashed against my forehead. Blood was boiling in my nose. And somewhere in the distance I could hear a woman's voice calling out to me with a kind of urgency that sounded like . . . Could it really be?

She was calling: *Angus!*

———

There was the roaring of machinery.

There was a cold wetness on my face. The woman was leaning close. There was rag-wrapped ice against my forehead. No. It was snow. Cold, refreshing. Melting. Wet. Snow.

I was desperate to pee.

I need to pee.

And the man's voice was saying, *Let me help you with that snowsuit, sonny.*

Hands delicate on a sticky zipper.

–Hurry.

But suddenly the nice man who was helping me was gone. Snatched away. And now he was struggling on the floor. An insect on its back. Legs flailing horribly. My father standing there, red-faced.

And I am losing my pee. Losing it, and the warmth is spreading in my snowsuit and I will be in trouble with my mom . . .

I was running now. Running toward the daylight that hurt my eyes. And the noise that hurt my ears.

And someone was screaming: *Angus!*

And falling down.

Time folds around itself. Absorbs itself. I am confused. There is motion. There is a wailing sound. I am cold and I am warm, swaddled in a blanket, but I know that I am warm from having pissed myself. And there is the familiar flood of grief and fear and shame. There is so much trouble when I pee in my snowsuit or in my bed. So much trouble for my mom, who has to wash my clothes and bedding on a scrubbing board and hang them on the line outside, and it is winter when nothing dries without freezing first, but she is leaning over me and her face is terrified and her eyes are wet and red-rimmed as I have never seen them and she is not angry. She is afraid. And she is not my mom.

Byron!

She is Annie.

I am in an ambulance. The oxygen mask. The hanging accessories around me, swaying with the motion. The ambulance is screaming and snarling, surging and halting through mid afternoon gridlock. Annie is speaking, but the racket makes it impossible to hear what she is saying. I know where I am, but I don't know how I got here. I remember the picture of the Russian. Even his name—Nick. I struggle to sit up, but now there is a man restraining me, and Annie is helping him.

–Whoa, whoa, I say, I don't need this. I want out of here.

Then we lurch-stop and the back door swings open. People walking quickly, turning, curious, briefly glancing in, disappearing. Two men drag the gurney I am strapped to toward the light. And I am struggling again.

–Let me go, for Christ's sake! This is . . .

Annie's voice is no longer chilled, but gentle.

–Hush now. Everything is under control.

Glass doors whoosh and I am being wheeled inside, down a corridor, past hurrying people and stationary gurneys under searing fluorescent lighting, pale-green faces, indifferent loudspeaker squawking, into a quiet anteroom. Curtains all around. And a young man in a white coat. Friendly. Interested.

–So, what's your story? he asks.

The question is important. The answer is important.

I needed to pee. Somebody was helping me, but he fell down. And then I fell down. And everyone was mad . . .

But Annie is telling another story.

–He just, sort of, went quiet and pale, then he gagged on a mouthful of coffee and I'd jumped up to get a paper towel or something. And when I came back, he was on the floor.

–You didn't hear anything? Like a bang? A clunk?

–I don't think so.

–We'll need to check to make sure he didn't strike his head on anything. Has he fainted before?

–There was an accident when he was little. On a farm. It was fairly serious. It left his leg badly injured. He can be unsteady on his feet sometimes. He suffered a head injury then too, I think. He's never spoken much about it.

–You are his . . .?

–Wife. Anne. Annie.

–Okay, Anne. We need to keep him for a little while, do some tests. At his age and with the earlier injury, it's worth exploring what's going on in his brain. You're unaware of anything like this happening recently?

–This is new.

–Well. We'll check him out to make sure it's nothing major. Let's get him out of this wet stuff.

–I think it's just the coffee he spilled on himself.

–No big deal. Nothing to explain. Any family history that you know of?

–His dad died fairly young from what they believed was a stroke. His mom died of Alzheimer's.

The doctor frowns and makes a note.

–Good to know. I'll order an MRI.

We were alone. I could feel her hand on my hands, which were folded on my chest. I opened my eyes.

–There you are, she said.

I smiled at her.

–I want to go home, I said.

–Soon.

She patted my hand, kissed me lightly on the forehead and went away.

23.

It felt like such a long, long time, but it was only two or three days. Two or three days filed away in a generic folder with all the other days I'd spent in other hospitals. Two or three days that felt like weeks misplaced among the weeks that felt like months and years.

On that last occasion in the hospital, I was ready to go home by noon the next day. And, mercifully, the doctor told me that I could be discharged the following morning, on day three. They were reasonably certain my little episode was an isolated event.

–We just need to wait for test results confirming that.

I told him I'd just had my DNA analyzed.

He looked surprised.

–People do it now for genealogy. But, because of my mother, I thought, who knows. There was a company offering to look for the risk of getting Alzheimer's.

He didn't respond.

–Actually, my test indicated I am at risk.

He sighed.

–If you have anything to worry about, we'll spot it. What can you tell me about that accident, when you were five?

–Not much. I was knocked unconscious, so there was obviously a head injury. But people were more interested in whether I would lose my leg. Whether I would ever walk again.

–After we have all the results, we'll talk. Okay?

He stood up, shook my hand.

Annie and Peggy must have been waiting just outside the door. The doctor was hardly gone when they came in.

Peggy was the one to kiss me, while Annie stood back, arms folded.

–You're looking a whole lot better, Peggy said.

–They're saying I can leave tomorrow morning. I won't bother you. I can manage it myself.

–No, no, I'll come and get you. They won't let you leave on your own anyway, said Annie.

–Where will I be going?

They exchanged quick glances, then looked back at me.

–We think you should stay with Peggy for another little while, Annie said.

–Okay. Sure.

Peggy was blinking rapidly.

–It's about Allan, Annie said.

–What about Allan?

–I should go, Peggy said. I left him on his own.

–Before you go, is there something I don't know?

Annie said,

–There's a lot you don't know, darling.

–Like, who is this Nick?

–Okay, I'm away, said Peggy.

She kissed me again. She and Annie embraced. And then there was just the two of us in a silence broken only by the universal sounds of hospitals.

–About Nick . . .

She ignored me.

–Allan is slipping, she said.

–How bad?

She hesitated for what felt like a long time.

–You can see for yourself tomorrow.

–I meant to tell you something the other day, before this happened.

I tried to stop myself. This wasn't something that I wanted anyone to know. But I couldn't help it. Couldn't help this shameful reaching out. I needed something. I was desperate for something.

–I mentioned that I was having my DNA checked for the possibility of Alzheimer's or whatever.

She was looking everywhere but at me.

–I wouldn't want to hold you up if you have more important things to do, I said.

–Let's not play games, Byron.

–Well. My DNA analysis indicates early-onset Alzheimer's.

She sighed, stared toward a window.

–I think we need a more scientific opinion than a mail-order test before we panic, she said.

–Yes, you're right.

–Meanwhile. There's Allan. There's no pretty way to put this, Byron. I'm afraid our Allan's done.

–Allan is *not* done. Allan is a long way from done.

–Face the reality, Byron, and believe me . . . We're all under stress. Not just you. Focus on the here and now, and what we have ahead of us.

I was ready to go, sitting on the side of the hospital bed in sweats, a T-shirt and my leather jacket. Running shoes. No socks. Shaving gear, toothbrush and a book in a backpack on the floor. Annie had taken away the clothes I had been wearing when I fell.

Did I really piss my pants?

There was a quick rap at the door and two doctors came in—the one who had been treating me and one who was considerably younger. I missed the name of the younger one but caught the fact that he was a medical geneticist. He explained that he was part of a very large international investigation of dementia. The causes. How it advances in a patient. How it changes people.

The study involved thousands of individuals. Men and woman. People of various ethnic and cultural and geographic backgrounds. Ages, physical abilities, intelligence.

–So you want to study me.

–We're not sure yet. But given the family history, your symptoms and the childhood concussion, maybe. You say you've had this ancestry test. We don't consider those tests conclusive, but they often give reliable indicators. So, we'll put you down as a possible participant. Okay?

I made a comment about making lemonade from lemons, and nodded.

As a first step, the younger doctor said, I was to come back to the hospital in a week or so for more tests, to establish a scientific baseline.

Fine with me.

The first thing Peggy said after Annie dropped me off was that Annie had told her about my DNA results.

–I'm not sure she was supposed to.

–I was going to tell you anyway. Not sure where we go from here.

She put her arms around me.

–Goddam dementia. A fucking plague.

–I'm okay, really, I said.

I stroked her back, her hair, kissed her softly.

–I'm okay, I repeated. It's not official yet. Annie's right. I have to focus on what's happening in front of us.

She stepped away, produced a tissue, blew her nose.

–You should go see Allan. We'll talk afterwards.

Allan was asleep. I moved a chair next to the bed and it scraped along the floor. His eyelids fluttered open. He stared my way briefly. His eyes closed.

No way he doesn't recognize me, I thought. Not a chance.

I sat there. Sounds from the living world seeped through the windows, the walls. He was very, very pale, his mouth hanging open. I found myself watching his chest to be sure that he was breathing. There was an occasional sound from somewhere in his throat, more snarl than snore.

I shut my eyes, leaned back. Hoped for sleep, my refuge.

And then I was seeing Allan, taller than everyone, crashing

through a crowd, the men around him falling down like bowling pins, Allan with sunglasses pushed up on his head, racing along a freeway in a vintage car, Allan swimming like he owned the sea.

Crumpled in the grass, folded like a fetus.

The Great Chase. Now nearly over.

And then something woke me, a silent flutter somewhere. I jerked upright. He was staring at me. He crooked a finger, moved his head slightly. *Come here.*

I moved closer.

—The drawer, he whispered.

With another small movement of his head, he indicated his desk.

—Top right.

—No, I said.

—Yes. It's time.

—No.

He closed his eyes. Sighed. I thought that he had gone back to sleep, but he opened them again. Whispered.

—Don't forget.

The strange snarling snore resumed. Then stopped. But his chest still rose and fell.

In the clutter of the desk drawer I found the doctor's business card. Beside it, the USB he'd showed me in the pub.

Which of these am I supposed to use? The key to his treasury? Or his ticket to eternity?

I looked back to where he was sleeping. Breathing normally.

I put the USB drive in my pocket.

———

I asked Peggy,

–What happened?

–Another stroke. And this time he fell hard.

–Why isn't he in hospital?

–He made me promise not to take him. Anyway, there's nothing they could do there that we can't do here. I've made arrangements for home care. There are people who come every day to tend to him. And there's a nurse.

–Still, it's too much stress for you.

She smiled.

–But I have you now.

I was not surprised that night when she came to my bed just as I was drifting off. She slipped in behind me, draped an arm over my shoulder. Snuggled close.

–I want to sleep here, she said.

I started to turn to her, but she stopped me.

–No, not that.

–Sorry, I said.

–We'll just sleep, okay?

–I understand.

–You always do.

And I lay there wondering if it was a good thing or my great misfortune to always understand her.

I suppose I wasn't surprised when I opened the file he had stored on the second thumb drive only to find another puzzle, in this case a passage from the Bible.

For the Lord Himself will come down from heaven with a loud command, with the voice of the Archangel and with the trumpet call of God, and the dead in Christ will rise first. After that, we who are still alive and are left will be caught up together with them in the clouds to meet the Lord in the air. And so we will be with the Lord forever.

I sat back, staring at the screen.

Somewhere in it or around it was information that would reveal the whereabouts of bank accounts. The name of an offshore company, perhaps. I had a password, *thepigswere-cedrics*, but what bank? What username?

Do you even care enough to go to all the trouble?

The appointment with the DNA detectives ate half a day. It started in a terrifying MRI machine that was like a noisy coffin.

Later, they took blood and saliva samples. Urine, too. Checked my blood pressure. Tapped my knees. Tickled my feet. Basically, a full checkup. I hadn't had one for a while.

And they asked me many questions about the accident.

–Mom was learning to drive a snowmobile. I got in the way. My leg got mangled, as you can see. I was knocked out for a while, they say.

–How long a while?

–I have no idea.

They took notes of everything I said, asking me from time to time to stop until they caught up.

I talked and talked. Maybe I was hoping that the talking would bring something deep to the forefront. I tried to impress them with my insights. I've been in hospitals a lot. They seemed to be determined to stick to their list of questions. They'd be shitty lawyers, I thought. No curiosity.

As I was leaving, they told me it would probably be months before they'd need me for the next round of tests.

–I'm happy to wait, I said.

And every night, Peggy came to me and we slept warmly nested into one another, like children. Dreaming about childhood.

Allan's vital signs remained strong. Somewhere in the corrupted flesh, the spirit of the football player was still fighting.

I said to Peggy,

–This could go on for quite a while.

–I know.

–I think it's time for me to face facts and start shutting down back home.

She nodded.

–How much are you going to shut down?

–Certainly the law practice. Maybe even the farm.

–That would be hard.

–Maybe not so very.

The last time I sat with him, Allan seemed to be awake, but he didn't respond when I spoke. I had the feeling that he recognized me but that he was finished with engagement. Just waiting now. I picked up his hand before I left and he gripped mine briefly, stared at it, then looked away. People who are dying seem resentful near the end.

I hardly remember the airport, the long drive home. Early December. I know I'd missed the autumn colours in Barney's River, Marshy Hope, Brierly Brook, and no longer felt the music in the place names. There was a shorter route, but I took the long one, delaying the inevitable.

The darkened hills along the highway seemed menacing. Even the sky was anxious, impatient with its undelivered snow. I thought about a long-dead local poet and a phrase in one of his impenetrable Gaelic songs: *the gloomy forest.*

When I stopped in the driveway, I hoped for the surge of energy that was once part of my arrival home. Waiting vainly for the magic from the crystals in the bedrock. Mom claimed she always felt that magic coming home, a psychic boost. Not that she ever went away that much. All I felt was the silent weight of isolation.

I sat at the kitchen table with my coat on. The air was heavy with the damp staleness of an old house that hadn't been lived in for a while. I knew that I could mitigate the gloom by turning on a light, turning on the radio, turning on the heat, lighting the wood stove. I remembered a bottle of whisky in my office. I told myself: *Start with that.*

My bed was made. I climbed in with my clothes on.

Penetrating morning light. Somehow, before I'd fallen asleep, I'd lit a fire. Half-empty whisky bottle on the table. A glass of water at the bedside.

I spent the morning on the phone with clients, asking for clearance to hand their business off to other lawyers. Everybody knew I'd been away. Everybody wondered why without asking.

I drove to town for groceries, dropped in to see a real estate agent, who listened sympathetically. He had the manner of the undertaker I had dealt with after Mom died. Mournful.

–Sad to see old places changing hands. It's been in your family for—what?

–Seems like forever, but I don't know.

–I'll find out when we search the title.

–Of course. It'll all be there. The information. The history.

In the drugstore, I saw Shirley. I had rarely spoken to her since my mother's passing. I'd been avoiding her as I have tended to avoid most people here and the casual encounters that always leave me feeling false. I was scanning the shelves, distracted by the effort to remember what I was looking for. And then we were face to face.

–Well, look at yourself, she said, instantly effusive.

–And you . . .

There were a few more of the usual pleasantries, and excuses made.

–I never hear from anybody, she said, but she knew that Annie was living in Toronto.

I suggested coffee. She looked uncertain, but supposed that she had time for a fast cup of tea.

–You've been gone awhile, she said when we were settled at a table in the local café.

–I pretty well shut the old place down. You'll never guess what I found when I was cleaning out a closet in Mom's room.

She stared at me blankly.

The old photo albums, I said. And an old newspaper

clipping, about a trial for assault involving my father. It didn't say who he assaulted.

She looked confused, or ready to get up and leave.

–Can you imagine my father assaulting anybody? I said, and laughed.

I shook my head.

–But it seems he got off. Not guilty.

She looked at her wristwatch, fidgeting.

–What I couldn't figure out was who he hit. Who was it, anyway?

–It was such a long time ago, she said at last.

–I'd heard there was friction with my uncle, Mom's brother.

–Angus, she said, nodding.

I waited.

–It was a misunderstanding, she said.

Her voice was trembling and I noticed that her eyes were wet.

–I didn't mean to upset you.

–They were bad times. I don't like thinking about them, she said, and stood, abandoning her half-drunk tea.

I stood too.

–I must go, she said.

We hugged. She stepped back, fished a tissue from a pocket and blew her nose, and backed away.

I walked the land. I stood where I had once explained to Allan how one winter night the ice moves in mysteriously, without warning, turning St. Georges Bay into a vast plain that reaches out from here, for all we know, to the Magdalen

Islands, to Gaspé. Montreal. Toronto. And then one morning, just as spring arrives, it's gone. The bay becomes its essence once again.

There was a racket in my jacket pocket. Around me, nature settled down for winter. Time stopped. Waiting for the ice. The phone was buzzing and vibrating. I considered ignoring it, to hang on to this moment of liberating stillness, but I fished it out. I saw Allan's number in the display.

It was Annie.

–Where are you?

–I'm at the farm.

–You sound outside.

–I am outside.

–How soon can you come back?

–That depends. I'm trying to arrange things here.

She paused, and in the pause there was nothing. Just dead air.

–Allan's gone, she said.

I phoned the real estate guy.

–Let's put everything on hold, I said.

PART FIVE

THE

GREAT

CHASE

24.

And now I know neither where I am nor why. Suddenly awak-
ened as if from a coma. Clearly on an airplane. On the aisle,
where I always try to be when I'm on airplanes. I stare past the
passenger beside me, out the starboard window, and see a wall
of black skyscrapers rising, and then the tower. The landmark
tower. We are floating down the black skyscrapers and the
tower and there is grey, flashing water rising up to meet us.
Then the tower is gone and all the dancing water and there is
sudden land and the violent bump of it, the drag, the reluctant
slowness. Finally, the purposeful acceleration. To the end.

Allan died.

Knowledge still far ahead of comprehension. Understanding
frozen.

Slowly, the perimeter of consciousness expands. A little. I
made phone calls. I packed. I found the unfinished Scotch and
finished it. No thought, just feeling. Fatigue, weariness. Self-
pity bordering on rage. I don't remember driving. Somehow,
I am standing at a ticket counter looking for a flight.

And then I'm in the air, all buckled in.

Something has ended. An epic narrative, concluded. The
finality of judgment.

—

The carousel had stopped. The room was empty, silent. There was one bag on the belt. It looked familiar. My name was on the tag.

Sitting somewhere in the terminal, I tell myself: *You are not insane.* The evidence is that I know now why I am here.

My friend is dead. My friend who wanted me to be him.

I know Allan's address. Allan is no longer there, but I must go there *because* he is no longer there.

Annie said she'd meet me at the airport. And now the phone is ringing in my pocket.

—*Where the fuck are you?*

—In the airport. I'll come out.

—*I'm in the airport. I've looked everywhere.*

—I'm not sure where I am. But I'm here somewhere.

—For Christ's sake. Do you know where you're going?

—I'm going to Allan's.

—Do you remember the address?

—Yes. Of course.

—Say it.

—Listen. I'm not . . .

—Just take a taxi, then. I'll see you there.

—Sorry.

—Never mind sorry. Just get in a cab.

Intoxicated, Annie told me once, is another word for poisoned. The brain is poisoned and ill, intoxication a self-induced mental illness.

That's all it is. I got drunk and I'm not good at it. I got

drunk at home. I got drunk waiting at the airport. They served wine on the plane. Everything went dark.

I can explain to myself at least.

Peggy opened the door before I rang the bell. She was frowning.

–Where's Annie? She was supposed to meet you.

–She's on her way.

I walked past her, into the living room. Left my boots on. Deliberately but for no particular reason. Feeling pissed. At everything. Everybody. Peggy stood in the doorway, arms folded, looking up and down the street.

–There she is, she said.

I knew Annie well enough that I could feel her frustration even before she came through the door. She removed her gloves slowly, deliberately, said to her sister,

–Wrong. Air. Port. Someone didn't bother telling me he was landing at the island. So naturally, I went to the one he always lands at.

–I called. I told you.

–No, you didn't. You called with the arrival time, but you didn't say where you were landing.

–I got the only flight available. I didn't ask where it was going to land.

–Well, we're all here now, said Peggy.

–Where's Allan?

The sisters stared at me, then stared at each other.

–Allan died, Peggy said.

–I know that. I want to see him, I said.

–I need a drink, Annie said. I think we all could use a drink.

She left the room. Peggy came to me, sat on the arm of the chair, took my hand in hers.

–Are you sure you're all right, Byron? You look wiped.

–I need to see him. Where's the funeral home?

–Allan left very particular instructions. There's no funeral home.

I stood so quickly Peggy almost fell. My bad leg felt numb, like the old days. Unreliable. I passed Annie coming through the doorway from the kitchen with a tray and three drinks.

–You shouldn't go in there, she said.

I yanked open Allan's door. The steel bed was gone. His desk was clear. I hobbled over, opened the top-right drawer, still cluttered, but I could see the doctor's business card was gone. I slammed it shut.

I was shouting as I stormed back to the living room.

–You called that fucking doctor. You put him down like an animal.

They were stricken, staring at me. I wanted to rewind the whole arrival. I wanted to be me and not this stranger. But the stranger was now in charge and out of words.

Annie led me to a chair and handed me my drink. I sat and stared into the drink for what felt like a long time. My mind cleared slowly. I raised my head and looked around. There was just me and Annie.

–Where did Peggy go?

–Upstairs.

–I don't know what's happening, Annie.

–We need to get you some help, Byron.

–No, I said.

–You need help.
–I know where help leads.
–We'll take care of you.
–I have to lie down.
–That's a good idea. You lie down. We'll talk later.

I sat up suddenly, pulse pounding. When I laid my head on the pillow, I could hear my terrifying heart.

The slender hands were fumbling with the zipper on my snowsuit.

–Hang on. Just a second.

–I can't hold it

Then the sickening sound.

Wallop.

Someone rolling, whimpering on the floor.

Someone standing, fists clenched. Warm piss now flooding out of me.

Allan? Someone murdered Allan.

Peggy gently shook my arm. The room was lit by the morning sun.

–I need to pee, I said.

She almost laughed.

–Byron, you know where the bathroom is.

I almost didn't make it. Squirting everywhere. Struggling for control, of everything. I was still disoriented when I returned to the bedroom to find her waiting.

–There's someone downstairs who wants to see you. Are you feeling up to it?

–Yes. Of course. Where did Annie go?

–She's downstairs too. She's staying here for a few days. To help with . . .

–Allan.

–Yes. To help with Allan. Come down, now.

He'd put on weight, but I knew him right away.

–Nick, he said.

–Yes. I know.

His eyes were animated, the expression warm. He was seeing into me, but in a friendly way. His hand was large, strong. The hand of an athlete.

–I dropped in just for a minute. To make sure everyone is okay. My condolences on your loss. I know he was your good friend.

I nodded. Of course, he would have known Allan. This man was a bigger part of the business than I could have known, part of the invisible dimension. Even if he was just the limo driver. Eyes and ears are everything in business.

–Annie told me just this morning, he said.

–We'll be fine.

–Yes. Of course. Annie will have everything in good shape.

–I remember you from—when was it? Two years ago?

–Yes, when you took my picture.

He laughed.

I shrugged.

–I'm a lawyer, I said.

–You would have made good spy.

–You know spies?

–No, no. But I was once in Russian military, where all the

time we heard about spies. It was a flattering photograph, actually. I thank you.

He poked my shoulder. He was irresistibly likeable.

–I have to leave now. I'll leave you to your privacy.

Limo driver my ass. He was one of those people who fill a room, who, after they've departed, leave a palpable emptiness.

–So that's Nick, I said.

The women were waiting for more.

–Allan said he was a limo driver, or owner.

–Yes, but a bit more than that in the larger scheme of things, Peggy said.

–I can imagine.

–You've obviously heard the gossip about him and me, Annie said.

–Gossip? I saw the pictures.

–Pictures?

–At the condo. The happy threesome.

She waved a hand.

–I just want to get it out of the way.

–It's none of my business.

–I'm your wife.

–You're not my property.

She stepped back, laughed lightly.

–Well, that's progressive.

–That's reality.

I hadn't noticed Peggy's absence. I was a bit disappointed when I realized she'd tactfully stepped out. I had been performing as much for her benefit as my own.

–We're just friends. Whether you want to believe it or not, Annie said.

–Like I said . . .

–There's another thing to get out of the way. We did not "put Allan down," as you so elegantly put it.

Peggy returned with mugs of coffee.

–I'll let that remark pass, though, because you were obviously distraught. Or drunk. Or both.

–Since I'm obviously mentally ill, drunk or sober doesn't matter.

–Let's move on, said Annie.

I sipped my coffee carefully. It was hot.

–I'll let Peggy explain what happened while you were gone.

Allan had put everything in writing. Peggy handed me the document. It was explicit. No resuscitation. No ambulance or hospital. Assisted death. It had been arranged with his doctor contact, only waiting for a signal that it was the right time.

–And when was it supposed to be the right time?

–When he could no longer communicate.

Mind stumbling. *How do we communicate when we can no longer communicate?*

–But what if he wanted to communicate a change of mind?

–We thought of that. I raised it with him, but, in any case, it became moot.

–Moot.

–He was comatose all day. When I went in to check before I went to bed, I just knew he was gone. I called the doctor. And he came and confirmed it. His heart just blew up. The doctor certified the cause of death. Massive coronary thrombosis. Everything is kosher. Legally. Byron, he wanted it this way. He's been ready ever since that first stroke, with you.

–And then what?

–Allan's instructions were that he be taken straight to a crematorium. That's where he is. His ashes.

Her eyes were now flooding, lower lip trembling. I wanted to be kind. But kindness was no longer in me.

–It's all very convenient, I said.

Annie stood so quickly, her coffee splashed on her lap. She brushed at it.

–I fucking can't believe you said that.

I wanted to say, *I can't believe it either.*

I wanted to say, *Please forgive me.*

I wanted to say, *I have no idea what's happening to me.*

But I couldn't say anything. I couldn't speak at all. There was a blizzard raging in my head. I stood, put my mug down, made a futile empty-handed gesture and went back upstairs.

I tried to sleep. I got up. I came back downstairs. They were sitting, chatting quietly with drinks, the room in semi-darkness. They fell silent and stared at me. I turned around and went back to my room.

When I came down again, the house felt empty. Abandoned. I poured a drink from their nearly empty bottle.

It felt like poison burning down. What drinking lye would feel like. I poured another. And then another. I went back upstairs.

—

The goddamned dreams. In all the dreams, I'm trying to go somewhere but keep getting lost. And needing to piss. Constantly. Bladder shot.

To the bathroom then back. Just lying there in bed, remembering the night before the last golf game. We didn't know it then. We never know when anything will be the last.

I never met a woman I couldn't disappoint.

Is that what we really had in common? Was it our fate to disappoint anyone who thought she understood us? Thought she knew us? Failed to see our future failures?

It is deep into night. I can feel it, though there is no clock anywhere that I can see. And I am gone again.

Thinking about sex. The weapon loaded.

Allan said it once. The weapon. I laughed. Then.

It sounded funny, then.

Peggy is now behind me in the bed, whispering, *I know what you meant. You didn't really mean "convenient." I understand. We're all hurting, Byron dear. Don't worry. We'll take care of you.*

I don't want anybody taking care of me . . .

I turned and faced her.

–I don't want your pity anymore. *You're just trying to be nice.*

I was dreaming, but I was awake. I touched her shoulder, touched her cheek. Her softness was real. My awful need was real.

Her face. I could see the sun sparkle on rivulets of water, the flash in her eyes. *If we were in a movie . . .*

I pressed myself against her. She moved away from me.

–No, she said.

I reached out to draw her to me. She pushed me away. I grabbed her wrist.

–I need you to be closer, I said.

–No.

–I never understood you. You just thought I did. I understand you now. I know what you wanted from me.

–Wait.

–No. I've waited too long.

I caught her other wrist, pulled her to me. She was so light. Light as air. I was over her now, holding her wrists firmly. Why was she resisting me?

–Byron, stop, right now.

Her tone was harsh. It isn't what she really feels, I told myself. For more than forty years she's been waiting, assuming I'm not like other men. Disappointed.

I was now on top, my good, strong knee forcing hers to separate. She bucked briefly, squirmed under me and tried to roll away. Then, suddenly, she stopped. Lay still.

–I don't want this, she said.

–*It's all there is*, I whispered.

–No.

She turned her face away. Just lay there, staring at the wall. Then she grimaced, gasped.

–Yes, I said.

–It hurts.

She was whispering. Something I couldn't hear.

The voice inside was screaming at me now: *Get it over with. Forty years of disappointment.*

In the end, less than a minute.

I felt a careful movement behind me. Was momentarily confused. Heard her leave the room. Heard her gently close the door.

I felt sick. I tried to be asleep. I wanted to be Allan. He said he wanted me to be him. I never was. But now I envied him. His being beyond all of this, all of us, beyond all disappointment. Dead.

Maybe I did sleep.

I stayed in bed until I knew the house was empty.

I called a taxi.

–I want to go to a hotel, I told the driver.

–Any place in particular?

–Somewhere cheap, I said.

–How cheap?

–There's a place on Jarvis.

–I think I know the one.

Annie phoned at least half a dozen times before I turned my phone off. I stared out the hotel room window. The day was fading fast. I went back to bed but once again couldn't sleep.

The room had a small balcony with a low railing. I tried the sliding door and it opened. I grasped the railing, looking down. Nothing moving on the street. An expectant silence. I felt my stomach turn to slime. Went back to bed. Got up again. Tried the sliding door again.

It's always an option, I thought. The possibility brought a tiny flutter of relief.

The magnitude of what my uncle did. I never realized his bravery.

When I turned the phone back on, there was a text.

I don't know where you are, but please check in. The hospital has been trying to reach you.

The hospital?

The phone rang just as I was staring at it. *Annie* in the display.

I accepted, but I didn't speak.

–I know you're there, she said. I can hear you breathing. What you're doing isn't fair.

I listened for anger, condemnation.

–I understand what you're going through. But this is no time to be alone. We need you. You need us. This isn't just about you.

She doesn't know, I thought.

Then Annie said,

–Have you got a pen and paper? There's a couple of things you should write down.

–Wait, I said.

I fumbled through a drawer. There was hotel stationery. A pen that was dry. I found my jacket. A pen in the pocket.

–Take this down, she instructed, then read out the doctor's name and number. Also, we have to sit down with the board. Can you be at the office tomorrow morning? Say about eleven?

–Not likely, I said.

–Byron, you must come home.

I laughed.

–Home, I said.

–I mean it. Come to the condo. Are you listening?

–I'm listening.

–I'll expect you. Get your shit together.

The doctor asked if I could be at his office the next morning for a quick meeting. Say around eleven?

–I'll be there.

There was a pub downstairs, just off the lobby, I walked past it half a dozen times. It was a little grungy but always looked inviting, obviously a local for some offices nearby. Bustling at noon, into mid-afternoon. Media by the look of some of the clientele. Noisy students in the evenings, babble rising. Then stopping suddenly. Quiet now, I'm sure.

There is no reason not to.

The waiter dropped a menu. I ordered a double. Scotch. Whatever bar Scotch he had going. I checked the menu, felt nauseous.

You should eat.

Maybe, after a drink or two, I'll feel like it.

Back home, when Annie and I first lived together, mealtime conversations were about our work, about people we vaguely knew and their manageable troubles with the law, the tax authorities. Mom knew most of the clients better than we did, but we didn't feel a need to be discreet. Mom really wasn't interested, wasn't likely to retain enough context to make the gossip interesting to anybody. The only work that Annie wouldn't talk about was what she did for Allan. She didn't volunteer. I never asked.

In time, as Mom became more distant, the conversations were mostly about her. Good days, bad days, in-between days, measuring the progress of what could not be reversed, finding too much hope in what seemed like small remissions.

Mom sat through it all like we were talking about someone else, a stranger to her.

I read a lot about Alzheimer's then. And somewhere I learned that the span of time between diagnosis and death was normally about five years. But nobody knew for sure. Each case was unique.

Annie refused to believe the five-year prognosis.

—Nobody can pin that down for an individual case, she said.

But as the good days became rare, five years began to seem like a terribly long time, even to Annie.

The stalwart, plain-spoken women who came every day saved us from the worst of it. I could eventually ignore the bathroom murmurings, the repeated toilet flushing, the hurried, furtive visits to the laundry room, clothes and bedding bundled carefully. Mom serene, sitting in her chair, studying her fingers.

Do we become immune to humiliation or is it deeply felt, beneath awareness and yet still painful?

Even dogs seem to feel embarrassment and shame.

At some point the waiter came and took away the menu.

—The kitchen is closing, he said.

—That's okay. Bring me the same.

And how will I react? I knew a man whose treatment for some ailment led to temporary incontinence. After it had passed, he could laugh about it, describe standing on his doorstep fumbling with keys as his bowels exploded.

—A shit-hemorrhage.

He said that it was worse in public. But you gradually become shameless, stuffing your shat-in underwear in public washroom waste cans.

—Imagine the poor bastard who encountered that at closing time.

Since it was temporary, it was educational. Amusing, looking back.

But when it's permanent? I should hope for less than the five-year sentence. Or hope for the courage of my uncle Angus. From whom I took my name. Perhaps my destiny.

It seems that I stumbled, returning from the washroom.

The barman had a helpful hand on my arm. I stared at the hand, then his face. He was young and muscular and fit.

—Maybe you've had enough. How about I ring you up?

—What do you mean?

—You're staggering, sir.

—I didn't fucking stagger.

—I'm not going to argue.

—Maybe you should go back to waiter school and learn the difference between a stagger and a limp.

His face flushed.

—Sir, you have to leave.

I lurched around in the darkness of the room. My head felt clear. How can I be drunk if I'm aware of everything? I bent to remove my shoes and lost my balance. Crashed into a dresser. Made it to the bed. The goddam limp.

I lay there fuming. The bastard cut me off for limping. Outrageous. I've seen fit young guys knocking over furniture in bars, spilling drinks, ruining the scene for everybody else. Fucking backwards ball caps on indoors. Even eating. I'd outlaw indoor ball caps. I'd outlaw ball caps altogether.

They should spend some time in my shoes. Coping with the shoe with the four-inch sole before the operation that immobilized me for a year. See how long they'd last without whining.

The stares and whispers.

Mom would say, *They're just making fun of you, Angus*, as if that made everything okay.

And it was the Winter sisters who started with the Byron. I should go back to Angus. He was crazy too, but in the end he had the balls to.

Jump.

I looked out over Jarvis Street, then down. Cars moving quickly in the night the way they do when everything else slows down. Hunting slow pedestrians at the crosswalks. How I know it.

How I stare the bastards down. How I make them hit the brakes.

And what happened in the barn? My uncle hit the brakes. My father hit my uncle.

Bravado, the stopper in a bottle filled with fear. Victims of molestation everywhere you look now, wearing their ball caps backwards.

I refuse to be a fucking victim. Nothing happened in the barn.

At the last minute, they *always* hit the brakes. They hit something. Or are hit by something.

He hesitated.

He said, You're all set now. You can pee now.

He stood. And then my father, roaring.

I lay down again, hauled the blankets up.

I felt better.

Nothing happened in the barn. Nothing happened in the bedroom.

There is a cause for everything, a crack in everything.

I wish I'd said that first. I could have, looking back, seeing all the cracks in everything.

That's how the light gets in.

Yes. Fucking right, Leonard. The light gets in. Sooner or later.

I sat up, swung my legs over the side of the bed and turned on the light. Enlightened. All clear now.

So, I have Alzheimer's and I know where it came from. And I know now why I've been the way I've been. Never had a chance. From day one. Anybody wants to talk about victimhood. I'm the guy. The snowmobile was destiny.

Early fucking onset, they said.

Well, bring it on. The earlier the better.

The sooner it begins, the sooner it is over.

25.

The doctor kept me waiting. At 11:20 my phone rang. It was Annie.

So I assume you aren't coming.

–I'm at the doctor's office.

–You should be here.

She was almost whispering.

–Things are happening. We have to make changes. Involving your position.

–I'm sure you can handle it.

–Call as soon as you get out of there. We need your input.

–My input?

–Did Allan give you any indication, when you talked to him, about banking?

–Banking?

–Offshore.

–I have to go now.

The doctor stood in his doorway, called me in. He was looking cheerful, and placed a friendly hand on my shoulder as I passed him.

–So, how are you feeling about everything today?

–I'm okay.

He sat behind the desk, looking at me. After a pause, he opened a folder, studied it.

–Permit me a cliché opening, then. We have good news and we have bad news, from our point of view.

He smiled, looked down briefly, then up. Removed his glasses.

–I'm afraid we have to exclude you from the study.

–I flunked the tests?

He laughed.

–Yes. You flunked the tests.

He picked up some papers from the folder, scanned them briefly.

–There is no evidence in your DNA of any abnormality. I think you referred to PSEN1 mutation. I guess you did some online research . . . *DNA for Dummies*. Correct?

He paused and smiled, shifted in his chair, put the glasses on again.

–Simply stated, this PSEN1 mutation reduces learning and memory capacity fairly quickly. Symptoms appear as early as in your forties. You're, what . . .?

He flipped through the pages.

–Late fifties?

He looked up, took the glasses off again.

–There's nothing here. Your DNA is boring.

–What about my mother?

–Maybe an anomaly. These things sometimes jump a generation. Luck of the draw.

–So, the episodes . . .

–I think what you experienced was a fainting spell.

–Okay. But there have been other things, little blackouts.

–We're not saying that everything is great with you. You could be depressed or suffering some delayed post-traumatic stress from that terrible childhood accident you described. A loss of consciousness is always problematical and you had a very serious bump on the head. We know a little more now about something called post-concussion syndrome from working with former athletes.

I Ie studied his papers again briefly.

–There is nothing innocuous about concussion and you show some brain lesions that are consistent with what we're learning about football injuries. It's impossible to draw conclusions. But for the time being . . .

He shrugged and closed the folder.

–The good news is that we have ruled out any genetic precondition that could cause dementia. Maybe, instead of thinking early-onset Alzheimer's, you should be worried about late-onset mid-life crisis.

He smiled. Chewed the end of his Sharpie.

–You might consider other avenues for investigation . . .

–Like what?

–Psychotherapy might be one place to start.

–It's all in my head?

–Anything in our heads that affects our ability to function is serious. Let me ask you something. Alcohol?

–What about it?

–Might it be a factor?

–I hardly drink at all.

–Think about it.

He stood then. Put the glasses and the Sharpie in his pocket. Smiled.

The light outside was blinding and the street noise deafening. People surging at me from all directions on the sidewalk. A cyclist nearly took me out when I hesitated in a bike lane.

The city, in the past hour, had come alive again. Or maybe I had simply become conscious once again of the world around me, released from where I had been for at least a week, maybe months, maybe longer. I fled into a coffee shop. The place was just as noisy as the outside. Loud chatter, manic laughter. Espresso maker sounding like a steam engine from another century.

Life. Blaring.

Life restored.

But what I felt was anything but restoration.

I ordered a large something. Found a tiny table in a corner. What now? I am denuded of a label.

In the early days after Mom's diagnosis, she no longer had to perform whoever people thought she was. No more artifice. She didn't need excuses anymore since she had an explanation that would cover everything. Before her life went dark, she felt a lightness.

I no longer have a condition to explain the unavoidable humiliations of an ordinary life, to justify what I am becoming, what I will become. What I will do. What I have done.

I dialed Peggy's number.

She answered.

–I'm busy, she said, and disconnected.

Yes. She's at the meeting I should be at and would be at if it wasn't for.

Peggy.

I stared at the dead telephone and asked myself what I intended to say to her.

Hey Peggy, I have great news. There's nothing wrong with me!

Oh, wonderful. That's fantastic, Byron. So that was really you who raped me? What a relief!

Almost too late, I remembered one of Allan's iron rules: Never Explain Yourself. To Anybody.

My DNA is boring. I am normal. That will be my secret. Let them think I'm crazy. Let that explain me.

They were waiting in the hotel lobby. I saw them before they saw me. Annie and Peggy. They were standing near the front desk with their coats on. I had an overwhelming impulse to run, but Annie spotted me and started walking quickly in my direction. Peggy stayed behind.

I turned away, but Annie shouted.

–Wait.

I stopped. I didn't want to see her. I didn't want to see Peggy.

–Byron! Look at me.

She turned me until I was facing her. I looked past her. I expected to see rage in Peggy's face, but I saw only sorrow mixed with fear.

There is no Byron. I must remember that.

–Byron? What the fuck is going on? You can't just . . . You look like shit, Annie said.

I could see the glint of tears on Peggy's cheeks.

Annie had my arm, but she spoke to Peggy.

–Wait here. We'll be right back.

She steered me toward the elevator.

–We're going to your room. Where's your key?

I fumbled in my pocket, staring at the floor. No speech possible. No resistance.

–We're going to get your things, Byron. And you're coming home with me. Do you understand?

–How did you find me?

–Nick tracked you down.

Nick. I might have laughed, but there was a terrible ache in my bad leg. The leg resisted movement, and when it did move, I sagged on that side. Annie came around.

–Lean on me, she said.

In my room, she just said,

–Holy shit.

When we stopped in front of the condo building, I stared up at it. I had no memory of being there before, of being carried out of there.

Then Annie came around and opened the car door, caught my hand.

–Come on, you're home now.

There was kindness in her tone. Or pity.

26.

I watch the vast lake just outside my window. Soon enough
it would be blustery with sails again, sparkling with pleasure.
Maybe then, time will have dulled the edge of memory. But
I have only half the memory. What about the other half?

Where is she now? What is Peggy thinking? I closed my
eyes. The only refuge now.

I woke to the ringing of my phone.

I didn't recognize the number but answered anyway. I didn't
recognize the voice. A man's voice. *The doctor again. Another
change in the diagnosis.* Then he said my name, bureaucratically,
and the word "Police."

–Tom. Yes, I remember. You were at the farm with another
fellow.

–Yes. Getting on to four years ago . . .

–Was it only four?

He laughed.

–I'd like to pick up where we left off . . .

–I'm not at the farm just now, and I'm not sure when . . .

–There's a little diner just down the street from where

you're at. Okay? Harbourfront. I could meet you there. When might you be available?

–You've been doing your homework.

–It's what they pay me for.

–Maybe you can give me a hint at what you're interested in this time.

–Well. You know telephones. Why don't we just arrange a mutually convenient time?

I spotted him before he saw me. He was at a corner table for four. Room for two of us plus documents. He seemed to be working on a crossword puzzle.

–You do the crossword? I said.

He didn't look up.

–Usually cryptic, but it's hard to find a good one. They're mostly all British. Full of cricket and the like. You?

–I started, for the mental exercise. But I couldn't quite get into it.

He looked at me and smiled. Folded the paper. Stood and offered his hand. I grasped it, and sat across from him.

–And I could never get the hang of the cryptic clues, I said.

–There's a particular technique you have to know. You have to have a certain kind of memory, too, what I call a sticky brain.

–Sticky, I said.

He was looking at me, hard, calculating.

–How have you been?

–Good. So, you're still at it. I'm trying to remember a name. I remember the project. The condo building, Halifax.

–Water Street Lofts.

–I've been having memory problems. My brain isn't that sticky anymore.

He smiled. He picked up a small leather case from the empty chair beside him, zipped it open, removed a file folder. He extracted a photograph and slid it toward me.

–You might remember him.

Albert Rose.

–I acted for him in that condo transaction. Albert something?

–Rose.

I studied the photograph. Tom was studying my face.

–As I said the last time, it was fairly straightforward. I did the paperwork for incorporation and we went our separate ways.

–You haven't seen him since?

–Well. I believe there was a meeting here when he was selling the property to someone. I'd have to check as to whether I was here for it.

–Just the one property.

–In Halifax. There could have been others. I could check.

He pulled another photo from his folder. I could only see the back of it.

–This guy would have been at the meeting with this Albert Rose?

He dropped it in front of me.

–You know this guy, right?

Allan.

–I've known him since back in university. In Nova Scotia. Allan.

–Allan what?

–Chase.

He nodded. He looked around the room, rubbed his chin.

–I'm going to heat up my coffee. Will you have one?

–I'm okay. How long do you think this is going to take?

–That depends.

He walked away slowly. I studied Allan's photograph, trying to identify where he was when it was taken. It was definitely not posed, something shot by someone on the sly. He was talking to someone off camera. He was smiling, relaxed. The surroundings were out of focus.

The policeman was back. I was still studying the photo.

–Where was this taken? I asked.

–I don't know where. It was a while ago.

–It must have been, because Allan has been pretty well laid up for the last year or so. You probably know he recently passed away.

–So I understand. He had a stroke, right?

–Yes. It was a heart attack that took him.

–Started on a golf course. You were with him?

–Yes. You're up on things.

I laughed, but felt the warning tingle.

–You knew him for a very long time?

–Since we were in university. But why is he of interest?

–He dropped out of university after a year or two, I understand.

–Yes.

–He was a football player.

–Yes.

–Did you ever meet his folks?

–Actually, no. I came here to Toronto to visit him once, but he was living on his own by then. Had his own place. In Kensington Market, I think. I didn't know the city then.

—So you never met parents, siblings or any relative of his.

—No. I gathered he was from a well-off family. He never mentioned brothers or sisters. But why all the interest in Allan?

—So, he went east to study and to play football.

—Yes. He said he was recruited from high school.

—Actually, no. He was a walk-on. He just showed up during training camp. It happens occasionally. Somebody asks for a tryout. Seems he made the right impression. He was good. I heard he was even scouted.

—I really didn't follow sports. Still don't.

—So, you wouldn't know much about before. What high school he went to. What his dad did for a living.

—Allan told me that his dad was in trucking.

—So we understand. But you never met the dad?

—I'm sure I'd remember if I had. Honestly, Allan never talked much about family, or growing up.

—That doesn't surprise me.

He was studying my face intensely.

—Here's the thing, Byron. When I tried to find out *anything* about your friend, before you met him in university, I quickly ran out of runway. You see, Allan Chase died of a drug overdose in 1977, two years before you say you bumped into him.

—Some other Allan Chase.

—There was only one.

I stared at him in silence, then looked down at the photo. With my forefinger, I moved it closer, then picked it up. For the first time in nearly forty years, I saw a stranger.

I put the photo down.

–I should tell you something, I said.

He was nodding.

–Maybe you should.

–I've been tested for dementia. Early-onset Alzheimer's.

–I understand.

–You do?

–The thing *you* have to understand, Byron, is that since the last time we spoke, we've made a lot of progress. We know a lot now that we didn't know then. So, it's extremely important that you're straight with me. I know about your issues. And I know that time might be a factor here.

–Pointless question, probably, but how do you know so much?

–I don't mind telling you, he said.

He placed his forefinger on the photograph of Albert Rose.

–This guy has decided to be co-operative.

–Albert Rose.

–No. He's not Albert Rose. This is Albert Rose.

And he reached across the table and put his finger on the photograph of Allan.

I froze. I felt a mental and emotional paralysis that could have passed for calmness. Then remembered: *I'm a lawyer*. I sat back in my chair, cleared my throat.

–Well, well. So who's the guy I've been calling Albert Rose?

–A loser. Ex-cop. Failed lawyer. He doesn't matter in the larger scheme of things. We're interested in the real Albert Rose. You with me?

I studied Allan's photograph. The expression on his face

was one of intimacy. It was Allan maybe two years back. Who was he talking to? There was a faint tremor of recollection. Quiet hotel lounge near the airport.

–Who was he with, when this was taken?

–Three guesses.

I sipped my coffee. Stalling, I suppose. Tom gave me time, slowly picked up the photographs, returned them to his folder. Laced his fingers together while he studied me.

–By the way, what was it with you guys and names? Your name is Angus, right? But everybody calls you Byron.

–Byron was a high school nickname. Because I limped. The poet, Lord Byron, was lame. Some of the kids started calling me Byron. I wasn't offended. The name stuck.

He laughed.

–You wouldn't get away with that today, a nickname drawing attention to a handicap or whatever.

27.

Ego and greed. Weaknesses that turn good judgment into recklessness. It had been the core of Allan's corporate philosophy: avoid ego and greed at all costs. In the end, it seems, he was felled by playfulness.

Tom explained.

–He was doing good at keeping a low profile. Then he resurrected his real name. Albert Rose. Being playful. Giving us the finger. Started hanging his real name on cut-out characters, people he'd invent for fake transactions.

The policeman looked me in the eye and in a serrated voice declared,

–You say you didn't know a darn thing about any of this.

I could only shake my head.

–And it isn't just your fading memory?

–I'm flabbergasted. I do not bloody care if you believe me. I'm trying to compute where I stand legally.

–That's very wise, he said.

–So, what got all this started, Tom?

–Fraud. But it's part of a much bigger thing now, Byron. International in scope. Drugs and money laundering. You follow?

I tried to understand whether Tom's confidence, his poise, was based on knowledge or the instincts of a first-rate poker player.

I concluded: either way, I'm in another world here.

–These things start real small sometimes. Some low-life drops a name. It happens all the time. We're good with names, Byron. A name like Allan Chase got stuck in some cop's ear years ago. At the time, he was just some low-level dope dealer, not worth the bother of an arrest. But the name became relevant at some point.

He shrugged.

–Serendipity. I always say, serendipity and old-fashioned shoe leather. A formula for everything in life.

–But you're a bit late now, aren't you?

–How so?

–Allan's dead, I said.

–Oh yes, said Tom. He's definitely dead. But you aren't, are you. And of course, the Winter ladies. You three are very much alive.

Serendipity or not, it was clear as he laid the story out for me that Tom had done his homework.

Both Allan Chase and Albert Rose had attended a well-regarded Catholic high school in Toronto. Both were very good at football. It was because of an award for playing football that the police first found out that Allan Chase had died in 1977, a few weeks after graduation.

But for a long time that was all they had. A few newspaper clippings about high school sports. All his academic records had mysteriously vanished, no one could say precisely when. It was years later, in the course of searching for the missing files on Allan Chase, that investigators learned another student file had also disappeared—the academic records of a kid named Albert Rose.

Rose had been a model student and, like Chase, a great all-round athlete. But in the spring of 1978 his life went off the rails. Just before his graduation, he was arrested for dealing drugs.

He wasn't really selling drugs, just using. But he knew the dealers and he'd sometimes pick up dime bags for his friends. And when he was busted, he was carrying enough to warrant prosecution for trafficking.

The friends were suddenly invisible. Albert who?

The school expelled him just weeks before he was to graduate. Even his folks cut him loose. Hard-nosed discipline types, his mom and dad. For all intents and purposes, they disowned him.

The judge was a bit more sympathetic. He made a good impression in the courtroom. A clean-cut guy and athlete with no previous record who deserved a second chance. He was eighteen. It was adult court. He got off with a suspended sentence. But still, he had a record that would haunt him for the rest of his days.

That was how young Albert saw it, anyway. His life was finished. So, he decided to switch places with the dead guy. At least on paper.

He dug up Allan Chase and he buried Albert Rose.

—

–So, let's say that you were in the dark the same as everybody else. But you must have had suspicions, Tom said.

–Nothing.

–Your friend had some fairly hefty associates in the drug business down in the States, and also Mexico. At a certain point the DEA came to us for help in finding him.

–And Albert Rose?

–That's where serendipity comes in.

An Allan Chase had briefly been a football hero at a university in Nova Scotia. He dropped out, and in the summer of 1980 an Allan Chase, with the same birthdate as the dead guy, qualified for a licence to drive trucks all over North America.

Then, somewhere along the way, Allan Chase became invisible and stayed that way until somehow, just a few years back, his name popped up on the fringes of a deal that was of interest to the US Drug Enforcement Agency.

–Once we determined that the real Allan Chase was actually dead and that someone had stolen his identity, the obvious villain was the other kid whose high school records had gone missing at the same time. Albert Rose. And then, when we were running out of leads, Albert surfaced in some dodgy real estate transactions.

Tom sighed. He leaned back in his chair, stared at me with a sad expression that might have passed for sympathy.

–I want to believe you, Byron, because I'd hate to think of what will happen to you if you're just stringing me along. But the other thing worth contemplating is that maybe someone has been stringing you along.

—

Who are you?

Allan obviously wasn't going to answer. Allan, now Albert, had been reduced to a kilogram or so of what looked like cat litter, contained in a black plastic box resting on the mantel in Annie's condo beside a tasteful arrangement of fresh-cut flowers. And, of course, a photograph. Something posed. From when he and Peggy married.

He'd been on the mantel for a week, since Annie brought him home from the crematorium, the subject of many conversations rooted in the certainty that he was the person that he always said he was.

–You don't mind him being here?

–I don't mind, but what about Peggy?

–Peggy's having difficulty with everything.

Annie arrived home late. When she asked how my day was, I was noncommittal. She wandered around a bit, tidying. Had a coffee.

–How are you feeling?

–Okay.

–I've been looking into medication for you. I'm hearing there's been some progress in Parkinson's, with miraculous results for some people. There might be something new for dementia. It's worth a try.

–I wouldn't waste a lot of time on it.

–Maybe you need something for your attitude.

–Maybe we should talk about the business.

–Yes. Peggy's coming by a little later.

–It's already late, I said.

–We can't put it off any longer. You're up for it?

–Do you want to give me a heads-up?

–I'm going to pour a drink. You?

–Nothing for me, thanks.

She sat, legs tucked under her, her drink on a side table, flipping through a document.

–What is it you have there?

She ignored me. Flipped another page. Reached for the drink. Contemplated for a moment. Sipped.

–Oh my, she said.

–What are you reading? I asked.

No response.

And I was remembering when Mom became invisible, and we would talk as if she wasn't there.

The difference is that she really wasn't there. She was in her own space, and we in ours, and the two spaces were bubbles, in a real way exclusive.

I am present. I am here.

Or am I?

Maybe someone has been stringing you along.

And suddenly Peggy was here too, in the bubble.

I struggled to stand, but she waved at me to stay put. Annie went into the kitchen to fetch a drink for Peggy. In her absence, I started to say something, I wasn't sure what. I must have stammered. Peggy waved her hand at me again.

–No. Don't say anything.

Annie returned with Peggy's drink. When they were sitting, I said,

–I want to say I'm sorry I haven't been pulling my weight lately.

–It's understandable, Annie said.

–Before we get started, I want to ask about Albert Rose. When was the last time . . .

Peggy interrupted.

–He's been out of the picture for quite a while now, as you should know.

–Since when?

They exchanged puzzled glances. Annie said,

–Since we unloaded that Halifax property and those Albert Rose companies you put in place way back when.

–You know that, said Peggy.

–I think his name was on a lot of properties, I said.

–Not anymore. Why the interest? Annie said.

–Yes, why do we care about Albert Rose? Peggy said.

–His name came up.

–How so?

–I've had visits from the police. They asked about Albert Rose.

–From the police?

–I told Allan. He didn't think it was important.

–So?

Annie was looking puzzled rather than alarmed.

–So, nothing. They first showed up at the farm, some years back. But I had another call the other day. Same cop. Asking about Albert Rose again. I indicated he was out of things and had been for some time. I was surprised by some of what he had to say.

There was a long silence. They stared at me. I stared at them. They stared at each other. There was so much silent communication, it was overwhelming.

–Byron?

–*Byron!*

It was Peggy.

–From now on, Byron, I think you should be very careful who you talk to. You should refer any inquiries about any part of our business to us. To me or Annie. Or, if neither one of us is available, to Nick.

–Nick?

–Yes, Nick. Annie, I think you should take it from here.

Annie's face was flushed, but she was steady. Man, she was as steady as a rock.

–There has been a decision by the board, Byron. And we've endorsed it. For the foreseeable future, you will be relieved of any company responsibilities.

–It's for your own good, dear, but it's for the protection of us all, said Peggy.

–We're in a very delicate phase now, the final stages of the transition, all according to Allan's instructions. Transferring all remaining assets into a trust.

–A charitable trust, I said.

–A trust.

–The plan was . . .

–The plan has changed.

–What about the old people?

–We're working something out with the old people. They aren't exactly welfare cases.

–And Allan's money . . .

–It's everybody's money, dear. We have a law firm looking for it, Bay Street people Nick knows.

–Nick again.

–Byron, I can feel you getting worked up. That's not helpful.

–We always counted on the fact that Allan was in charge, I said.

– It isn't your concern now, Peggy said.

– So, who's in charge now? Don't say fucking Nick.

–Basically, the board.

–And who is the name on the letterhead? The top dog? On paper anyway, where my name used to be?

–Mrs. Peggy Winter.

–Congratulations, Mrs. Winter.

–I'm sorry if this is all coming at you . . .

– So, who is really calling the shots?

–The board, with our participation.

–*Our* participation?

–Me and Annie.

–You don't know fuck all about the board.

–We know enough. Allan picked them. They're reputable.

I laughed. I stood up.

–I think I'll go now.

–Go where? said Annie.

–Home.

–You are home, honey.

She glanced at Peggy, her eyebrows raised. I looked around the room. I could imagine Allan laughing on the mantel. Telling me,

It's about context, Byron. Meaning comes from context. Context can lend humour. Context can lend drama. Your context is now dementia. Which lends nothing but humiliation. Each

small mistake is more confirmation of what they're already thinking.

As far as they're concerned, you're gaga, man. But that could be a good thing.

Explain nothing.

I think it was when Peggy called me "dear" that I decided to leave them in the dark. It wasn't so much the innocuous word, but the way she said it. I'd been called dear many times, just like that. In hospitals. By kind but ultimately mercenary strangers.

They could learn the truth themselves, the way I did.

And if I had any doubt about my true position in this three-way relationship, it disappeared when Annie called me "honey" for the first time in her life.

I was in the condo living room when the truth came home to roost. It was much sooner than I'd expected. Annie had gone to work early. My phone rang. I could hear a commotion around her, could hardly hear what she was telling me.

–What's going on? I asked.

–The place is crawling with policemen. They have search warrants. They're tearing everything apart.

–I'll come.

–No, stay there. They're also at Peggy's house. I think they're on the way to the condo place too. I've already called our lawyers.

There was pounding on the door as I disconnected. Someone shouted to open up. Shouted "Police" as if I didn't know already.

I stumbled to the door.

There was a policeman in uniform, holding up a paper, asking if I was who I was, advising me that they had a warrant and were about to search the place for evidence of fraud and money laundering and other things that, because of the confusion, I forget. There were half a dozen other cops behind him. I stepped aside and they walked in. Straggling behind, there was a plainclothes officer with a laminated ID tag hanging from his neck and a shit-eating grin plastered on his face.

–Hello, Byron, he said.

–Nick, I said. I think you know your way around.

28.

They ignored me as they ransacked the place. Eventually, Nick took me gently by the arm and led me to the rocking chair near the window overlooking Lake Ontario. There were foaming whitecaps. Planes from the island drifted down, lifted upwards. I became a non-being in the busy room, more or less like Allan on the mantel.

I looked toward his black plastic box and suddenly felt lighter. Remembered his confidence, how he respected the law, even when he broke it, and the truth, even when he lied.

Don't sweat this, I imagined him saying.

I'm not sweating it.

I could hear his chuckle and feel his utter confidence in me.

Bugger off, I told him.

After what seemed like quite a long time, Nick placed a comradely hand on my shoulder.

–Let's go somewhere quiet, he said.

He led me toward the small office beside the main bedroom. He really did know his way around, but he didn't seem to realize that this is where I slept. He pointed to a chair. I sat. He sat at the desk. In command.

–I'm sure I don't have to explain. You're an attorney.

–You needn't explain, I said.

–I need your phone, he said.

–My phone?

–Yes, please.

The questions would have been instinctive in other circumstances: *Is it in the search warrant? Am I under arrest?*

I decided on the spot to ask neither. I took the phone from my pocket and handed it to him. He had trouble trying to suppress the surprised look on his face.

–Password?

Oh, fuck you, I didn't say.

–It's *malignant2.* Small *m,* I said.

He chuckled. Poked the password in. Started scrolling. I assumed he was reviewing my phone log. He obviously didn't see anything of interest. He handed the phone back.

–We might want to take another look at some point.

–Whatever is appropriate. But can I call my wife?

–Soon.

I realized my hands were trembling and was surprised. Nerves? Normally, I'd have been disturbed by that. But in these circumstances, reacting like a normal person was probably a good thing.

–Could I have some water?

–Yeah, sure.

He left the room, returned with the water.

–What's in that black box on the mantel?

–Human remains, I said.

–I figured. The big guy, right?

–Allan.

–I only met him once, early on, when he pretended to be a flunky at a meeting, that day you took my picture. That was nicely done.

–There were reasons for that. Business considerations.

–I imagine.

He flipped through a notebook until he came to a blank page.

–So how is the ol' memory these days, Byron?

–That depends.

Yes. Memory always depends on the situation. Right?

–I'm not sure what you mean. I have days . . .

–So, let's start with the early days, with Albert, or Allan . . . We'll call him Allan. Were there other names?

–I only knew Allan.

–Since?

–I think it was 1979.

The challenge in the chat with Nick was restraining my normal impulse to meet questions with smarter questions that would substitute for answers. Suppressing curiosity. To keep one thing in mind: *you aren't a lawyer now.*

Revealing common things, like indignation, confusion, even fear—that would be okay. Sounding like the lawyer that I was—or used to be—could be fatal. I kept saying to myself: *This is not normal, I am a person of interest now.*

They all think that I'm not well.

They could be right.

To this policeman, who was acting as if he really knew me as a result of his obviously successful deception, I had become my disability—a country bumpkin with a limp, now diminished by an intellectual disorder. He assumed the upper hand because my brain was damaged, by disease or injury or both.

–So, let's go back. Try to remember the Allan you first met.

–The pigs were Cedric's.

–Come again?

–I was reading a book when we met. And we started talking about this guy named Cedric, a big landowner back in the Middle Ages. He had a bunch of people working for him. One of them was this guy who looked after the pigs. The guy's name was Gurth . . .

–Gurth?

–So anyway, the rest is vague. It's been a long time since I read the story, but the point of the story was . . .

Nick was standing, looking down.

–Could you excuse me for a minute?

–Sure thing, Nick.

He was gone for a few minutes. When he came back, he said,

–So, what does this pig story have to do with . . .

–You asked how I met Allan. Where's Annie?

–She's at the office.

–Her office?

–Yes.

–And Peggy. Where's Peggy?

–She's home. I'll be upfront, Byron. They're both having conversations with people, more or less like this one. Okay?

–Sure. They're honest women.

–I believe that too. And I believe that you're an honest guy. And you know as well as I do that as long as everybody is truthful, the conversations are all pretty well going to lead to the same place.

–What place?

–Reality, Byron. Fantasy will get us nowhere.

He grinned, the smile that made him so damned likeable.

–So how about we talk about where we stand, going forward.

–Oh. Please. Don't ever say that to Annie, Nick.

He gestured his confusion with his hands. Big thick policeman hands. Big handsome blank policeman face.

–I don't get it.

–She fuckin freaks out when anybody says "going forward." Don't ask me why, but when somebody says that in front of her, the conversation is o-ver.

–Everybody says "going forward."

–That's the point.

He was frowning now, flipping through the pages of his notebook.

–So let's get back to your friend.

–Yes. Gurth.

–Who?

–I was explaining. I always used to think that Allan saw himself as Cedric. But one day he told me, "No, I'm Gurth." His reasoning, when I asked him why, was he'd always rather be the underdog. In the end, as long as the underdog plays his cards right and doesn't get too crooked or too greedy, he'll always get a fair share.

–Of what?

–The pairings.

–The pairings of fucking what?

–I have no idea. I always assumed of the pigs. He'd get a couple of breeding pairs and be able to start his own herd.

–Okay.

He sighed.

–Obviously, Allan didn't follow his own advice, did he?

–How so?

–He got crooked, didn't he. And greedy too.

–How was he crooked?

–You don't think that smuggling drugs and laundering money and fuck knows what else is crooked?

–But I don't know anything about that.

–Excuse me. I have to take a whiz.

–I know the feeling.

He stared at me with the expression sophisticated folks reserve for fools.

–Like a dozen times a day, I said.

I stole a glance after he'd walked into the living room. I saw him standing, hands spread, as if he was trying to explain something to the other officer, who was looking at the floor, chin in hand.

When he returned, I said,

–I have a question for you, Nick. Who is Albert Rose?

–You're saying you don't know?

–I mean the guy who was using the name, the guy who's working with your crowd.

–That'll come out in due course. For now, just some schmuck who was afraid of your virtuous friend, this so-called Allan. Did you ever think you had any reason to be afraid of Allan?

–God. No. Or . . . well . . . maybe once.

–What was that about?

I waited while he opened his notebook to a fresh page.

–I once got the impression that Allan thought I had the hots for his wife. Peggy. You know Peggy?

–And did you?

–And did I what?

–Did you have the hots for Peggy?

–Actually, yes. Even though I introduced them way back when. Although it never went anywhere with me and Peggy. You want to know why?

–Why what?

–Why it never went anywhere with me and Peggy.

–Sure.

–I think back then she thought that I was queer.

I wish I had a picture of the expression on his face. He was scratching at his head, just beside his ear. There was dandruff drifting to his shoulder. I wanted to reach over and brush it off.

–Why would she think that?

–Think what?

He sighed.

–Think that you were queer.

–Because I didn't try to fuck her when I had the chance. I'm surprised Annie didn't tell you all about that.

His face flushed and he stiffened. He closed his notebook, put his pen away. Sat back, stared at me for a while.

–I have some advice for you, Byron. Don't overplay your hand. Okay?

–I'm listening.

–You have a good hand. I don't want anything bad to happen to you. Or to your wife.

–Did you fuck my wife, Nick?

He stood. Stared down at me. I thought for a moment he might grab me.

–You aren't obliged to answer, I said.

He walked away, stopped in the doorway, turned back, face blazing.

–Isn't that the way it works, Nick? Fuck everyone you can, every chance you get?

I smiled.

He checked whatever he was going to say, then left.

Chaos settles down, even when it's unresolved. We tidy up our physical surroundings and we retreat into a reasonable contemplation of practical solutions to a specific set of challenges. We fret. But we never call them problems anymore. The big things are challenges. The little things are issues.

After the raids, Annie announced that she was going to stay at Peggy's for a while. Peggy needed her, she said, and she wanted distance from the condo. I think she also wanted distance from Allan's ashes and from me. She suspected there would be other visits from the police. She came home briefly to collect some clothes, her toothbrush, a makeup bag.

–I have to distance myself, she said.

–From me.

–No, from here.

–Nick?

–I'll explain sometime.

–You don't have to.

–I had no idea he was anybody. He was nobody. You have to understand that. I thought that I was using him, making sure the Russians were playing straight with us. So believe me, I deserve what's happened. But you don't deserve this. I hope you understand.

–I understand that everybody is somebody, always needing something.

–Yes. Maybe you do.

–How is Peggy?

–You can imagine. This, just after Allan.

–Lucky Allan.

–Please, Byron.

–Timing is everything, he always used to say.

If she thought that I was my normal self, she'd have snapped at me, but now, here, she just seemed sad.

–We're not supposed to talk too much, Byron. But just tell me, is there anything important that I should know?

–How would I know that? You three ran everything. I have no idea what you know and don't know.

–You were his friend, she said.

–Peggy was his wife. Talk to her.

–I hear you.

At the door, she paused and turned. Her eyes were full of questions. I almost went to her. So much she needed, so much she wanted me to say.

–Try to get some sleep, I said.

—

And then I was alone—a lot. It wasn't tactical. I just didn't matter. I attended a meeting with a team of lawyers. Then there was a session in a boardroom with the prosecutors. Tom was on the sidelines with some other men who looked like cops.

Nick was there too, but it was as if he couldn't see me. As far as Nick was concerned, I was out of it. Before he'd left that first day, he came up behind me at the mantel, where I was checking Allan's flowers. I could see him coming—there was a mirror above the mantel. I started speaking—to Allan.

—Here comes trouble. You let me do the talking.

Nick stopped. He opened his mouth, but no words came out. He walked away.

I was asked, frequently at first, about my medical issues. They knew everything, it seemed, except the results of my last meeting with the doctor.

Nick's undercover investigation had been thorough, but his files were incomplete. And so they treated me the way wounded people are so often treated—talked at in a loud and mannered way, smiled at kindly, or at least the way strangers imagine kindness looks.

And then I'd find myself alone, with no one talking to me at all, which wasn't necessarily a bad thing. All things considered.

Annie often answered for me. A childhood injury. Family history. Recent physical collapse. A hospital. Early-onset dementia.

I would just sit there, nodding seriously.

As we were all finding out, Annie insisted, there was a whole world of deception beyond anything we knew about Allan's businesses. A whole history about which we were unaware.

The system that he put in place was hard enough to figure out when one's brain was working normally.

–Even for his accountant, she said.

Her smile, as usual, was pure vulnerability, which was probably why she rarely let it show.

One of the lawyers frowned.

–Your husband knew him since forever, as did you. While Byron might not have been part of the conspiracies, it's really hard to imagine that you or he never picked up on things along the way. Think back now, Anne. Even if it didn't register as criminal behaviour at the time, things might take on different significance now that we have a clearer picture.

–I'll let Byron speak for himself.

All eyes turned toward me.

I fiddled with my most expensive pen, a Montblanc. Made a quick note on a pad. Cleared my throat.

–I've been a lawyer for many years, as you all know. My friend, Allan Chase, has been, from time to time, a client. Real estate transactions. The like. I acted as his proxy CEO during some complex business deals, mostly taking care of negotiations, or making small decisions on the fly. My dealings were with bankers, brokers, other lawyers.

–He must have had a lot of faith in you.

–Yes, he did.

–Surprising that, at some point, he didn't confide . . .

–Actually, he did confide in me. Let me tell you a little story. I think it is a useful allegory. I think, in retrospect . . . maybe. Anyway. Let me run it by you. In the Middle Ages, there was a wealthy landowner whose name was Cedric. He had a lot of people working for him and one of them was a guy named Gurth, his swineherd. Cedric had a lot of pigs, you see, and he delegated all the dirty work . . .

And so on.

They were courteous, always.

Annie caught me by surprise, after one exhausting day.

–Peggy isn't doing well.

–Really?

–I think we'd all be better off if we were together at the condo. She isn't sleeping. She keeps reliving the moment she discovered Allan. She'd be better here, I think. She's always been more relaxed when you're around.

She poured drinks. I accepted mine. I hadn't had a drink for what felt like weeks by then. Maybe it was even longer.

–She'll be with us only for a little while.

I pretended I was thinking deeply.

–Will you be okay with that?

–Yes, of course, I said.

–She needs us, Byron. We're going to need each other, all three of us.

I sipped briefly, then said,

–That means *you'll* be coming home to stay.

–Yes.

–That's good, I said.

So we three were together then, a little family. And when they talked, I listened, which was easy given they didn't seem to notice I was there.

It's odd how a single adjustment in perspective on what we know about a person can overwhelm everything we've previously known.

Misplacing a book or car keys or a pen; forgetting why I was in the pharmacy; losing track of time; taking a wrong turn on my way home. All meant something different now, something ominous and burdensome for everyone around me.

I knew that they'd soon suggest I shouldn't drive. And now, with Peggy in the condo, it was just a matter of time before power of attorney was broached—legal custody.

I was pretty sure they were already thinking long term. Assisted living. Nursing home. Crematorium.

I came out of the bathroom one morning. Annie hissed,

–You forgot to pull your zipper up.

I looked down. She was right. I zipped up and said,

–At least I remembered to pull it down.

Once, they would have laughed their heads off.

Any time I'd stumble,

–*Sure as hell he's going to fall again.*

–*Here, dear, let me take your arm.*

–*Fuck off and leave me alone. And stop calling me dear.*

Dramatically shrinking away from me, from every outburst, then exchanging glances full of meaning.

There he goes again.

Goes where?

I could have told them everything I knew. I could have walked them through my last lunch with Allan, the last meeting with the doctor, but it would not have mattered. Anything

I said was now evidence that I was in denial, which was evidence that I was disconnected from reality.

I could have walked them through my meetings with Tom, the cop.

But somewhere deep in my consciousness, I heard Allan, loud and clear.

—Get serious! Or better still, don't get serious.

Like Allan, I was gone for good.

.

I said to Annie, when we were alone one evening,

—The thing we have going for us is that we're telling them the truth. The truth is shatterproof if it has consistency. With consistency, the truth survives everything, even if it consists of lies. Conversely . . .

She was staring at me as if I were a dog who had just recited a line from Homer.

—Where's that coming from?

—Just something Allan told me long ago.

—So, what else did Allan tell you long ago?

—He used to talk a lot about trusting people.

—Do you trust us, Byron?

—If I may say so, I'm not so sure about Peggy.

—Not so sure about what?

—Her consistency.

—Go to bed, Byron. You need your rest.

29

My phone was ringing. It hadn't rung for ages. First, I thought it was for someone else, but I was home alone. I answered and it was Tom, the policeman. I feigned confusion. I apologized.

–I'm terrible with names.

–Tom, he said.

–Right. Tom. What can I do for you today, Tom?

–Can you remember where we had our coffee, a short while back?

–Remind me, Tom.

–Just down the street . . .

–Yes, yes, Harbourfront.

–I was wondering if we could maybe have another coffee.

–Well, I don't know. Maybe I should ask a lawyer.

–You're a lawyer, Byron.

–Yeah, but . . .

–Listen. I'm not playing tricks. I want to lay things out for you. Anything we say will be just between the two of us. Anyway, you can always play the dementia card.

–The what?

–Forget I said that. How about it?

—

He was sitting in the same place. Table for four in the corner. Room for documents.

He fetched the coffee. And then he sat for a while staring at me as if he wasn't sure where to begin. One of the older tricks. Nothing like silence to get someone else to break the ice. He took a sip of the coffee.

–So, we're going to talk man to man here, Byron. We're going to stick to the meat and potatoes. No more stories about pigs. Okay?

–I never told you the story about Cedric . . .

He held up a hand.

–I've heard it from enough other people. Trust me.

–But can I tell a different one . . .

–Okay, but make it short . . .

–This one's about horseshit.

–Well, I'm used to that.

–Okay. Here goes. In university, there was a professor high up in the business department. Economics and statistics and accounting and the like. He had a PhD from Harvard or MIT or somewhere. Each summer he'd go home to the little place where he grew up. He loved horses, this professor, and there was a track there. And every summer he'd volunteer around the track. One day he's in the horse barn, shovelling manure. Two guys show up in suits. Shoes-with-tassels kind of guys. They want to know who's in charge. He tells them everyone's gone home but him. What can I do for you? he asks. They say they want to see the books. He says he can show them. They produce ID—they're auditors from some government outfit. He takes them to the office, hauls out the books. Leaves. An hour or so later the two suits are back in the horse barn, where he's finishing up. We're done, they say, you might want to put the ledgers back in the safe. That was quick, the professor says. Everything okay? Actually, the books are impressive, they say. Pristine. Do you know who does the books for them? Yes, he says. I do the books. They look him up and down. Rubber boots. Scruffy clothes. Horseshit splattered over everything. He points to the top of his head. Don't let the ball cap fool youse, he says.

Tom is nodding.

–That's a good one.

–Whenever I'd be interviewing people to be witnesses or whatnot, I'd always remember that. We never know who we're talking to, do we, Tom.

He rubbed his hands together. Took another sip of coffee, which was getting cold.

–Okay, Byron, let's talk turkey.

–But first, Tom, who the hell is Nick?

–Ah, Nick. I can't tell you too much, Byron. Just that he's one of us, another cop, which you already know, but he's an American.

–An American?

–Mob specialist. FBI. Seconded to the RCMP. He has a Russian background. Russian organized crime guy. That should tell you something, Byron.

–Like what?

–You were on the edge of something very big and very tricky, maybe even dangerous, my friend. A word of advice: don't fuck with Nick.

–But Nick fucked with me. You know about my wife.

–That's something we might have to deal with down the line, but for now . . .

–I'm thinking about professionalism, Tom.

–Let's move on.

–Sure.

–And for the sake of this conversation, all due respect, Byron, I'm going to pretend that you're just as compos mentis as I am. That might not be saying much, eh?

–For sure. I'm grateful.

–So we agree. No more stories. You're good with the stories, Byron. Maybe someday over a beer. But for now, meat and potatoes. Got it?

–Got it.

–The focus now is money. You know all about the law regarding proceeds of crime. From our investigation, there is hard evidence of crime—drug smuggling and money laundering. I don't have to spell it out. So, what's the bottom line? What do you think?

–Depends on a lot of things. The kind of evidence you have. Accountability, I suppose.

–Byron, trust me, we have evidence. The Americans had been trailing your dead friend for years.

–So why didn't they bust him years ago?

–Because, in the larger scheme of things, he was small fry. He was, basically, bait. Low end of the food chain. He was more useful out there, so they just let him do his thing. They'd have grabbed him sooner or later, when he was no longer useful. But, of course, he fooled us all, made the great escape.

–Right. So now what?

–He couldn't take his money with him.

–True enough. And the law is big on confiscation, I know from reading cases.

–It's called accountability, Byron. Your word. But there's a relationship between the accountability and the so-called confiscation. People who help with the confiscation tend to avoid much of the accountability.

–That sounds right.

–The guy that's most accountable here is beyond the law. Our law, anyway. So Allan gets a free pass. The Russians he was mixed up with are another story. But for now, there's quite a cast of smaller fish.

–Uh huh.

–There's you.

I sighed. I interlaced my fingers and studied them. I looked him in the eye and said,

–I know, Tom.

–So, Byron. I'm going to spell it out. I'm going to pretend that I don't like you. I'm going to suggest that you allowed yourself to front a modest criminal operation that happens to be connected to something serious.

–Like how serious?

–Like big-time international-level serious. Like Mexican drug cartel serious. Like Russian mafia serious.

–That does sound serious, Tom. Maybe we shouldn't be talking at all.

–Maybe. But for now, let's say we're on the same side. Okay?

–Whatever.

—And don't be offended if I say we think you guys are pretty Mickey Mouse, okay? We're all more interested in what you know than what you've done.

—And in Allan's money.

—Yes, and the money. So, I'm clear?

—I'm going to tell you truthfully, Tom, I don't have a clue what you're talking about.

—You know nothing about dope.

—You already know that when Allan was young, he sold pot like everybody did.

—What do you know about his American years?

I shrugged.

—You didn't have much contact for quite a while.

—I was for many years a small-time lawyer, working out of my farmhouse and looking after Mom, who had Alzheimer's. You knew that, about Mom?

—I heard that. I could relate to that, Byron. My dad went the same way.

—I'm sorry to hear that.

He waved a hand.

—So, I can understand. You were pretty well tied up for quite a while. But Peggy was in the picture for a lot of that time. Right?

—I'd want to be precise about that. I could check.

—Where and when did they get married?

—I'm not sure. It was in Mexico, I think.

He laughed.

—Of course it was. Pretty hard getting any information out

of that place. You wouldn't know how much contact Annie had with her sister in those days?

–I don't think much. Annie was with me on the farm. She had her own business back then and was tied up with Mom the same as I was. She started working for Allan almost casually, doing basic bookkeeping.

–What did you think when he started getting you involved?

–I found it strange. But he made it clear that he only needed me for Canadian stuff. I think Annie was the same. Nothing to do with the States or offshore.

–Offshore. What do you know about offshore?

–I don't know anything about offshore.

–Let me jog your memory. So, on and off, you're the lawyer on a series of real estate deals. A dozen or so properties flipped. Allan's company walks away with about thirty million dollars after the final sale. You with me?

–I don't remember how much.

–Annie has confirmed the thirty mil.

–She'd know.

–She also confirms that, a couple of years ago, the thirty million was invested in some major projects, jointly owned with Russian financial interests.

–I don't know about that.

–You were the CEO.

–Okay. But I'm pretty sure that somebody else handled the details.

–Your friend Allan.

–I guess so.

–So. Here's where the bells go off for us. About a year ago, the big partners, the Russians, they buy you out for about eighteen million. An investment of thirty million shrinks to eighteen. A loss of twelve million for you guys.

–I'd have to check.

–You don't need to check. Annie has already confirmed that. What's interesting to us is that these partners who bought your stuff at eighteen million, they flipped it just weeks later to some other people with similar last names for thirty-six million.

–I didn't know that.

–So, here's the thing. We smell the fabric softener here.

–You smell what?

–Did you ever do a load of wash, Byron?

–Hah. I get it.

–Either you guys got screwed out of eighteen mil, or you ended up with eighteen mil that, before this, was useless money because it smelled like shit. You follow?

–Whoa.

–Drug money, illegally repatriated and buried in low-profile Canadian real estate. Then flipped and reflipped. Textbook money laundering, Byron. Take some time to think it through. Lots of people figure you and the two women are up to your neck in this. I'm not so sure.

–This is mostly all news to me, Tom.

–And anyway, we'd have a hard time prosecuting a guy with your medical history and prognosis. Plus, I think you're pretty straight, Byron.

–Thank you. That's a relief.

–There's a shady board of directors, though. We'll be taking a closer look. And there's Annie.

–Yes. Annie.

–She's being a good soldier, Byron. The Crown and our guys, they think she's the cat's ass. Almost one of us now. She's one sharp cookie, that wife of yours. And anyway, even if there was a possibility of prosecuting her, I think Nick kind of compromised any possibility of that. But I don't want to get into that here.

He stared, eyes hard and angry.

–How do you feel about all that, Byron?

–All what?

–Tell you the God's truth, Byron. I don't have a lot of time for stick men. I have some personal history. But that's a story for another day.

–What about Peggy? I asked.

–Peggy. That's a hard one. You see, she might have the key to the big mystery here, Byron.

–And what's the big mystery?

He leaned in, eyes narrowed, face about ten inches from mine. I now noticed the dark half moons beneath his eyes; the bristles poking out of ears and nostrils; the smell of coffee on his breath. My heart felt like it had stopped.

–Where the fuck did the eighteen million go, Byron?

I stood at the mantel. *I hope you're enjoying this.*

I took him from his place, held him carefully in two hands. Thinking: This is what it all comes down to. Dust to dust.

And money, he replied. *They only care about the money,*

Byron. They let me pile it up for years, knowing that, when I was no longer useful to them, they could take me out and take my money. Proceeds of crime, they call it. I call it deferred taxation.

But you were way ahead of them, weren't you?

All the way.

Which was why you planned to give it all away. You knew that they'd come after it.

What happens now is up to you, my friend.

I went to sit in the rocking chair, looking out on Lake Ontario. It was a windy day. I could imagine St. Georges Bay, back home. I missed back home. Allan was so right: Why would anybody need more than what I had?

How often I'd heard Mom say: *There's more to life than the life we know. If I didn't believe that, there would be no point in anything.*

Kitchen table wisdom. What if Mom was right?

And then there's the reality in the black plastic box now sitting on my lap. Dust. Minerals. Plastic.

What about money?

Okay, Al. We have some unfinished business.

I pried the lid off the box. *You never told us what we should do with what's left of you.*

Maybe off a boat, when summer comes?

Anything but a cemetery.

I reached into the box. Was about to remove the tiny plastic baggie . . .

—Are you talking to him?

Peggy?

I jerked around. She was standing near the dining table, looking shocked.

–Byron, for God's sake.

I jammed the lid back on the box. Stood.

–I didn't hear you coming in.

–I was here. I was in the kitchen. I heard someone out here talking.

–Sorry.

–Jesus, Byron . . .

–It's okay. I was just having a moment. I was wondering what we're going to do with this. We just can't keep him here forever.

–That's the least of our worries, she said.

I returned him to the mantel, made sure of the symmetry between him and the flowers and the photograph.

–Maybe in the summer. We'll get someone with a boat.

I could sense that she was close behind me. I turned to face her. She folded her arms and stepped back. I jammed my hands into my pockets.

–If you don't mind me asking, does he ever answer when you talk to him?

–All the time.

She laughed.

–There was a time when he'd answer me too. That was quite a while ago.

–I'm sorry, I said.

–About what?

–About everything.

–Poor Byron, she said.

–No. Not poor me. Poor everyone but me.

Her face was empty. Everything about her, emptied.

–I should have been talking to you, not him, I said.

–To say what?

–Basically, what I just sort of said. I'm sorry? But then I ask, sorry for what? And the answer is, really, I'm sorry that you're mad at me. That's kind of like self-pity. Isn't it?

–I'm not mad at you, Byron.

–I don't believe that.

–I'm mad at whatever turned you into every man I've ever known.

–Yes.

–But that isn't fair. Why should you *not* be like everybody else?

–So what's everybody else like?

–Selfish. Violent. Corrupt. What the world considers normal.

–I thought it was a problem that I *wasn't* normal. I thought normal was the thing to be. I guess it doesn't matter now.

–I tried to tell you. It was a gift to be different from everybody else.

–How was I supposed to know what you were telling me?

–That's always been our problem, Byron.

She kissed my cheek. And walked away.

30

I waited until I was sure she wasn't coming back. I went back to the mantel, pried the top off the plastic box, reached inside, found the baggie. I removed the two thumb drives and put them in my pocket, put the baggie in the garbage, making sure that it didn't have any particles of Allan in the folds.

I locked the office door behind me and plugged the first drive into a USB port on my computer and opened it.

Having talked to Allan over lunch, it was straightforward now. The numbers were definitely all bank accounts. The password and username were now obvious to me. Too weird to make any sense to anyone else, but for me they were brilliant.

It took a bit more work to identify a bank, but I got there. I'll keep that process to myself. They had a lovely home page, sand and sky and azure water, lithe bodies, of all pigmentations from gold to chocolate, frolicking. Everybody deliriously happy on an island that I'd never heard of. Dominica.

I logged on to the e-mail account that Allan had given me for emergencies. It was easy to remember: malignantcove@hotmail .com. I entered the name of the bank and, when prompted, the username and password. And there I was.

I clicked on Banking and was asked to enter another password. And now my mind was blank.

Everything I needed was somewhere in the drives. Obviously, the second password was to be the biggest challenge, but I was meant to find it. It would be something obvious to me. Or maybe not so obvious, but something that I could figure out. Maybe only me. But Allan couldn't have anticipated my confusion. The strange state that I find descending, or rising up, without warning and, from time to time, cloaking me in a dark mist.

Perhaps not Alzheimer's, but definitely something out of order in my head. Maybe, like everybody else, I was just being mauled by time.

I could hear voices in the living room. I quickly entered the information that I now had—password, username, name of the bank—and saved it to the first thumb drive. I shut the laptop down.

Annie and Peggy were sitting close together on a sofa. Annie had her arms around her sister, holding her tightly, making soothing sounds as Peggy sobbed on her shoulder. I walked by, close enough to touch, but they didn't see me. Maybe I *have* become invisible, the ghost of Byron past. I pinched my hand. I am here. Substantial flesh. I walked to the rocking chair by the large picture window and I sat. The lake was black, lights garlanded around it.

And then Peggy blew her nose and declared,

–I know I'll be all right. It's just the shock of everything.

–You must keep reminding yourself, it's all a game now. It's all about the almighty dollar. It's how much they can terrorize us to get as much as possible.

–They keep saying we have tens of millions. Billions. Where's that coming from, Annie?

–It's all tactics. We're telling them the truth and we just have to keep doing that.

–But Annie, just six million and change? Even I don't believe that. I know there's a ton more somewhere.

–Peggy, listen to me. You do *not* know there's a ton more. You *suspect* there should be tons more, just like they do. But you don't *know* anything but what the numbers tell us at this point. Cash on hand. Some equity.

–Do you know?

–That's neither here nor there. I'm doing my best to help them find whatever we can find.

–I wish I was more like you. You're just so cool about everything.

Annie laughed, a mirthless chuckle.

–Be careful what you wish for.

–They're threatening to charge me . . .

–Fuck that, don't even go there. Charge you with what?

–Fraud. Conspiracy. Money laundering. False this and that.

–All words. They're pulling scary words out of their assholes. Don't fall for it.

–But our homes. My house. This place.

–No court will let them put us on the street.

I stood. They still didn't notice me.

–I wouldn't be so fucking sure of that, I said.

Now they saw me.

–How long have you been there? Annie said, sounding edgy, like I'd been spying on them.

I laughed.

–I live here at your insistence, I said.

–How much did you hear?

–I heard everything, not that anything surprises me.

–You should have said something.

–I goddamned near tripped over you walking to this chair. See, here's the problem. You've decided that I'm wacko, and wacko means invisible . . .

–Nobody said you were . . .

–Shut the fuck up for a change.

I could feel the words rushing forward, like a tsunami, but then hauling back to a trickle. I knew the phrases would soon come rushing back in waves, but I was no longer sure about what garbage they might carry with them, what meaning, what misunderstanding. I felt tear-pressure building, the paradox of anger, evidence of weakness when passion makes you strongest.

Without another word, I turned away from them. I went to where I slept. I went to the office, where there was a pull-out daybed I'd been sleeping on for weeks. I went to the office, where there was an unopened bottle of whisky in the deep bottom drawer of an antique desk beside the miserable, lumpy goddamned pullout daybed. I locked the door behind me.

I thought I heard someone try the door sometime later in the night. A doorknob turning once. Twice. Then nothing.

I slid back down the dream slide to where the man was waiting to help me with the snowsuit zipper.

Here, I think I've got it. Hang on.

Wallop.

I ran outside, toward the safety of daylight. And ended up in darkness.

The pressure on my bladder was desperate. I sat up. To go to the bathroom, I would have to leave this sanctuary. I would have to risk an encounter with one of them. Not now. Ideally, not ever.

I switched on the desk light.

The empty whisky bottle . . .

I grabbed it. Why the hell not. It's all the same colour anyway.

I listened as they left the condo early the next morning, off to their meetings with lawyers and policemen.

I returned to the computer. I was in my underwear, but so what. I stared at the enigmatic second drive, read the biblical passage. Over and over. And I was thinking of another story, one I heard from an old lawyer in Halifax, about a worker at the navy dockyard. Every Friday evening he'd arrive at the main gate to go home for the weekend and he'd have a wheelbarrow loaded with straw. The guards on the gate would stop him every time. Find nothing in the straw. And wave him through, only to discover in an audit that there were several dozen wheelbarrows unaccounted for.

Now why was that playing in my head?

A part of my brain that wasn't working properly was still sending signals just the same, like one of those beacons triggered in an aircraft after it has crashed. It was saying, *Look at the big picture. It should be obvious to you.*

Two things I know about computers: When all else fails with the technology, reboot. When in doubt about the data, google.

I googled. I started typing. *For the Lord Himself will come down from heaven with a loud command . . .*

Google popped up with Saint Paul to the Thessalonians. I typed a few more words and the whole selection jumped into the frame, along with a citation.

1 Thessalonians 4:16–17.

After studying it until I almost knew it off by heart, I told myself: *There is absolutely nothing in the wheelbarrow.*

It's just straw.

And then I thought: *Look again.*

I played with the citation for an hour. And when I eventually typed in *1thes41617*, I hit the jackpot. Literally. Eighteen million dollars and change, littering fifteen bank accounts in the middle of the Caribbean.

I just stared.

You are one piece of work, my friend.

My phone was ringing. I checked to make sure it wasn't Annie. Certainly not Peggy. It was Tom, returning my call.

–Hey, Tom.

–Byron. What's up?

–Tom, are you up for another coffee? I've done a lot of thinking about our last conversation.

–Me too. Same place?

–Sounds good.

After I finished talking, Tom said,

–In principle, I have no problem. But I'm going to have to run it up the pole. I only wish I knew more.

–You're better off in the dark, I said.

–Can I have a hint as to your source of information?

–Come on, Tom. You know better. Our lives often depend on sources. Trust me a little.

–Let me understand. You can bring the eighteen million to the table . . .

–Correction, someone can . . .

–Someone can bring the missing eighteen million dollars to the table, voluntarily, if we agree to . . . Just run it by me one more time.

–One: Don't touch the homes. Annie's condo and Peggy's house. My farm. Two: Stop threatening Peggy with prison time. If there's a criminal case against Peggy, make it go away.

–What if they just double down, hang you up by the balls until you produce the money? They have ways of doing that, my friend.

–First, I trust you, Tom. I think you're a reasonable man. You know in your gut that they will never find that money. They'll have what they've dug up already. Five or six million, I understand. They'll have a few million from the personal property. They'll be feeding and housing Peggy in some institution for God knows how long, and probably support-ing her one way or another at public expense for the rest of her life because of what jail will do to her.

–Or?

–Or they carry off roughly twenty-five million in ill-got-ten gains and put it to work for the well-being of the citi-zenry. Peggy and Annie get on with their lives as two smart, productive, law-abiding citizens with many contributions to make to society in future years.

—Not bad for a guy with early-onset dementia, Byron.

—Let me know their response.

—You'll get a text from me. Two words in either case. *Nothing doing.* Or, *Green light.*

—I'll be waiting, Tom.

—Whatever happens, it's been interesting, Byron.

Annie was late.

—Where's Peggy?

—I'm not sure.

—Byron, we have to talk. About last night.

—What about last night?

—Surely you remember. Your behaviour was unacceptable. I'm not sure that this is a viable arrangement.

—Neither am I. I've been gathering my stuff. By the way, I found this in a jacket pocket. I don't know how long it's been there.

I held up a thumb drive. I passed it to her. She looked at it with a puzzled expression.

—What's this?

—A USB thingy . . .

—I know that. Did you look at it?

—Yes. It's just a bunch of numbers. It looks like a list of bank accounts. Could be passwords.

She grabbed a laptop and headed for her bedroom.

I checked my phone. There was a single text.

Green light, it said.

31

I was staring at the lake from my usual lookout in the rocking chair beside the big picture window. The little planes were coming and going, trying not to make a noise. The condo dwellers were always listening, always poised to raise a stink if they should hear airplane sounds coming from an airport.

It was a windy day in late spring, but there were a few early sailboats out riding waves about a metre high. It was one of those days when Mom would squint into the wind and say we might as well go in. Always, when she saw whitecaps, *We might as well go in. The poor critters will still be in the traps tomorrow.*

I couldn't remember the last time I was on a boat. Strange, I thought. I was really good at driving a boat. And good at getting around on board. Even in the shitty weather, I was like everybody else. As Mom would say, *When the water's rough, everyone is lame.*

I was glad that Allan saw me drive the boat. I think he was impressed that I was good at something.

Mom would never tell me I was good, but I could tell she too admired the way I handled it. The way I read the wind and worked with the tide when we were in the harbour. The way I let the boat and Mother Nature have their way in the channel, and how I knew when to make the subtle mechanical adjustments that we all could live with, me and Mom and Nature and the boat.

The fishermen would all tell me: *You can't fight Mother Nature, boy. She'll kill you if you try.*

It struck me like a fist, sitting in that rocking chair.

I'm going home.

Annie rubbed my shoulders.

–How are you today, Byron?

–Good as gold, I said.

She laughed.

–You are indeed.

–Were you able to make head or tail out of that thing I gave you? That whatchamacallit?

–The whatchamacallit. Thumb drive.

–Yes.

–Yup. We made head or tail of it for sure.

–Now what?

–Now nothing.

She was studying me. She was uncertain, possibly for the first time in our lives. Uncertain what was in my mind. If anything.

–Good, I said. I'm glad things got sorted out.

–You don't remember where you got that?

–Got what?

–The thumb drive.

I shrugged.

–It was in a pocket.

She came around and crouched in front of me, clasped my hand. She was really giving me the eye.

–No clue, eh? It just showed up in a pocket? Like the fairies put it there.

–Allan must have given it to me. It's the only explanation. When or where is anybody's guess. What did you do with it?

–I made a proposition to the Crown. It was like they were waiting for it. Go figure.

–Proposition to do what?

She just stared, a smile spreading.

–You're crazy, Byron. Like I am.

–I wouldn't know about that. Where did Peggy get to?

–She didn't tell you? She's moving back to her own place.

–Oh.

–Yes. We'll miss her.

–What's she going to do?

–I'm not sure. I'm not sure what any of us will do. What are you going to do, Byron?

She mussed my hair and laughed the way she hadn't laughed in years.

–I'm going home, I said.

–Sure you are, she said.

She laughed again, lightly. Her sexy laugh. She walked away. I watched her, thinking of an expression Mom would use. She *sauntered*.

At security, the guy was holding up my backpack.

–Whose is this?

–It's mine, I said.

–Do you mind opening it?

–No problem.

I unzipped it and held it open.

–What's in the box?

–Human remains, I said.

–I thought so.

–Is that a problem?

–No. It's just that it has to go through on a different tray. By itself.

–Sure.

I lifted Allan out of the backpack and handed him to the security officer, who was wearing elastic gloves. He walked away briefly, then returned with Allan sitting on a tray that looked just like all the other trays. I watched as Allan and his tray disappeared into the X-ray machine.

–What's special about that tray?

–I have no idea, the guy said. It's just the one we always use.

–You get a lot of dead people coming through?

–More than you think.

–So, it's kind of like a little hearse, the special tray.

–You got it. This person someone close to you?

–Yes. Very.

Before I turned the phone off on the plane, I saw the text: *Where are you Byron? We're worried.*

I texted back: *I told you, heading home. Don't worry. I'll be in touch.*

I spent two days in Halifax. I spent an hour, one afternoon, on the bridge. The Angus L., they call it. Interesting, I thought. My uncle, the bridge and I, all called Angus. It's not such a bad name. I peered over the side. There was a tugboat passing underneath. There was a ferry, bucking whitecaps as it crossed the harbour. The bridge was rattling with passing cars, sounding almost flimsy.

The water, even from where I was standing, high above it, chilled me. My stomach shrivelled. I could feel pressure in my bowels. Acrophobia. I've heard it isn't so much a fear of heights as it is an irrational fear of the urge to jump. Eternity, right there before my eyes. Answers to so many impossible questions. Tempting.

I had a sudden urge to piss. Strange how, every time I feel anxiety, that's my natural reaction. I looked both ways. Nobody in sight. I unzipped and let it flow. I watched the wind unravel the unsteady stream, dispersing droplets in all directions.

I relaxed.

I tried to imagine my uncle standing here, but I couldn't picture him. He couldn't have been more dead.

How totally fucked up would you have to be to . . .

Man. That poor bastard.

We're almost there, sonny. Darned zipper. Hang on. You can do it.

I zipped up and walked on.

I bought a truck while I was in Halifax. A Ford. F-150. I'm going to be a country boy again. I felt half the age I really am, just driving off the lot behind the wheel of that pickup truck that smelled just like the showroom where I found it.

I stopped in my driveway and I felt the crystals or whatever. Definitely something lurking in the land. Most likely in the rock below the thin topsoil that nourished so many generations for so many years, stingy and impoverished though it was.

When I got inside, I placed Allan on the guest room windowsill where he could see everything. I could almost hear his voice: *Sure hasn't changed much since I was here last.* That would have been for Mom's funeral.

And he did come all the way for my college graduation. May 1982, it was. He roared down the lane in a two-tone Mustang, black and yellow. Said he drove straight through from Toronto. Sixteen hours. Stopping only for a coffee and a stretch.

–You were flying, man.

–Found a shortcut through the Miramichi, straight to Moncton. Bypassed all the trucks between Edmundston and Fredericton. Saved two hours.

–I thought you were a fan of trucks.

–Not when I'm stuck behind one in a hot rod on a sunny day.

Though it was graduation day, Mom and I still had to haul the traps as usual. It was too nice a day not to go out. The night before, Allan and I had gone to town just to see the action. It was like Mardi Gras, streets teeming with students and their friends and families.

Allan knew we couldn't stay out late. Mom and I were determined to be on the water by five. He was okay with that.

–I might go out with you, in the morning, he said.

–Neat. I'll find you something warm to wear. Some of the old man's coats and sweaters are still around. He was about your size.

–If I'm not up when you're leaving, don't bother waking me.

Before we'd turned in that night, I said,

–Just think, if you'd stayed on at the books, we'd both be celebrating now.

–But we are celebrating, he said.

–What are you celebrating, Allan?

–Same as you, Byron. Life. And the time we have and the freedom to make something out of it.

He wasn't up when Mom and I went out the next morning.

The sun rose slowly. The sky turned magenta then pink, and the night retreated and the day took over all the land behind us, the sea around us. The other fishing boats materialized. Running lights, little dots of red or green, took on dark shapes and we were soon waving at people we knew bobbing in the near distance.

Halfway through the haul, Mom poured coffees from our Thermoses. I was on the wheel as usual.

–So. Today's the big day, she said.

–Feels like any other day.

–He'd have enjoyed being here, your dad.

–I imagine.

–He had high hopes.

–We never talked much about school or anything.

–He did, though, just the same. He had high hopes.

Allan was at the stove when we came in, the house full of the smell of bacon and toast and coffee.

–I took the liberty, he said.

–God bless you, said Mom.

He poured hot coffee.

–I figured you'd be hungry. I wanted to go with you. But I just couldn't get my aging body out of the sack.

He grinned and shrugged.

–It's how I feel every morning, but there you go, said Mom.

–The will is strong, but the flesh is weak, he said.

–You can say that again, said Mom.

Later, when he was in the shower, she said, That's a fine young man there, your friend.

Spring is usually just a concept here. We can have snowstorms in May. It's a bonus for the fishermen if May is gentle, and this one was. The mornings were cold and damp, but the winds were light and by noon the air was warm enough to permit a pleasant walk with a Thermos full of coffee through the fields, toward the shore.

I wasn't hearing much from the women in Toronto. They were creating a new accounting partnership, hunting for some office space. I got the sense that they were relieved to be on their own, free of Allan and our mysteries, free of spooky Russians and their intrigues. I assumed that Nick was back where he belonged. The Excited States, as I liked to think of it.

Then Annie called.

After some small talk, she said,

–Listen, Byron, one day soon I'd like to discuss a business proposition.

–Any time you're ready, I said.

–I think you have the right idea. It's time to go home. This place is unaffordable and almost unlivable.

–I hear you. How does Peggy feel about this?

–It's always been her plan. To go home. Eventually.

–Yes. She mentioned something once. We were on the boat.

–A summer day.

–Yes. A perfect summer day. You mentioned business.

–Just a thought. Maybe the three of us, in a little practice. Simple stuff. Wills, deeds, uncomplicated taxes.

–You really think Peggy's up for this?

–I'll find out. But you think about it.

And I did, for days. I thought about it. And about how we remember and how, sometimes mercifully, we don't remember.

How we forget. How we forgive.

I bumped into Shirley again, while on a grocery shopping trip in town. This time she seemed keen for tea and a little chat.

Do you ever hear from Annie?

–Well, of course. We're still married, you know.

–Well, thank God, she said. I didn't like to ask.

–You can ask me anything, Shirley.

Her eyes grew misty. She grabbed her teacup, met my eyes over the top of it, then dropped her eyes and sipped.

–You know, when you were younger, you looked just like your uncle. He was very good-looking.

–I don't remember anything about him, I said.

She put the cup down. I reached across and caught her hand. She wouldn't look at me. Then,

–He would never have harmed anybody. Certainly not you.

I just nodded.

–I think there was something in that old barn. Something evil. Something that got into everybody.

–Maybe.

–Your mom thought so. She said the devil lived out there. She even mentioned calling in the exorcist. The diocese had one then, you know.

–But Dad did the job himself. The exorcism. Burned the devil out.

–Maybe. But sometimes the devil isn't so easy to get rid of.

She seemed to drift away for a minute. Then she said,

–I should have stopped poor Angus. Before he went to Halifax.

–You couldn't have known the future.

–Yeah. But I did. I knew.

The waiter came with the coffee pot. We shook our heads simultaneously. He walked away. She breathed deeply and sighed and then smiled.

–He wanted to marry me, you know.

I just stared.

–He told me we'd get married when he came back from the city. He didn't want me to be hurt by all the crazy talk. He said we should wait until everything blew over. But I knew it. I knew he wasn't coming back.

–I'm sorry about all this, Shirley.

–And I just let him go.

She caught my hand.

–He was a little bit different, is all.

–Yes.

–Some things we just can't do anything about.

We finished our coffees, said our goodbyes, and I watched her walk away. I know she was significantly younger than my mother, but somehow she seemed so much older.

I told the real estate guy that maybe it was time to list the farm. Leave all the devils in the past.

–I suppose you'll be looking for something in town. I can watch for a nice single-family place on one of the older streets. Something quiet.

–As a complete hypothetical, what would be the chance of something a little bit more spacious than a single-family?

How spacious are you thinking?

–Say, something that would accommodate three seniors with enough space to keep them out of each other's hair. And maybe room to run a small business. And maybe, down the road, some live-in help.

–Small business, eh.

–Say a law office and a couple of accountants.

He laughed.

–You'd probably have to build something.

I laughed too.

–Keep your eyes open, I said.

The next time she called, Annie seemed distressed.

–Everything okay?

–I talked to Peggy. I don't think she's ready. I was surprised.

–Ready?

–To go back home.

She sighed.

–I thought it just made sense, moving back. But Peggy is in her own space these days. The shock of what she went through, it's a big adjustment. So she just wants to put everything on hold for now.

–Of course.

–She's going to need me for a while. You know Peggy.

–I do. I understand completely.

–But I'll be there when *you* need me.

–I know you will, Annie. I know.

–You stay in touch, now.

–Goodbye, Peggy.

–Byron? Are you sure you're okay?

–Why do you ask?

–You just called me Peggy.

–I didn't.

–You did.

–Sorry.

–By the way, what are you going to do with Allan's ashes?

–I'll think of something.

–You'll let us know.

–Yeah. I'll let you know. Bye, Annie.

–Bye for now, Byron.

DUST

TO

DUST

32.

The guy at the pro shop asked if I needed golf clubs. I said I didn't.

–Just the cart.

He rang it in, returned the credit card.

–Just drop it where you found it when you're finished.

It was a warm, slightly hazy day in early September. The greens and fairways seemed deserted. I was sitting just behind the tenth tee when two carts whirred up and stopped.

I had two little ones from the hotel mini-bar with me. I had just opened one of them. I waved, gestured. Told them in golfer sign language that they should play through.

They clambered out, the four of them. Three seemed to be in their early forties. Good-looking, beefy, at that lovely point in life when the dream still feels totally realistic, just before the normal shit starts happening.

The clothes were perfect. The shirts, the pants, the golf shoes. Ball caps tightly moulded to perfectly rounded skulls. Definitely golf gloves somewhere. They were friendly, nodded greetings as they walked past. One asked if I was waiting for someone. I said I was.

–Couldn't get a better day, he said.

–I feel sorry for all the people who aren't here, I said.

–You got that right.

One by one, the first three teed off and took their shots, and it was wonderful to behold the grace and precision. And how cool they were. Each of the three balls just vanished in the distance. And yet there were no high-fives, there was no triumphal teasing. Just guys doing what was expected and feeling good about it.

Then the fourth guy took his position. He was very young, perhaps a student about to begin his first year at a university. I related to his hesitancy. You could almost smell the fear as he approached his tee and clumsily placed the ball.

One of the three, obviously his dad, was muttering instructions. The kid shuffled his feet around. I noted he was wearing running shoes. He took a couple of practice swings. Then he swung hard, and missed.

–Fuck, I heard him say.

Now his dad came nearer, leaning slightly on his driver. The head on the driver was the size of a boot. He was obviously a perfect dad. You could tell by the calm restraint. *Feet a bit more apart, son. Keep your arms straight. Don't forget to follow through. No, don't look at me, look at the ball. Breathe deep.* And so on. I'd heard it all before.

The kid swung. The ball hopped about five feet. He was not enjoying this. I knew everything that was going on inside him. I wanted to hear him say, *Fuck this*, toss the club aside and walk away.

The dad was now behind him, reaching around his skinny torso, positioning the kid's hands precisely on the shaft of the golf club, speaking softly. The other two members of the foursome had wandered off, were standing, chatting, with their backs to what was going on.

The kid looked in my direction. I pretended to be reading something on my lap. Dad stepped away. The kid was rigid as he slowly raised the club. I'd bet money that he closed his eyes as he began the swing. He couldn't not. I couldn't not. To be able to do what everybody told you—keep your eyes on the ball and NOT where you want the ball to go—requires a special favour from nothing less than God almighty.

The kid swung hard. There was a crack. He opened his eyes. The ball was gone, carried off on a swell of music from an angel choir, disappearing. Somewhere. Who cares where? The kid was shouting.

—Yeaaaaaaah.

The dad was pumping his fist. The other two were now ambling back, grinning happily.

The kid looked in my direction. I gave him a thumbs-up. He just nodded, remembering to be cool, like Dad, like the other two fanatics. They climbed back in the carts, looking serious.

I watched as they silently worked their way down the fairway. Three of them were at the distant green in about two strokes. It took the kid a little longer. But he got there in maybe five.

There was a small grove of birch just across from where I was parked in my cart. I was trying to imagine the trajectory of the ball I'd nailed the last time I was here. The last golf ball I'd hit or would ever hit. Just after Allan had hit the last one that he would ever hit. It would never have crossed our minds as we climbed out of the golf carts, just about where I was sitting, that this would be the end of something.

I sipped on the second little one.

I couldn't be bothered dragging myself out of the golf cart to take a closer look at those birch trees. Had Allan not fallen, what happened here that day would have been a hilarious story for afterwards, or on all subsequent golf outings. How Byron scored a hole-in-one in the golf cart cupholder.

Even I thought it was funny. But it was a story that never would be told.

It was right over there that I tried to pick him up. Until the doctor told me to put him down.

I finished off the second little one. I was relieved it wasn't bigger, and that I hadn't brought another one.

I drove down the fairway, slowly. There was a rotten sand trap about two-thirds of the way to the green, a second pit off a little farther to the right. I picked the larger of the two, and parked beside it.

I removed Allan from the backpack. I looked around. It was like the whole world was suddenly deserted. I limped in the direction of the sand, then down into it.

I pried the lid off the black plastic box.

Here we are.

I saw a rake on the far side of the pit. I put Allan down, fetched the rake. I moved some sand aside, made a small depression, and then I poured him out. The colours didn't quite match. Allan was darker than the sand. So I raked it until I could hardly notice any difference. I told myself it wouldn't matter. The last thing on a golfer's mind in a sand trap is the colour of the sand.

Sorry I don't have anything left for a little toast.

I swear he replied, *Bad planning, Byron. You have to learn to look ahead.*

I could hear the wheels of a large truck howling past on the nearby highway. I'd never seen Allan drive a truck, but I believed that he was good at it. He had that Class A trucker's licence for more than twenty years, according to what the investigators turned up.

I gave the sand another little rake. Now he was completely blended in, one fundamental element indistinguishable from all the other minerals. *Earth to earth. Ashes to ashes. Dust to dust.* They never mentioned sand. But Allan would have liked this. I knew him well enough to say that with considerable confidence, even though, if we added up all the time that we were actually together, it wouldn't come to much.

Maybe a single year in total. Maybe less.

The very best of friends don't necessarily live in each other's pockets. Right?

We were a strange pair. Two guys who didn't have a thing in common. Except that we both thought that we were disappointments to almost everyone who mattered—everyone except each other, I think. We can never know for sure.

There was a soft thump nearby and I saw a golf ball rolling down a slight incline into the sand pit. It rolled right in and stopped. I looked around. There were people far away. I walked toward the ball. I remembered to use the rake to erase my footsteps.

It was a cheap golf ball—even I could tell. I remembered how Allan always had a supply of cheap balls in his bag for me to use because I was always losing them. And how he would make me crazy wasting time looking for lost balls in the bushes beside the fairway so I wouldn't lose his fancy ones.

–Gonna take a leak, he'd say.

And then he'd vanish into the woods and gullies and be gone for maybe fifteen minutes. And come back, pockets bulging with other people's golf balls.

–Pissing golf balls, are you now, I'd say, and he'd give me his weary, patient look.

–These are just for you. If I catch you using my good ones, I'll break your hand.

He was joking. I know he could scare you joking. Maybe some people were afraid of him. But I don't think he really had it in him to hurt anybody. I know that if anything really bad had happened to the careless Newfoundlander, Mike, it wouldn't have been Allan who did it, no matter how badly Mike had disappointed him.

Time to go, I said.

Don't be a stranger, he replied.

I picked up the stray golf ball. Brushed off the sand, put it in my pocket. The owner would never miss it, I told myself. He'd probably find half a dozen others while he was looking for it.

Anyway, golfers always carry tons of golf balls with them, everywhere they go.

I wheeled the golf cart toward the trail that winds between the greens, around the fairways, past the water features and the sand traps, past the groves of inconvenient trees. Heading home.

ACKNOWLEDGEMENTS

For my scant familiarity with the game of golf, I am grateful to the Celtic Music Interpretive Centre of Judique, N.S., and their annual fund-raising tournaments, in which I awkwardly participated for many years.

Byron's private search for information about Alzheimer's is partly informed by a feature story published in the *New York Times* on September 15, 2018, called "23andMe Said He Would Lose his Mind. Ancestry Said the Opposite. Which Was Right?"

I could not imagine having finished this manuscript without, once again, the steady editorial direction of Anne Collins, her patient discipline and penetrating eye. I'm grateful for the whole team at Random House Canada, from the book's designer, Terri Nimmo, to my longtime collaborator, Scott Sellers. I'd also like to thank both Matthew Sibiga and Marion Garner for their long-time support.

My agent, Shaun Bradley, raised important warning flags about narrative missteps in an original draft while my first reader, Carol Off, showed courage and persistence helping me recover from the early story-telling stumbles.

Derek and Barbara Kennedy were generous with time and timely encouragement as the narrative evolved. Danielle

Stone provided insight into the challenges that confront young lawyers at the start of a career.

I regret that a close friend to whom I dedicate the book didn't live to see the final product. He would have been, at the very least, amused.

LINDEN MACINTYRE'S bestselling first novel, *The Long Stretch*, was nominated for a CBA Libris Award and his boyhood memoir, *Causeway: A Passage from Innocence*, won both the Edna Staebler Award for Creative Non-Fiction and the Evelyn Richardson Award. His second novel, *The Bishop's Man*, was a #1 national bestseller, won the Scotiabank Giller Prize, the Dartmouth Book Award and the CBA Libris Fiction Book of the Year Award, among other honours. The third book in the loose-knit trilogy, *Why Men Lie*, was also a #1 bestseller as well as a *Globe and Mail* "Can't Miss" Book. His novels *Punishment* and *The Only Cafe* were also national bestsellers, as was his 2019 work of non-fiction, *The Wake*. A distinguished broadcast journalist, MacIntyre, who was born in St. Lawrence, Newfoundland, and grew up in Port Hastings, Cape Breton, spent twenty-four years as the co-host of *the fifth estate*. He has won ten Gemini awards for his work. MacIntyre lives in Toronto with his wife, CBC radio host and author Carol Off. They spend their summers in a Cape Breton village by the sea.